ROUNDUP

ROUNDUP

EDITED BY
STEPHEN OVERHOLSER

DOUBLEDAY & COMPANY, INC.
GARDEN CITY, NEW YORK
1982

Library of Congress Cataloging in Publication Data
Main entry under title:

Roundup.

1. Western stories. 2. American fiction—West (U.S.)
3. American fiction—20th century. I. Overholser,
Stephen.
PS648.W4R68   813'.0874'08
ISBN: 0-385-17947-2   AACR2
Library of Congress Catalog Card Number 81-43728
Copyright © 1982 by Western Writers of America
All Rights Reserved
Printed in the United States of America
First Edition

This volume is dedicated
to the memory of

Lewis B. Patten
1915–1981

Western Novelist
and
Charter Member of
Western Writers of America

CONTENTS

INTRODUCTION

Behind the Western short story lies a long and rich tradition, one that echoes the voices of our pioneer men and women. Tales swapped around the dancing flames of a campfire were based on real experiences and embodied the genuine human drama of people traveling to an uncharted and sometimes hostile land to make a new start in life.

These stories, often much embroidered, found their way into periodicals of the nineteenth century. So strong was reader interest that more were published over the years, written with authenticity varying from gritty truth to the fanciful fictions of a West that existed only in the minds of Eastern writers. By the turn of the century this mixture of literary realism and sheer invention had evolved into a highly popular genre, one that was uniquely American.

Western short stories and novels flourished through the first half of the twentieth century. Pulp and slick paper magazines alike published "Westerns." From shoot-'em-ups to slice-of-life narratives, these stories were devoured by readers who hungered for tales of the West.

With the advent of television in the early 1950s the magazines declined. Western magazines died out altogether as readers turned to series Westerns on TV for a new and exciting way of experiencing our mythical past. But these "televised short stories" ran their course, too. Western dramas were replaced by adventure dramas with contemporary settings.

The loss has been felt, and today we are seeing a renewed interest in Western stories. Heroic characters are in demand, and the hero has always been at the heart of the Western. We like to read about an individual who can bring about order from chaos, who can make things right.

In the stories here you will meet men and women of this caliber. Every story is new, written for today's readers by today's authors. The authors are members of the Western Writers of America, and these stories are their contribution to an important literary tradition.

You will recognize some of the writers because they have published well-known novels and have won awards for them; others may be new to you because their careers are young. All are top-notch storytellers.

In "The Last Indian Fight in Kerr County," Elmer Kelton tells the gripping story of a young couple caught in their remote Texas cabin by a band of marauding Indians. Jeanne Williams writes of hard life and agonizing death in a westward-bound wagon train in "The Debt."

Any woman who has ever packed her family's belongings and moved to a new home will appreciate the frustrations and share the anger of Emma Sanders in "Such Brave Men," by Carla Kelly. Elmore Leonard tells the surprising story of a marked, shunned woman in the Southwest who is met, and befriended, by a notorious Mexican bandit in "The Tonto Woman."

A cowhand's love for a schoolteacher is the theme of Wayne D. Overholser's story "The Wooing of Rosy Malone." And Benjamin Capps writes humorously of a trail boss's woes after the herd is delivered to the railhead in Dodge City in "The Disgraceful Affair of Turpentine Jackson."

Here in *Roundup* you will be amused and amazed by these and other stories. Read on!

STEPHEN OVERHOLSER
EDITOR

ROUNDUP

THE LAST INDIAN
FIGHT IN KERR
COUNTY

Elmer Kelton

In later times, Burkett Wayland liked to say he was in the last great Indian battle of Kerr County, Texas. It happened before he was born.

It started one day while his father, Matthew Wayland, then not much past twenty, was breaking a new field for fall wheat planting, just east of a small log cabin on one of the creeks tributary to the Guadalupe River. The quiet of autumn morning was broken by a fluttering of wings as a covey of quail flushed beyond a heavy stand of oak timber past the field. Startled, Matthew jerked on the reins and quickly laid his plow over on its side in the newly broken sod. His bay horse raised its head and pointed its ears toward the sound.

Matthew caught a deep breath and held it. He thought he heard a crackling of brush. He reached back for the rifle slung over his shoulder and quickly unhitched the horse. Standing behind it for protection, he watched and listened another moment or two, then jumped up bareback and beat his heels against the horse's ribs, moving in a long trot for the cabin in the clearing below.

He wanted to believe ragged old Burk Kennemer was coming for a visit from his little place three miles down the creek, but the trapper usually rode in the open where Matthew could see him coming, not through the brush.

Matthew had not been marking the calendar in his almanac, but he had not needed to. The cooling nights, the curing of the grass to a rich brown, had told him all too well that this was September, the month of the Comanche moon. This was the time of year—their ponies strong from the summer grass—that the warrior Comanches could be expected to ride down from the high plains. Before winter they liked to make a final grand raid through the rough limestone hills of old hunting grounds west of San Antonio, then retire with stolen horses and mules—and sometimes captives and scalps—back to sanctuary far to the north. They had done it every year since the first settlers had pushed into the broken hill country. Though the military was beginning to press in upon their hideaways, all the old settlers had been warning Matthew to expect them again as the September moon went full, aiding the Comanches in their nighttime prowling.

Rachal opened the roughhewn cabin door and looked at her young husband in surprise, for normally he would plow until she called him in for dinner at noon. He was trying to finish breaking the ground and dry-sow the wheat before fall rains began.

She looked as if she should still be in school somewhere instead of trying to make a home in the wilderness; she was barely eighteen. "What is it, Matthew?"

"I don't know," he said tightly. "Get back inside."

He slid from the horse and turned it sideways to shield him. He held the rifle ready. It was always loaded.

A horseman broke out of the timber and moved toward the cabin. Matthew let go a long-held breath as he recognized Burk Kennemer. Relief turned to anger for the scare. He walked out to meet the trapper, trying to keep the edginess from his voice, but he could not control the flush of color that warmed his face.

He noted that the old man brought no meat with him. It was Kennemer's habit, when he came visiting, to fetch along a freshly killed deer, or sometimes a wild turkey, or occasionally a ham out of his smokehouse, and stay to eat some of it cooked by Rachal's skillful hands. He ran a lot of hogs in the timber, fattening them on the oak mast. He was much more of a hogman and trapper than a farmer. Plow handles did not fit his hands, Kennemer claimed. He was of the restless breed that moved westward ahead of the farmers, and left when they crowded him.

Kennemer had a tentative half smile. "Glad I wasn't a Comanche. You'd've shot me dead."

"I'd've tried," Matthew said, his heart still thumping. He lifted a shaky hand to show what Kennemer had done to him. "What did you come sneaking in like an Indian for?"

Kennemer's smile was gone. "For good reason. That little girl inside the cabin?"

Matthew nodded. Kennemer said, "You'd better keep her there."

As if she had heard the conversation, Rachal Wayland opened the door and stepped outside, shading her eyes with one hand. Kennemer's gray-bearded face lighted at sight of her. Matthew did not know if Burk had ever had a wife of his own; he had never mentioned one. Rachal shouted, "Come on up, Mr. Kennemer. I'll be fixing us some dinner."

He took off his excuse of a hat and shouted back, for he was still at some distance from the cabin. "Can't right now, girl. Got to be traveling. Next time maybe." He cut his gaze to Matthew's little log shed and corrals. "Where's your other horse?"

"Grazing out yonder someplace. Him and the milk cow both."

"Better fetch him in," Kennemer said grimly. "Better put him and this one in the pen closest to the cabin if you don't want to lose them. And stay close to the cabin yourself, or you may lose more than the horses."

Matthew felt the dread chill him again. "Comanches?"

"Don't know. Could be. Fritz Dieterle come by my place while ago and told me he found tracks where a bunch of horses crossed the Guadalupe during the night. Could've been cowboys, or a bunch of hunters looking to lay in some winter meat. But it could've been Comanches. The horses wasn't shod."

Matthew could read the trapper's thoughts. Kennemer was reasonably sure it had not been cowboys or hunters. Kennemer said, "I come to warn you, and now I'm going west to warn that bunch of German farmers out on the forks. They may want to fort-up at the best house."

Matthew's thoughts were racing ahead. He had been over to the German settlement twice since he and Rachal had arrived here late last winter, in time to break out their first field for spring planting. Burk Kennemer had told him the Germans—come west from the older settlements around Neu Braunfels and Fredericksburg—had been here long enough to give him sound advice about farming this shallow-soil land. And perhaps they might, if he could have understood them. They had seemed friendly enough, but they spoke no English, and he knew nothing of German. Efforts at communication had led him nowhere but back here, his shoulders slumped in frustration. He had counted Burk Kennemer as his only neighbor—the only one he could talk with.

"Maybe I ought to send Rachal with you," Matthew said. "It would be safer for her there, all those folks around her."

Kennemer considered that for only a moment. "Too risky traveling by daylight, one man and one girl. Even if you was to come along, two men and a girl wouldn't be no match if they jumped us."

"You're even less of a match, traveling by yourself."

Kennemer patted the shoulder of his long-legged brown horse. "No offense, boy, but old Deercatcher here can run circles around them two of yours, and anything them Indians is liable to have. He'll take care of me, long as I'm by myself. You've got a good strong cabin there. You and that girl'll be better off inside it than out in the open with me." He frowned. "If it'll make you feel safer, I'll be back before dark. I'll stay here with you, and we can fort-up together."

That helped, but it was not enough. Matthew looked at the cabin, which he and Kennemer and the broken-English-speaking German named Dieterle had put up after he finished planting his spring crops. Until then, he and Rachal had lived in their wagon, or around and beneath it. "I wish she wasn't here, Burk. All of a sudden, I wish I'd never brought her here."

The trapper frowned. "Neither one of you belongs here. You're both just shirttail young'uns, not old enough to take care of your-selves."

Matthew remembered that the old man had told him as much, sev-eral times. A pretty little girl like Rachal should not be out here in a place like this, working like a mule, exposed to the dangers of the thinly settled frontier. But Matthew had never heard a word of com-plaint from her, not since they had started west from the piney-woods country in the biting cold of a wet winter, barely a month married. She always spoke of this as *our* place, *our* home.

He said, "It seemed all right, till now. All of a sudden I realize what I've brought her to. I want to get her out of here, Burk."

The trapper slowly filled an evil black pipe while he pondered and twisted his furrowed face. "Then we'll go tonight. It'll be safer travel-ing in the dark because I've been here long enough to know this country better than them Indians do. We'll make Fredericksburg by daylight. But one thing you've got to make up your mind to, Matthew. You've got to leave her there, or go back to the old home with her yourself. You've got no business bringing her here again to this kind of danger."

"She's got no home back yonder to go to. This is the only home she's got, or me either."

Kennemer's face went almost angry. "I buried a woman once in a place just about like this. I wouldn't want to help bury that girl of yours. *Adiós,* Matthew. See you before dark." He circled Deer-catcher around the cabin and disappeared in a motte of live-oak timber.

Rachal stood in the doorway, puzzled. She had not intruded on the conversation. Now she came out onto the foot-packed open ground. "What was the matter with Mr. Kennemer? Why couldn't he stay?"

He wished he could keep it from her. "Horsetracks on the Guada-lupe. He thinks it was Indians."

Matthew watched her closely, seeing the sudden clutch of fear in her eyes before she firmly put it away. "What does he think we ought to do?" she asked, seeming calmer than he thought she should.

"Slip away from here tonight, go to Fredericksburg."

"For how long, Matthew?"

He did not answer her. She said, "We can't go far. There's the milk cow, for one thing. She's got to be milked."

The cow had not entered his mind. "Forget her. The main thing is to have you safe."

"We're going to need that milk cow."

Impatiently he exploded, "Will you grow up, and forget that damned cow? I'm taking you out of here."

She shrank back in surprise at his sharpness, a little of hurt in her eyes. They had not once quarreled, not until now. "I'm sorry, Rachal. I didn't go to blow up at you that way."

She hid her eyes from him. "You're thinking we might just give up this place and never come back . . ." She wasn't asking him; she was telling him what was in his mind.

"That's what Burk thinks we ought to do."

"He's an old man, and we're young. And this isn't his home. He hasn't even got a home, just that old rough cabin, and those dogs and hogs . . . He's probably moved twenty times in his life. But we're not like that, Matthew. We're the kind of people who put down roots and grow where we are."

Matthew looked away. "I'll go fetch the dun horse. You bolt the door."

Riding away, he kept looking back at the cabin in regret. He knew he loved this place where they had started their lives together. Rachal loved it too, though he found it difficult to understand why. Life had its shortcomings back in east Texas, but her upbringing there had been easy compared to the privations she endured here. When she needed water she carried it in a heavy oaken bucket from the creek, fully seventy-five yards. He would have built the cabin nearer the water, but Burk had advised that once in a while heavy rains made that creek rise up on its hind legs and roar like an angry bear.

She worked her garden with a heavy-handled hoe, and when Matthew was busy in the field from dawn to dark she chopped her own wood from the pile of dead oak behind the cabin. She cooked over an ill-designed open fireplace that did not draw as well as it should. And, as much as anything, she put up with a deadening loneliness. Offhand, he could not remember that she had seen another woman since late in the spring, except for a German girl who stopped by once on her way to the forks. They had been unable to talk to each other. Even so, Rachal had glowed for a couple of days, refreshed by seeing someone besides her husband and the unwashed Burk Kennemer.

The cabin was as yet small, just a single room which was kitchen, sleeping quarters and sitting room combined. It had been in Matthew's mind, when he had nothing else to do this coming winter, to start work on a second section that would become a bedroom. He would build a roof and an open dog run between that part and the original, in keeping with Texas pioneer tradition, with a sleeping area over the dog run for the children who were sure to come with God's own time and blessings. He and Rachal had talked much of their plans, of the additional land he would break out to augment the potential income from their dozen or so beef critters scattered along the creek. He had forcefully put the dangers out of his mind, knowing they were there but choosing not to dwell upon them.

He remembered now the warnings from Rachal's uncle and aunt, who had brought her up after her own father was killed by a falling tree and her mother was taken by one of the periodic fever epidemics. They had warned of the many perils a couple would face on the edge of the settled lands, perils which youth and love and enthusiasm had made to appear small, far away in distance and time, until today. Now, his eyes nervously searching the edge of the oak timber for anything amiss, fear rose up in him. It was a primeval, choking fear of a kind he had never known, and a sense of shame for having so thoughtlessly brought Rachal to this sort of jeopardy.

He found the dun horse grazing by the creek, near a few of the speckled beef cows which a farmer at the old home had given him in lieu of wages for two years of backbreaking work. He had bartered for the old wagon and the plow and a few other necessary tools. Whatever else he had, he and Rachal had built with their hands. For Texans, cash money was still in short supply.

He thought about rounding up the cows and corraling them by the cabin, but they were scattered. He saw too much risk in the time it might take him to find them all, as well as the exposure to any Comanches hidden in the timber. From what he had heard, the Indians were much less interested in cattle than in horses. Cows were slow. Once the raiders were ready to start north, they would want speed to carry them to sanctuary. Matthew pitched a rawhide *reata* loop around the dun's neck and led the animal back in a long trot. He had been beyond sight of the cabin for a while, and he prickled with anxiety. He breathed a sigh of relief when he broke into the open. The smoke from the chimney was a welcome sight.

He turned the horses into the pole corral and closed the gate, then poured shelled corn into a crude wooden trough. They eagerly set to crunching the grain with their strong teeth, a sound he had always enjoyed when he could restrain himself from thinking how much that corn would be worth in the settlements. The horses were blissfully unaware of the problems that beset their owners. Matthew wondered how content they would be if they fell into Indian hands and were driven or ridden the many long, hard days north into that mysterious hidden country. It would serve them right!

Still, he realized how helpless he and Rachal would be without them. He could not afford to lose the horses.

Rachal slid the heavy oak bar from the door and let him into the cabin. He immediately replaced the bolt while she went back to stirring a pot of stew hanging on an iron rod inside the fireplace. He avoided her eyes, for the tension stretched tightly between them.

"See anything?" she asked, knowing he would have come running.

He shook his head. "Not apt to, until night. If they're here, that's when they'll come for the horses."

"And find us gone?" Her voice almost accused him.

He nodded. "Burk said he'll be back before dark. He'll help us find our way to Fredericksburg."

Firelight touched her face. He saw a reflection of tears. She said, "They'll destroy this place."

"Better this place than *you*. I've known it from the start, I guess, and just wouldn't admit it. I shouldn't have brought you here."

"I came willingly. I've been happy here. So have you."

"We just kept dancing and forgot that the piper had to be paid."

A silence fell between them, heavy and unbridgeable. When the stew was done they sat at the roughhewn table and ate without talking. Matthew got up restlessly from time to time to look out the front and back windows. These had no glass. They were like small doors in the walls. They could be closed and bolted shut. Each had a loophole which he could see out of, or fire through. Those, he remembered, had been cut at Burk Kennemer's insistence. From the first, Matthew realized now, Burk had been trying to sober him, even to scare him away. Matthew had always put him off with a shrug or a laugh. Now he remembered what Burk had said today about having buried a woman in a place like this. He thought he understood the trapper, and the man's fears, in a way he had not before.

The heavy silence went unrelieved. After eating what he could of the stew, his stomach knotted, he went outside and took a long look around, cradling the rifle. He fetched a shovel and began to throw dirt onto the roof to make it more difficult for the Indians to set afire. It occurred to him how futile this labor was if they were going to abandon the place anyway, but he kept swinging the shovel, trying to work off the tension.

The afternoon dragged. He spent most of it outside, pacing, watching. In particular he kept looking to the west, anticipating Burk Kennemer's return. Now that he had made up his mind to it, he could hardly wait for darkness, to give them a chance to escape this place. The only thing which came from that direction—or any other—was the brindle milk cow, drifting toward the shed at her own slow pace and in her own good time for the evening milking and the grain she knew awaited her. Matthew owned no watch, but he doubted that a watch kept better time than that cow, her udder swinging in rhythm with her slow and measured steps. Like the horses, she had no awareness of anything except her daily routine, of feeding and milking and grazing. Observing her patient pace, Matthew could almost assure himself that this day was like all others, that he had no reason for fear.

He milked the cow, though he intended to leave the milk unused in the cabin, for it was habit with him as well as with the cow. The sun was dropping rapidly when he carried the bucket of milk to Rachal. Her eyes asked him, though she did not speak.

He shook his head. "No sign of anything out there. Not of Burk, either."

Before sundown he saddled the dun horse for Rachal, making ready. He would ride the plow horse bareback. He climbed up onto his pole fence, trying to shade his eyes from the sinking sun while he studied the hills and the open valley to the west. All his earlier fears were with him, and a new one as well.

Where is he? He wouldn't just have left us here. Not old Burk.

Once he thought he heard a sound in the edge of the timber. He turned quickly and saw a flash of movement, nothing more. It was a feeling as much as something actually seen. It could have been anything, a deer, perhaps, or even one of his cows. It *could* have been.

He remained outside until the sun was gone, and until the last golden remnant faded into twilight over the timbered hills that stretched into the distance like a succession of blue monuments. The autumn chill set him to shivering, but he held out against going for his coat. When the night was full dark, he knew it was time.

He called softly at the cabin door. Rachal lifted the bar. He said, "The moon'll rise directly. We'd better get started."

"Without Burk? Are you really sure, Matthew?"

"If they're around, they'll be here. Out yonder, in the dark, we've got a chance."

She came out, wrapped for the night chill, carrying his second rifle, handing him his coat. Quietly they walked to the corral, where he opened the gate, untied the horses and gave her a lift up into the saddle. The stirrups were too long for her, and her skirts were in the way, but he knew she could ride. He threw himself up onto the plow horse, and they moved away from the cabin in a walk, keeping to the grass as much as possible to muffle the sound of the hoofs. As quickly as he could, he pulled into the timber, where the darkness was even more complete. For the first miles, at least, he felt that he knew the way better than any Indian who might not come here once in several years.

It was his thought to swing first by Burk's cabin. There was always a chance the old man had changed his mind about things . . .

He had held onto this thought since late afternoon. Maybe Burk had found the tracks were not made by Indians after all, and he had chosen to let the young folks have the benefit of a good, healthy scare.

Deep inside, Matthew knew that was a vain hope. It was not Burk's way. He might have let Matthew sweat blood, but he would not do this to Rachal.

They both saw the fire at the same time, and heard the distant barking of the dogs. Rachal made a tiny gasp and clutched his arm.

Burk's cabin was burning.

They reined up and huddled together for a minute, both coming dangerously close to giving in to their fears and riding away in a blind run. Matthew gripped the rawhide reins so tightly that they seemed to cut into his hands. "Easy, Rachal," he whispered.

Then he could hear horses moving through the timber, and the crisp night air carried voices to him.

"They're coming at us, Matthew," Rachal said tightly. "They'll catch us out here."

He had no way of knowing if they had been seen, or heard. A night bird called to the left of him. Another answered, somewhere to the right. At least, they sounded like night birds.

"We've got to run for it, Rachal!"

"We can't run all the way to Fredericksburg. Even if we could find it. They'll catch us."

He saw only one answer. "Back to the cabin! If we can get inside, they'll have to come in there to get us."

He had no spurs; a farmer did not need them. He beat his heels against the horse's sides and led the way through the timber in a run. He did not have to look behind him to know Rachal was keeping up with him. Somehow the horses had caught the fever of their fear.

"Keep low, Rachal," he said. "Don't let the low limbs knock you down." He found a trail that he knew and shortly burst out into the open. He saw no reason for remaining in the timber now, for the Indians surely knew where they were. The timber would only slow their running. He leaned out over the horse's neck and kept thumping his heels against its ribs. He glanced back to be sure he was not outpacing Rachal.

Off to the right he thought he saw figures moving, vague shapes against the blackness. The moon was just beginning to rise, and he could not be sure. Ahead, sensed more than seen, was the clearing. Evidently the Indians had not been there yet, or the place would be in flames as Burk's cabin had been.

He could see the shape of the cabin now. "Right up to the door, Rachal!"

He jumped to the ground, letting his eyes sweep the yard and what he could see of the corrals. "Don't get down," he shouted. "Let me look inside first."

The door was closed, as they had left it. He pushed it open and stepped quickly inside, the rifle ready. The dying embers in the fireplace showed him he was alone. "It's all right, Rachal. Get down quick, and into the cabin!"

She slid down and fell, and he helped her to her feet. She pointed and gave a cry. Several figures were moving rapidly toward the shed. Matthew fired the rifle in their general direction and gave Rachal a push toward the door. She resisted stubbornly. "The horses," she said. "Let's get the horses into the cabin."

She led her dun through the door, though it did not much want to go into that dark and unaccustomed place.

Matthew would have to admit later—though now he had no time for such thoughts—that she was keeping her head better than he was. He would have let the horses go, and the Indians would surely have taken them. The plow horse was gentler and entered the cabin with less resistance, though it made a nervous sound in its nose at sight of the glowing coals.

Matthew heard something *plunk* into the logs as he pushed the door shut behind him and dropped the bar solidly into place. He heard a horse race up to the cabin and felt the jarring weight of a man's body hurled against the door, trying to break through. Matthew pushed his own strength upon the bar, bracing it. A chill ran through him, and he shuddered at the realization that only the meager thickness of that door lay between him and an intruder who intended to kill him. He heard the grunting of a man in strain, and he imagined he could feel the hot breath. His hair bristled.

Rachal opened the front-window loophole and fired her rifle.

Thunder seemed to rock the cabin. It threw the horses into a panic that made them more dangerous, for the moment, than those Indians outside. One of them slammed against Matthew and pressed him to the wall so hard that he thought all his ribs were crushed. But that was the last time an Indian tried the door. Matthew could hear the man running, getting clear of Rachal's rifle.

A gunshot sounded from out in the night. A bullet struck the wall but did not break through between the logs. Periodically Matthew would hear a shot, first from one direction, then from another. After the first three or four, he was sure.

"They've just got one gun. We've got two."

The horses calmed, after a time. So did Matthew. He threw ashes over the coals to dim their glow, which had made it difficult for him to see out into the night. The moon was up, throwing a silvery light across the yard.

"I'll watch out front," he said. "You watch the back."

All his life he had heard that Indians did not like to fight at night because of a fear that their souls would wander lost if they died in the darkness. He had no idea if the stories held any truth. He knew that Indians were skillful horsethieves, in darkness or light, and that he and Rachal had frustrated these by bringing their mounts into the cabin.

Burk had said the Indians on these September raids were more intent on acquiring horses than on taking scalps, though they had no prejudice against the latter. He had said Indians did not like to take heavy risks in going against a well-fortified position, that they were likely to probe the defenses and, if they found them strong, withdraw in search of an easier target.

But they had a strong incentive for breaking into this cabin.

He suggested, "They might leave if we turn the horses out."

"And what do we do afoot?" she demanded. Her voice was not a schoolgirl's. It was strong, defiant. "If they want these horses, let them come through that door and pay for them. These horses are *ours!*"

Her determination surprised him, and shamed him a little. He held silent a while, listening, watching for movement. "I suppose those Indians feel like they've got a right here. They figure this land belongs to them."

"Not if they just come once a year. We've come here to stay."

"I wish we hadn't. I wish I hadn't brought you."

"Don't say that. I've always been glad that you did. I've loved this place from the time we first got here and lived in the wagon, because it was ours. It *is* ours. When this trouble is over it will *stay* ours. We've earned the right to it."

He fired seldom, and only when he thought he had a good target, for shots inside the cabin set the horses to plunging and threshing.

He heard a cow bawl in fear and agony. Later, far beyond the shed, he could see a fire building. Eventually he caught the aroma of meat, roasting.

"They've killed the milk cow," he declared.

Rachal said, "We'll need another one, then. For the baby."

That was the first she had spoken of it, though he had had reason lately to suspect. "I shouldn't have put you through that ride tonight."

"That didn't hurt me. I'm not so far along yet. That's one reason we've got to keep the horses. We may need to trade the dun for a milk cow."

They watched through the long hours, he at the front window, she at the rear. The Indians had satisfied their hunger, and they were quiet, sleeping perhaps, waiting for dawn to storm the cabin without danger to their immortal souls. Matthew was tired, and his legs were cramped from the long vigil, but he felt no sleepiness. He thought once that Rachal had fallen asleep, and he made no move to awaken her. If trouble came from that side, he thought he would probably hear it.

She was not asleep. She said, "I hear a rooster way off somewhere. Burk's, I suppose. Be daylight soon."

"They'll hit us then. They'll want to overrun us in a hurry."

"It's up to us to fool them. You and me together, Matthew, we've always been able to do whatever we set our minds to."

They came as he expected, charging horseback out of the rising sun, relying on the blazing light to blind the eyes of the defenders. But with Rachal's determined shouts ringing in his ears, he triggered the rifle at darting figures dimly seen through the golden haze. Rachal fired rapidly at those horsemen who ran past the cabin and came into her field of view on the back side. The two horses just trembled and leaned against one another.

One bold, quick charge and the attack was over. The Comanches swept on around, having tested the defense and found it unyielding. They pulled away, regrouping to the east as if considering another try.

"We done it, Rachal!" Matthew shouted. "We held them off."

He could see her now in the growing daylight, her hair stringing down, her face smudged with black, her eyes watering from the sting of the gunpowder. He had never seen her look so good.

She said triumphantly, "I tried to tell you we could do it, Matthew. You and me, we can do anything."

He thought the Indians might try again, but they began pulling away. He could see now that they had a considerable number of horses and mules, taken from other settlers. They drove these before them, splashing across the creek and moving north in a run.

"They're leaving," he said, not quite believing.

"Some more on this side," Rachal warned. "You'd better come over here and look."

Through the loophole in her window, out of the west, he saw a dozen or more horsemen loping toward the cabin. For a minute he thought he and Rachal would have to fight again. Strangely, the thought brought him no particular fear.

We can handle it. Together, we can do anything.

Rachal said, "Those are white men."

They threw their arms around each other and cried.

They were outside the cabin, the two of them, when the horsemen circled warily around it, rifles ready for a fight. The men were strangers, except the leader. Matthew remembered him from up at the forks. Excitedly the man spoke in a language Matthew knew was German. Then half the men were talking at once. They looked Rachal and Matthew over carefully, making sure neither was hurt.

The words were strange, but the expressions were universal. They were of relief and joy at finding the young couple alive and on their feet.

The door was open. The bay plow horse stuck its head out experimentally, nervously surveying the crowd, then breaking into a run to get clear of the oppressive cabin. The dun horse followed, pitching in relief to be outdoors. The German rescuers stared in puzzlement for a moment, then laughed as they realized how the Waylands had saved their horses.

One of them made a sweeping motion, as if holding a broom, and Rachal laughed with him. It was going to take a lot of work to clean up that cabin.

The spokesman said something to Matthew, and Matthew caught the name Burk Kennemer. The man made a motion of drawing a bow, and of an arrow striking him in the shoulder.

"Dead?" Matthew asked worriedly.

The man shook his head. *"Nein, nicht tod. Not dead."* By the motions, Matthew perceived that the wounded Burk had made it to the German settlement to give warning, and that the men had ridden through the night to get here.

Rachal came up and put her arm around Matthew, leaning against him. She said, "Matthew, do you think we killed any of those Indians?"

"I don't know that we did."

"I hope we didn't. I'd hate to know all of my life that there is blood on this ground."

Some of the men seemed to be thinking about leaving. Matthew said, "You-all pen your horses, and we'll have breakfast directly." He realized they did not understand his words, so he pantomimed and put the idea across. He made a circle, shaking hands with each man individually, telling him *thanks,* knowing each followed his meaning whether the words were understood or not.

"Rachal," he said, "these people are our neighbors. Somehow we've got to learn to understand each other."

She nodded. "At least enough so you can trade one of them out of another milk cow. For the baby."

When the baby came, late the following spring, they named it Burkett Kennemer Wayland, after the man who had brought them warning, and had sent them help.

That was the last time the Comanches ever penetrated so deeply into the hill country, for the military pressure was growing stronger.

And all of his life Burkett Kennemer Wayland was able to say, without taking sinful advantage of the truth, that he had been present at the last great Indian fight in Kerr County.

SUCH BRAVE MEN
Carla Kelly

"A little paint will make all the difference," said Hart Sanders as he and his wife surveyed the scabby walls in Quarters B.

Emma stood on tiptoe to whisper in her husband's ear. She didn't want to offend the quartermaster sergeant, who was leaning against the door and listening. "Hart, what *are* these walls made of?"

"Adobe," he whispered back.

"Oh."

Perhaps she could find out what adobe was later.

Hart turned to the sergeant lounging in the doorway. The man straightened up when the lieutenant spoke to him.

"Sergeant, have some men bring our household effects here. And we'll need a bed and table and chairs from supply."

"Yes, sir."

Emma took off her bonnet and watched the sergeant heading back to the quartermaster storehouse, then she turned and looked at her first army home again. Two rooms and a lean-to kitchen, the allotment of a second lieutenant.

Hart was watching her. He wanted to smile, but wasn't sure how she would take that.

"Not exactly Sandusky, is it?" he ventured.

She grinned at him and snapped his suspenders. "It's not even Omaha, Hart, and you know it!"

But she had been prepared for this, she thought to herself later as she was blacking the cookstove in the lean-to. Hart had warned her about life at Fort Laramie, Dakota Territory. He had told her about the wind and the heat and the cold and the bugs and the dirt, but sitting in the parlor of her father's house in Sandusky, she hadn't dreamed anything quite like this.

As she was tacking down an army blanket for the front room carpet, she noticed the ceiling was shedding. Every time she hammered in a tack, white flakes drifted down to the floor and settled on her hair, the folding rocking chair, and the whatnot shelf she had carried on her lap from Cheyenne Depot to Fort Laramie. She swept out the flakes after the blanket was secure, and reminded herself to step lightly in the front room.

Dinner was brought in by some of the other officers' wives, and they dined on sowbelly, hash browns and eggless custard. The sowbelly looked definitely lowbrow congealing on her Lowestoft bridal china, and she wished she had thought to bring along tin plates like Hart had suggested.

She was putting the last knickknack on the whatnot when Hart got into bed in the next room. The crackling and rustling startled her, and she nearly dropped the figurine in her hand. She ran to the door.

"Hart? Are you all right?" she asked. He had blown out the candle, and the bedroom was dark.

"Well sure, Emma. What's the matter?"

"That awful noise!"

She heard the rustling again as he sat up in bed.

"Emma, haven't you ever slept on a straw-tick mattress?"

She shook her head. "Does it ever quiet down?"

"After you sleep on it awhile," he assured her, and the noise started up again as he lay down and rolled over.

She had finished putting the little house in order next morning when Hart came bursting into the front room. He waved a piece of paper in front of her nose.

"Guess what?" he shouted, "D Company is going on detached duty to Fetterman! We leave tomorrow!"

"Do I get to come?" she asked.

"Oh no. We'll be gone a couple months. Isn't it exciting? My first campaign!"

Well, it probably was exciting, she thought after he had left, but that meant she would have to face the house alone. The prospect gleamed less brightly than it had the night before.

Company D left the fort next morning after Guard Mount. She was just fluffing up the pillows on their bed when someone knocked at the front door.

It was the adjutant. He took off his hat and stepped into the front room, looking for all the world like a man with bad news. She wondered what could possibly be worse than seeing your husband of one month ride out toward Fetterman (wherever that was), and having to figure out how to turn that scabrous adobe box into a home.

"I hate to have to tell you this, Mrs. Sanders," he said at last.

"Tell me what?"

"You've been ranked."

Emma shook her head. Whatever was he talking about? Ranked? "I don't understand, Lieutenant."

He took a step toward her, but he was careful to stay near the door. "Well, you know, ma'am, ranked. Bumped. Bricks falling?"

She stared at him, and wondered why he couldn't make sense. Didn't they teach them English at the Point?

"I'm afraid it's still a mystery to me, Lieutenant."

He rubbed his hand over the balding spot on the back of his head and shifted from one foot to the other.

"You'll have to move, ma'am."

"But I just did," she protested, at the same time surprised at herself for springing to the defense of such a defenseless house.

"I mean again," persisted the lieutenant. "Another lieutenant just reported in with his wife, and he outranks your husband. Yours is the only quarters available, so you'll have to leave."

It took a minute to sink in.

"But who? I can't . . ."

She was interrupted by the sound of boots on the front porch. The man who stepped inside was familiar to her, but she couldn't quite place him until he greeted her. Then she knew she would never forget that squeaky voice. He was Hart's old roommate from the Academy. She remembered that Hart had told her how the man spent all his time studying, and never was any fun at all.

"Are *you* taking my house?" she accused the lieutenant.

"I'm sorry, Mrs. Sanders," he said, and he didn't sound sorry at all.

"But . . . but . . . didn't you just graduate with my husband two months ago? How can you outrank him?" she asked, wanting to throw both officers out of her house.

He smiled again, and she resisted the urge to scrape her fingernails along his face. Instead, she stamped her foot and white flakes from the ceiling floated down.

"Yes, ma'am, we graduated together, but Hart was forty-sixth in class standing. I was fifteenth. So I still outrank him."

As she slammed the pots and pans into a box and yanked the sheets off the bed, she wished for the first time that Hart had been a little more diligent in his studies.

A corporal and two privates moved her into quarters that looked suspiciously like a chicken coop. She sniffed the air in the little one-room shack and almost asked the corporal if the former tenants she ranked out had clucked and laid eggs. But he didn't speak much English, and she didn't feel like wasting her sarcasm.

Emma swept out the room with a vigor that made her cough, and by nightfall when she crawled into the rustling bed, she speculated on the cost of rail fare from Cheyenne to Sandusky.

The situation looked better by morning. The room was small, to be sure, but she was the only one using it, and if she cut up a sheet, curtains would make all the difference. She hung up the Currier and Ives lithograph of sugaring off in Vermont, and was ripping up the sheet when someone knocked at the door.

It was the adjutant again. He had to duck to get into the room, and when he straightened up, his head just brushed the ceiling.

"Mrs. Sanders," he began, and it was an effort. "I hope you'll understand what I have to tell you."

Emma sensed what was coming, but she didn't want to make it easy on him.

"What?" she asked, sitting herself in the rocking chair and folding her hands in her lap. As she waited for him to speak, she remembered a poem she had read in school called *Horatio at the Bridge*.

"You've been ranked out again."

She was silent, looking at him for several moments. She noticed the drops of perspiration gathering on his forehead, and that his Adam's apple bobbed up and down when he swallowed.

"And where do I go from here?" she asked at last.

He shuffled his feet and rubbed the back of his head again, gestures she was beginning to recognize.

"All we have is a tent, ma'am."

"A tent," she repeated.

"Yes, ma'am."

"At least I didn't get attached to my chicken coop," she thought as she rolled up her bedding. She felt a certain satisfaction in the knowledge that Hart's roommate had been bumped down to her coop by whoever it was that outranked him. "Serves him right," she said out loud as she carried out the whatnot and closed the door.

The same corporal and privates set up the tent at the corner of Officers Row. It wasn't even a lieutenant's tent. Because of the increased activity in the field this summer, only a sergeant's tent could be found. The bedstead wouldn't fit in, so the corporal dumped the bed sack on the grass and put the frame back in the wagon. She started to protest when he drove away, but remembering his shortage of useful English, she saved her breath. He was back soon with a cot.

She had crammed in her trunks, spread the army blanket on the grass and was setting up the rocking chair when someone rapped on the tent pole.

She knew it would be the adjutant even before she turned around. Emma pulled back the tent flap and stepped outside.

"You can't have it, Lieutenant," she stated.

He shook his head. "Oh no, ma'am, I wasn't going to bump you again." He held out a large square of green fabric. She took it.

"What's this for?" she asked.

"Ma'am, I used to serve in Arizona Territory, and most folks down there line tent ceilings with green. Easier on the eyes."

He smiled at her then, and Emma began to see that the lot of an adjutant was not to be envied. She smiled back.

"Thank you, Lieutenant. I appreciate it."

He helped her fasten up the green baize, and it did make a difference inside the tent. Before he left, he pulled her cot away from the tent wall.

"So the tent won't leak when it rains," he explained, and then laughed. "But it never rains here anyway."

Since she couldn't cook in the tent, she messed with the officers in Old Bedlam that night. There were only three. The adjutant was a bachelor, Captain Endicott was an Orphan and had left his family back in the States, and the other lieutenant was casually at post on his way from Fort Robinson to Fort D. A. Russell.

The salt pork looked more at home on a tin plate, and she discovered that plum duff was edible. The coffee burned its way down, but she knew she could get used to it.

She excused herself, ran back to her tent, and returned with the tin of peaches she had bought at the post trader's store for the extortionate sum of two dollars and twenty-five cents. The adjutant pried open the lid, and the four of them speared slices out of the can and laughed and talked until Tattoo.

Captain Endicott walked her back to her tent before Last Call. He shook his head when he saw the tent.

"Women ought to stay in the States. Good schools there, doctors, sociability. Much better," he commented.

"But don't you miss your family?" she asked.

"Lord, yes," he began, then stopped. "Beg pardon, Mrs. Sanders."

He said good-night to her, and walked off alone to his room in Old Bedlam.

Emma undressed, did up her hair, and got into bed. She lay still, listening to the bugler blow Extinguish Lights. She heard horses snuffling in the officers' stables behind Old Bedlam. When the coyotes started tuning up on the slopes rimming the fort, she pulled the blanket over her head and closed her eyes.

She knew she was not alone when she woke up before Reveille the next morning. She sat up on the cot and gasped.

A snake was curled at the foot of her blanket. She pulled her feet

up until she was sitting in a ball on her pillow. She was afraid to
scream because she didn't know what the snake would do, and besides, she didn't want the sergeant at arms to rush in and catch her
with her hair done up in rags.

As she watched and held her breath, the snake unwound itself and
moved off the cot. She couldn't see any rattles on its tail, and she
slowly let out her breath. The snake undulated across the grass and
she stared at it, fascinated. She hadn't known a reptile could be so
graceful. "How do they do that?" she asked herself, as the snake
slithered into the grass at the edge of the tent. "I must remember to
ask Hart."

She pulled on her wrapper and poked her head out of the tent.
The sun was just coming up, and the buildings were tinted with the
most delicious shade of pink. She marveled that she could ever have
thought the place ugly.

Her first letter from Hart was handed to her three days later at
Mail Call. She ripped open the envelope and drew out a long, narrow
sheet. She read as she walked along the edge of the parade ground.

Dearest Emma,
    Pardon this stationery, but I forgot to take any along, and be-
sides, this works better for letters than in the outhouse.
    Good news. We're going to be garrisoned here permanently,
so you'll be moving quite soon, perhaps within the next few
days.
    Bad news. Brace yourself. There aren't any quarters avail-
able, so we'll have to make do in a tent.

Emma stood still and laughed out loud. A soldier with a large *P*
painted on the back of his shirt stopped spearing trash and looked at
her, but she didn't notice. She read on.

    It won't be that bad. The CO swears there will be quarters
ready by winter.
    Am looking forward to seeing you soon. I can't express how
much I miss you.

                                                    Love,
                                                    Hart

She was almost back to her tent when the adjutant caught up with
her.

"Mrs. Sanders," he began. His Adam's apple bobbed, and he
started to rub his head.

"It's all right, Lieutenant," she broke in, "I've already heard.
When am I leaving?"

"In the morning."

"I'll be ready."

As she was repacking her trunks that evening, she remembered something her mother had said to her when she left on the train to join Hart in Cheyenne. Mother had dabbed at her eyes and said over and over, "Such brave men, Emma, such brave men!"

Emma smiled to herself.

THE TONTO WOMAN

Elmore Leonard

A time would come, within a few years, when Ruben Vega would go
to the church in Benson, kneel in the confessional and say to the
priest, "Bless me, Father, for I have sinned. It has been thirty-seven
years since my last confession . . . Since then I have fornicated with
many women, maybe eight hundred. No, not that many, considering
my work. Maybe six hundred only." And the priest would say, "Do
you mean bad women or good women?" And Ruben Vega would
say, "They are all good, Father." He would tell the priest he had
stolen, in that time, about twenty thousand head of cattle but only
maybe fifteen horses. The priest would ask him if he had committed
murder. Ruben Vega would say no. "All that stealing you've done,"
the priest would say, "you've never killed anyone?" And Ruben
Vega would say, "Yes, of course, but it was not to commit murder.
You understand the distinction? Not to *kill* someone to take a life,
but only to save my own."

Even in this time to come, concerned with dying in a state of sin,
he would be confident. Ruben Vega knew himself, when he was
right, when he was wrong.

Now, in a time before, with no thought of dying, but with the same
confidence and caution that kept him alive, he watched a woman
bathe. Watched from a mesquite thicket on the high bank of a wash.

She bathed at the pump that stood in the yard of the adobe, the
woman pumping and then stooping to scoop the water from the basin
of the irrigation ditch that led off to a vegetable patch of corn and
beans. Her dark hair was pinned up in a swirl, piled on top of her
head. She was bare to her gray skirt, her upper body pale white, glis-
tening wet in the late afternoon sunlight. Her arms were very thin,
her breasts small, but there they were with the rosy blossoms on the
tips and Ruben Vega watched them as she bathed, as she raised one
arm and her hand rubbed soap under the arm and down over her

ribs. Ruben Vega could almost feel those ribs, she was so thin. He felt sorry for her, for all the women like her, stick women drying up in the desert, waiting for a husband to ride in smelling of horse and sweat and leather, lice living in his hair.

There was a stock tank and rickety windmill off in the pasture, but it was empty graze, all dust and scrub. So the man of the house had moved his cows to grass somewhere and would be coming home soon, maybe with his sons. The woman appeared old enough to have young sons. Maybe there was a little girl in the house. The chimney appeared cold. Animals stood in a mesquite-pole corral off to one side of the house, a cow and a calf and a dun-colored horse, that was all. There were a few chickens. No buckboard or wagon. No clothes drying on the line. A lone woman here at day's end.

From fifty yards he watched her. She stood looking this way now, into the red sun, her face raised. There was something strange about her face. Like shadow marks on it, though there was nothing near enough to her to cast shadows.

He waited until she finished bathing and returned to the house before he mounted his bay and came down the wash to the pasture. Now as he crossed the yard, walking his horse, she would watch him from the darkness of the house and make a judgment about him. When she appeared again it might be with a rifle, depending on how she saw him.

Ruben Vega said to himself, Look, I'm a kind person. I'm not going to hurt nobody.

She would see a bearded man in a cracked straw hat with the brim bent to his eyes. Black beard, with a revolver on his hip and another beneath the leather vest. But look at my eyes, Ruben Vega thought. Let me get close enough so you can see my eyes.

Stepping down from the bay he ignored the house, let the horse drink from the basin of the irrigation ditch as he pumped water and knelt to the wooden platform and put his mouth to the rusted pump spout. Yes, she was watching him. Looking up now at the doorway he could see part of her: a coarse shirt with sleeves too long and the gray skirt. He could see strands of dark hair against the whiteness of the shirt, but could not see her face.

As he rose, straightening, wiping his mouth, he said, "May we use some of your water, please?"

The woman didn't answer him.

He moved away from the pump to the hardpack, hearing the ching of his spurs, removed his hat and gave her a little bow. "Ruben Vega, at your service. Do you know Diego Luz, the horsebreaker?" He pointed off toward a haze of foothills. "He lives up there with his family and delivers horses to the big ranch, the Circle-Eye. Ask Diego Luz, he'll tell you I'm a person of trust." He waited a moment. "May I ask how you're called?" Again he waited.

"You watched me," the woman said.

Ruben Vega stood with his hat in his hand facing the woman who was half in shadow in the doorway. He said, "I waited. I didn't want to frighten you."

"You watched me," she said again.

"No, I respect your privacy."

She said, "The others look. They come and watch."

He wasn't sure who she meant. Maybe anyone passing by. He said, "You see them watching?"

She said, "What difference does it make?" She said then, "You come from Mexico, don't you?"

"Yes, I was there. I'm here and there, working as a drover." Ruben Vega shrugged. "What else is there to do, uh?" Showing her he was resigned to his station in life.

"You'd better leave," she said.

When he didn't move, the woman came out of the doorway into light and he saw her face clearly for the first time. He felt a shock within him and tried to think of something to say, but could only stare at the blue lines tattooed on her face: three straight lines on each cheek that extended from her cheekbones to her jaw, markings that seemed familiar, though he could not in this moment identify them.

He was conscious of himself standing in the open with nothing to say, the woman staring at him with curiosity, as though wondering if he would hold her gaze and look at her. Like there was nothing unusual about her countenance. Like it was common to see a woman with her face tattooed and you might be expected to comment, if you said anything at all, "Oh, that's a nice design you have there. Where did you have it done?" That would be one way—if you couldn't say something interesting about the weather or about the price of cows in Benson.

Ruben Vega, his mind empty of pleasantries, certain he would never see the woman again, said, "Who did that to you?"

She cocked her head in an easy manner, studying him as he studied her, and said, "Do you know, you're the first person who's come right out and asked."

"Mojave," Ruben Vega said, "but there's something different. Mojaves tattoo their chins only, I believe."

"And look like they were eating berries," the woman said. "I told

them if you're going to do it, do it all the way. Not like a blue
dribble."

It was in her eyes and in the tone of her voice, a glimpse of the
rage she must have felt. No trace of fear in the memory, only cold
anger. He could hear her telling the Indians—this skinny woman,
probably a girl then—until they did it her way and marked her good
for all time. Imprisoned her behind the blue marks on her face.

"How old were you?"

"You've seen me and had your water," the woman said, "now
leave."

It was the same type of adobe house as the woman's but with a
great difference. There was life here, the warmth of family: children
sleeping now, Diego Luz's wife and her mother cleaning up after the
meal as the two men sat outside in horsehide chairs and smoked and
looked at the night. At one time they had both worked for a man
named Sundeen and packed running irons to vent the brands on the
cattle they stole. Ruben Vega was still an outlaw, in his fashion,
while Diego Luz broke green horses and sold them to cattle companies.

They sat at the edge of the ramada, an awning made of mesquite,
and stared at pinpoints of light in the universe. Ruben Vega asked
about the extent of graze this season, where the large herds were that
belonged to the Maricopa and the Circle-Eye. He had been thinking
of cutting out maybe a hundred—he wasn't greedy—and drive them
south to sell to the mine companies. He had been scouting the Circle-
Eye range, he said, when he came to the strange woman . . .

The Tonto woman, Diego Luz said. Everyone called her that now.

Yes, she had been living there, married a few years, when she went
to visit her family who lived on the Gila above Painted Rock. Well,
some Yavapai came looking for food. They clubbed her parents and
two small brothers to death and took the girl north with them. The
Yavapai traded her to the Mojave as a slave . . .

"And they marked her," Ruben Vega said.

"Yes, so when she died the spirits would know she was Mojave
and not drag her soul down into a rathole," Diego Luz said.

"Better to go to heaven with your face tattooed," Ruben Vega
said, "than not at all. Maybe so."

During a drought the Mojave traded her to a band of Tonto
Apaches for two mules and a bag of salt and one day she appeared at
Bowie with the Tontos that were brought in to be sent to Oklahoma.
Among the desert Indians twelve years and returned home last
spring.

"It put age on her," Ruben Vega said. "But what about her husband?"

"Her husband? He banished her," Diego Luz said, "like a leper. Unclean from living among the red niggers. No one speaks of her to him, it isn't allowed."

Ruben Vega frowned. There was something he didn't understand. He said, "Wait a minute—"

And Diego Luz said, "Don't you know who her husband is? Mr. Isham himself, man, of the Circle-Eye. She comes home to find her husband a rich man. He don't live in that hut no more. No, he owns a hundred miles of graze and a house it took them two years to build, the glass and bricks brought in by the Southern Pacific. Sure, the railroad comes and he's a rich cattleman in only a few years."

"He makes her live there alone?"

"She's his wife, he provides for her. But that's all. Once a month his segundo named Bonnet rides out there with supplies and has someone shoe her horse and look at the animals."

"But to live in the desert," Ruben Vega said, still frowning, thoughtful, "with a rusty pump . . ."

"Look at her," Diego Luz said. "What choice does she have?"

It was hot down in this scrub pasture, a place to wither and die. Ruben Vega loosened the new willow-root straw that did not yet conform to his head, though he had shaped the brim to curve down on one side and rise slightly on the other so that the brim slanted across the vision of his left eye. He held on his lap a nearly flat cardboard box that bore the name *L. S. Weiss Mercantile Store.*

The woman gazed up at him, shading her eyes with one hand. Finally she said, "You look different."

"The beard began to itch," Ruben Vega said, making no mention of the patches of gray he had studied in the hotel-room mirror. "So I shaved it off." He rubbed a hand over his jaw and smoothed down the tips of his mustache that was still full and seemed to cover his mouth. When he stepped down from the bay and approached the woman standing by the stick-fence corral she looked off into the distance and back again.

She said, "You shouldn't be here."

Ruben Vega said, "Your husband doesn't want nobody to look at you. Is that it?" He held the store box, waiting for her to answer. "He has a big house with trees and the San Pedro River in his yard. Why doesn't he hide you there?"

She looked off again and said, "If they find you here, they'll shoot you."

"They," Ruben Vega said. "The ones who watch you bathe? Work for your husband and keep more than a close eye on you and you'd like to hit them with something, wipe the grins from their faces."

"You better leave," the woman said.

The blue lines on her face were like claw marks, though not as wide as fingers: indelible lines of dye etched into her flesh with a cactus needle, the color worn and faded but still vivid against her skin, the blue matching her eyes.

He stepped close to her, raised his hand to her face and touched the markings gently with the tips of his fingers, feeling nothing. He raised his eyes to hers. She was staring at him. He said, "You're in there, aren't you? Behind these little bars. They don't seem like much. Not enough to hold you."

She said nothing, but seemed to be waiting.

He said to her, "You should brush your hair. Brush it every day . . ."

"Why?" the woman said.

"To feel good. You need to wear a dress. A little parasol to match."

"I'm asking you to leave," the woman said. But didn't move from his hand, with its yellowed, stained nails, that was like a fist made of old leather.

"I'll tell you something if I can," Ruben Vega said. "I know women all my life, all kinds of women in the way they look and dress, the way they adorn themselves according to custom. Women are always a wonder to me. When I'm not with a woman I think of them as all the same because I'm thinking of one thing. You understand?"

"Put a sack over their head," the woman said.

"Well, I'm not thinking of what she looks like then, when I'm out in the mountains or somewhere," Ruben Vega said. "That part of her doesn't matter. But when I'm *with* the woman, ah, then I realize how they are all different. You say, of course. This isn't a revelation to you. But maybe it is when you think about it some more."

The woman's eyes changed, turned cold. "You want to go to bed with me? Is that what you're saying, why you bring a gift?"

He looked at her with disappointment, an expression of weariness. But then he dropped the store box and took her to him gently, placing his hands on her shoulders, feeling her small bones in his grasp as he brought her in against him and his arms went around her.

He said, "You're gonna die here. Dry up and blow away."

She said, "Please . . ." Her voice hushed against him.

"They wanted only to mark your chin," Ruben Vega said, "in the custom of those people. But you wanted your own marks, didn't you? *Your* marks, not like anyone else . . . Well, you got them." After a moment he said to her, very quietly, "Tell me what you want."

The hushed voice close to him said, "I don't know."

He said, "Think about it and remember something. There is no one else in the world like you."

He reined the bay to move out and saw the dust trail rising out of the old pasture, three riders coming, and heard the woman say, "I told you. Now it's too late."

A man on a claybank and two young riders eating his dust, finally separating to come in abreast, reined to a walk as they reached the pump and the irrigation ditch. The woman, walking from the corral to the house, said to them, "What do you want? I don't need anything, Mr. Bonnet."

So this would be the Circle-Eye foreman on the claybank. The man ignored her, his gaze holding on Ruben Vega with a solemn expression, showing he was going to be dead serious. A chew formed a lump in his jaw. He wore army suspenders and sleeve garters, his shirt buttoned up at the neck. As old as you are, Ruben Vega thought, a man who likes a tight feel of security and is serious about his business.

Bonnet said to him finally, "You made a mistake."

"I don't know the rules," Ruben Vega said.

"She told you to leave her be. That's the only rule there is. But you bought yourself a dandy new hat and come back here."

"That's some hat," one of the young riders said. This one held a single-shot Springfield across his pommel. The foreman, Bonnet, turned in his saddle and said something to the other rider who unhitched his rope and began shaking out a loop, hanging it nearly to the ground.

It's a show, Ruben Vega thought. He said to Bonnet, "I was leaving."

Bonnet said, "Yes, indeed, you are. On the off end of a rope. We're gonna drag you so you'll know the ground and never cross this land again."

The rider with the Springfield said, "Gimme your hat, mister, so's you don't get it dirty."

At this point Ruben Vega nudged his bay and began moving in on the foreman who straightened, looking over at the roper and said, "Well, tie onto him."

But Ruben Vega was close to the foreman now, the bay taller than the claybank and would move the claybank if the man on his back told him to. Ruben Vega watched the foreman's eyes moving and knew the roper was coming around behind him. Now the foreman turned his head to spit and let go a stream that spattered the hard-pack close to the bay's forelegs.

"Stand still," Bonnet said, "and we'll get her done easy. Or you can run and get snubbed out of your chair. Either way."

Ruben Vega was thinking that he could drink with this ramrod and they'd tell each other stories until they were drunk. The man had thought it would be easy: chase off a Mexican gunnysacker who'd come sniffing the boss's wife. A kid who was good with a rope and another one who could shoot cans off the fence with an old Springfield should be enough.

Ruben Vega said to Bonnet, "Do you know who I am?"

"Tell us," Bonnet said, "so we'll know what the cat drug in and we drug out."

And Ruben Vega said, because he had no choice, "I hear the rope in the air, the one with the rifle is dead. Then you. Then the roper."

His words drew silence because there was nothing more to be said. In the moments that Ruben Vega and the one named Bonnet stared at each other, the woman came out to them holding a revolver, an old Navy Colt, which she raised and laid the barrel against the muzzle of the foreman's claybank.

She said, "Leave now, Mr. Bonnet, or you'll walk nine miles to shade."

There was no argument, little discussion, a few grumbling words. The Tonto woman was still Mrs. Isham. Bonnet rode away with his young hands and a new silence came over the yard.

Ruben Vega said, "He believes you'd shoot his horse."

The woman said, "He believes I'd cut steaks, and eat it, too. It's how I'm seen after twelve years of that other life."

Ruben Vega began to smile. The woman looked at him and in a few moments she began to smile with him. She shook her head then, but continued to smile. He said to her, "You could have a good time if you want to."

She said, "How, scaring people?"

He said, "If you feel like it." He said, "Get the present I brought you and open it."

He came back for her the next day in a Concord buggy, wearing his new willow-root straw and a cutaway coat over his revolvers, the coat he'd rented at a funeral parlor. Mrs. Isham wore the pale blue and white lace-trimmed dress he'd bought at Weiss's store, sat primly on the bustle and held the parasol against the afternoon sun all the way to Benson, ten miles, and up the main street to the Charles Crooker Hotel where the drummers and cattlemen and railroad men sitting in their front-porch rockers stared and stared.

They walked past the manager and into the dining room before Ruben Vega removed his hat and pointed to the table he liked, one against the wall between two windows. The waitress in her starched uniform was wide-eyed taking them over and getting them seated. It was early and the dining room was not half filled.

"The place for a quiet dinner," Ruben Vega said. "You see how quiet it is?"

"Everybody's looking at me," Sarah Isham said to the menu in front of her.

Ruben Vega said, "I thought they were looking at me. All right, soon they'll be used to it."

She glanced up and said, "People are leaving."

He said, "That's what you do when you finish eating, you leave."

She looked at him, staring, and said, "Who are you?"

"I told you."

"Only your name."

"You want me to tell you the truth, why I came here?"

"Please."

"To steal some of your husband's cattle."

She began to smile and he smiled. She began to laugh and he laughed, looking openly at the people looking at them, but not bothered by them. Of course they'd look. How could they help it? A Mexican rider and a woman with blue stripes on her face sitting at a table in the hotel dining room, laughing. He said, "Do you like fish? I know your Indian brothers didn't serve you none. It's against their religion. Some things are for religion, as you know, and some things are against it. We spend all our lives learning customs. Then they change them. I'll tell you something else if you promise not to be angry or point your pistol at me. Something else I could do the rest of my life. I could look at you and touch you and love you."

Her hand moved across the linen tablecloth to his with the cracked, yellowed nails and took hold of it, clutched it.

She said, "You're going to leave."

He said, "When it's time."

She said, "I know you. I don't know anyone else."

He said, "You're the loveliest woman I've ever met. And the strongest. Are you ready? I think the man coming now is your husband."

It seemed strange to Ruben Vega that the man stood looking at him and not at his wife. The man seemed not too old for her, as he had expected, but too self-important. A man with a very serious demeanor, as though his business had failed or someone in his family had passed away. The man's wife was still clutching the hand with the gnarled fingers. Maybe that was it. Ruben Vega was going to lift her hand from his, but then thought, Why? He said as pleasantly as he was able, "Yes, can I help you?"

Mr. Isham said, "You have one minute to mount up and ride out of town."

"Why don't you sit down," Ruben Vega said, "have a glass of wine with us?" He paused and said, "I'll introduce you to your wife."

Sarah Isham laughed; not loud but with a warmth to it and Ruben Vega had to look at her and smile. It seemed all right to release her hand now. As he did he said, "Do you know this gentleman?"

"I'm not sure I've had the pleasure," Sarah Isham said. "Why does he stand there?"

"I don't know," Ruben Vega said. "He seems worried about something."

"I've warned you," Mr. Isham said. "You can walk out or be dragged out."

Ruben Vega said, "He has something about wanting to drag people. Why is that?" And again heard Sarah's laugh, a giggle now that she covered with her hand. Then she looked up at her husband, her face with its blue tribal lines raised to the soft light of the dining room.

She said, "John, look at me . . . Won't you please sit with us?"

Now it was as if the man had to make a moral decision, first consult his conscience, then consider the manner in which he would pull the chair out—the center of attention. When finally he was seated, upright on the chair and somewhat away from the table, Ruben Vega thought, All that to sit down. He felt sorry for the man now, because the man was not the kind who could say what he felt.

Sarah said, "John, can you look at me?"

He said, "Of course I can."

"Then do it. I'm right here."

"We'll talk later," her husband said.

She said, "When? Is there a visitor's day?"

"You'll be coming to the house, soon."

"You mean to see it?"

"To live there."

She looked at Ruben Vega with just the trace of a smile, a sad one. Then said to her husband, "I don't know if I want to. I don't know you. So I don't know if I want to be married to you. Can you understand that?"

Ruben Vega was nodding as she spoke. He could understand it. He heard the man say, "But we *are* married. I have an obligation to you and I respect it. Don't I provide for you?"

Sarah said, "Oh, my God—" and looked at Ruben Vega. "Did you hear that? He provides for me." She smiled again, not able to hide it, while her husband began to frown, confused.

"He's a generous man," Ruben Vega said, pushing up from the table. He saw her smile fade, though something warm remained in her eyes. "I'm sorry I have to leave. I'm going on a trip tonight, south, and first I have to pick up a few things." He moved around the table to take one of her hands in his, not caring what the husband thought. He said, "You'll do all right, whatever you decide. Just keep in mind there's no one else in the world like you."

She said, "I can always charge admission. Do you think ten cents a look is too high?"

"At least that," Ruben Vega said. "But you'll think of something better."

He left her there in the dining room of the Charles Crooker Hotel in Benson, Arizona—maybe to see her again sometime, maybe not— and went out with a good conscience to take some of her husband's cattle.

THE WOOING OF
ROSY MALONE

Wayne D. Overholser

I am not by nature a philosophical man, but I have often wondered about the part that fate plays in one's life. How much of our lives is determined by destiny, or how much depends on our decisions? Just being at a certain place at a certain time when a certain thing happens is the kind of thing I mean. My presence in Garnet when the Rawlins gang rode into town is a case in point.

My name is Jim Dance and I have a little spread a couple of miles south of Garnet. I own about fifty head of cattle, enough to scratch out a living along with the work I do for one of my neighbors. I've also planted an apple orchard and in another five years I should turn a profit. Of course I aim to build up my herd, too. I figure I'm about as well fixed as any young cowboy in the county.

I'm also in love with Rosy Malone, the Garnet schoolteacher, and I want to give her a comfortable life. The problem is she won't marry me. I thought she loved me and liked my place. She came out every week or so to clean it up and she always cooked a big meal for me when she was there, so I had trouble figuring out why she wouldn't marry me.

Rosy had other men chasing her, so she had plenty of choice, but I always thought I had the inside track. She'd give me phony excuses for saying no, like, "I'm not ready to give up my independence." Or, "The children need me." Or, "I just can't face the responsibilities of marriage."

That's the way it stood that October afternoon when I rode into Garnet to pick up my Winchester. I'd gone hunting the day before and had had two good chances to bring in some camp meat, but I missed both shots. I'm a good shot with a rifle and there was no excuse for missing either one, so I told myself my sights were off and I wanted the gunsmith in Garnet to check them.

I hated to admit it, but the truth was I'd got worked up over Rosy's last turndown. We'd been to a dance on Saturday night and I'd had a hell of a good time and I thought Rosy had, too.

The schoolhouse is on the edge of a thick growth of lodgepole pines north of town, and the teacherage, a one-room log cabin, sits behind the schoolhouse and is hidden from the road. I didn't like her living there by herself and had told her so more than once, but she said she wasn't afraid, the cabin was comfortable and free, and she had a gun and was a good shot. That ended the discussion.

When we got to her place after the dance, she made a pot of coffee and served me a slice of chocolate cake. Then I hugged and kissed her before I left, and she responded more than she usually did, so I thought that was a good time to ask her for the umpteenth time to marry me.

She pulled away from me and walked across the room and stood by the stove. She said, "Jim, I like you better than any other man I know, and I want to marry you, but I'm afraid to. You've got a violent streak in you that comes out once in a while and it scares me. Some day you're going to kill a man or be killed."

I stood there just kind of paralyzed and stared at her. I guess I stared about a minute, feeling as if she had taken a blacksnake to my back. She was a very pretty girl, with a figure that made men want to keep on staring at her. She had blue eyes and auburn hair that curled all over her head. I guess if I could have created a dream girl to marry, she would have looked just like Rosy Malone. Standing there just looking at her, I knew that for the first time she was giving me the real reason she didn't want to marry me.

I turned around and walked out. I mounted and rode home. The next day I hurt all over. I couldn't forget what she'd said. I thought it was unfair, and I wondered what kind of man she wanted. I just had never thought of myself as a violent man.

Sure, I had been considered a little wild when I was younger. I'd had my share of barroom brawls and I had a reputation for not taking anything off anybody, but I also knew I was steadier and worked harder and would give Rosy a better life than the other men she went with.

I didn't sleep any Saturday night. I steamed about it all day Sunday and on Monday I went hunting instead of staying home and working. Blaming those missed shots on my sights was an excuse and I knew it in my guts, but I sure as hell couldn't bring myself to admit it. I took my rifle into Garnet to check the sights and told the gunsmith I'd be back on Tuesday to pick it up.

That's how I happened to be in Garnet when the Rawlins bunch rode into town. I wasn't surprised when I walked into the store and the gunsmith laid my Winchester on the counter, saying, "Jim, there's nothing wrong with your sights. I wish all the guns I had in here shot as true as this one does. I'd like to buy . . ."

I was reaching down to pick up the Winchester when I heard two shots. It took a second or two for me to realize they came from the direction of the bank which was about half a block to the east. At least that was the way it sounded.

I grabbed the rifle up off the counter and ran out through the street door. Three horses were in front of the bank. One man was in the saddle, one was trying to mount, and a third one was coming out of the bank, a couple of bags of coins in one hand and a gun in the other that he was holstering as he ran.

Levering a shell into the chamber, I cut loose, taking the man who was leaving the bank. I knocked him flat, then fired at the man who had just stepped into the saddle and sent him sprawling as his boogered horse bucked once and took off down the street. By this time the third man was cracking steel to his horse and had reached the end of the business block when I got off my third shot. I should have saved my fourth bullet because the bank robber disappeared around the corner just as I was squeezing the trigger.

It was all over in about ten seconds. A dozen men boiled out of the doorways along Main Street and surrounded the two men lying in the dust, Doc Muller among them.

By the time I got there, Muller had examined both men and was standing up announcing that they were dead. Somebody demanded, "Who got 'em?"

The gunsmith who had run on ahead of me said, "Jim Dance done it. I seen it all. Best shooting I ever saw."

They shook my hand and told me I'd saved the bank and their money and that meant saving the town and the county. Then someone came out of the bank, white-faced and trembling, and announced that Vic Sorrel, the banker, had been killed.

"Trying to get his gun out of a drawer, looked like," the man said. "They just gunned him down."

By that time I'd had a good look at the men I'd killed. They were young and bearded, maybe twenty or twenty-one. One had a hole through his head, the other one in his chest. A lot of blood was on the ground.

I guess it was the blood that did it. I knew I was going to be sick, so I headed for my horse that was still hitched in front of the gun shop. I didn't quite make it to my horse, so I had no chance to get out of town. I stood there in the street beside the hitchrack throwing up everything I'd eaten for a week. At least it felt that way.

By the time I was over it, the preacher, Paul Adams, had reached me. He said, "Don't have any regrets, Jim. They were bad ones. They've killed a lot of men including Vic Sorrel who was a good friend to everybody in town."

I had a bitter taste in my mouth as I took my bandanna out of my pocket and wiped my lips. I wasn't thinking very straight, but I knew what the preacher said was true. Vic had loaned me the money to get started, saying it was good business to help young, hardworking men who dreamed about working for themselves.

"The community needs men like you, Jim," he said as he shook hands with me.

Rosy's words about me having a violent streak came roaring back into my mind as I stood looking at the preacher. I guess she was right because I hadn't thought about what I was doing. I'd just started shooting. But Vic Sorrel had had the same streak of violence, I thought. He'd tried to defend the bank and other people's money and he would have killed the outlaws if they'd given him a chance.

I stepped into the saddle and rode home, not even thanking the preacher for what he had said. I didn't work any that day, either, not anything important anyhow, just stood around repairing harness and cleaning out the corrals and doing any busywork I could find to keep my mind off those two young men I had seen lying in the street.

Just before dark the sheriff, Don Bailey, rode out from town. He said, "You done a good job, Jim. I was out at my ranch when I heard what had happened. By the time I got to town and rounded up a posse, old Bill Rawlins was long gone. We couldn't pick up his trail."

"Rawlins?" I asked.

I was a little shocked. The Rawlins gang was well known in Garnet because they holed up in the mountains to the west of town when they weren't out robbing banks. They never bothered anyone within fifty miles of town. I guess they figured that if they let us alone, we'd let them alone. Why they had changed their pattern was more than I could figure out, so I asked the sheriff.

"Hell, who knows how an outlaw's mind works," Bailey said. "Maybe they figured on leaving the country and this was their last big job before they headed for Mexico. Anyway, I'm glad you got the boys. Old Bill will probably leave the country, now that he's alone.

"Then again, maybe he won't. He's just naturally a mean son of a bitch. He's abused women until they've died. He's shot men in the back. He's tortured them until they've begged him to kill them."

He cleared his throat, then went on, "If he finds out who shot his boys, he'll be back to get you. I don't know what to tell you, I just don't have the deputies to keep one out here to protect you. I can send a man out for a couple of nights just to be sure Rawlins don't sneak up on you."

"No, I can look out for myself," I said.

"There's a reward out for the Rawlins boys," he said. "Five hundred dollars for each of 'em. I'll see you get it." He hesitated, then asked, "You sure you don't want any protection?"

"I'm sure," I said.

He rode off and I walked over to my front porch and sat down. While the sheriff was telling me about Bill Rawlins, a terrible thought had upset the hell out of me. Suppose Rawlins holed up somewhere around here or stopped at some ranch for supper and heard about me and Rosy being my girl. He might come after her, knowing that would be the way to hurt me.

I hated like hell to face Rosy. By now she'd probably heard what had happened and she'd remind me that she had told me what I was and now I'd proved it. I figured that saving the bank wouldn't cut any ice with her.

Still, if it did happen to Rosy, I'd never forgive myself, so I saddled up and rode to her place. When she opened the door to my knock and saw who it was, she backed up and an expression came over her face I had never seen before. I judged from the looks of her red eyes she had been crying.

"Go away, Jim," she said.

That wasn't what I expected her to say. I thought she'd tell me I had the mark of Cain on me, that I was born to hang, that she'd be afraid to ever be alone with me again. But she didn't say anything like that. I had a feeling she was grieving because her opinion of me was right and therefore she knew she could never marry me.

I wasn't going to be run off before I said what I had come to say, so I just stood there and said, "You're going to listen to me. Then I'll leave you alone. The men I shot were part of the Rawlins gang, the sons of old Bill Rawlins. He got away. The sheriff told me he was a bad one, the kind who would dry gulch me if he found out who shot his boys. We don't know where he is, but he may have circled back and stopped at some ranch for supper.

"This kind of news travels fast, so he may have heard who killed his sons. He may also have heard that you are my girl. If he did, I'd say the chances are he'll come after you. I want you to sleep in town for a few days until we know he's out of the country."

"I'm safe here," she said.

She stood her ground as if she were frozen, her face set and cold. I got sore then, thinking she didn't want to hear my side of it. I guess I yelled at her when I said, "Damn it, Rosy, I saved the bank and maybe saved a lot of people. Those men deserved to die. They murdered Vic Sorrel."

"A human life is worth more than a bank or the money people have put in it," she said. "I could never have done what you did. All I know is that you killed two men."

"Then you won't go?"

"No," she answered.

I turned and left the cabin, knowing she had a stubborn streak a yard wide and I could stand there all night and argue with her without changing her mind. I mounted and started home, then I began thinking that if Bill Rawlins did come back, I couldn't bear to think of what he'd do to Rosy. Her being stubborn wouldn't help her a damn bit. If she wouldn't save herself, then I'd have to do it.

I rode back and left my horse in the lodgepoles far enough from the teacherage so Rosy wouldn't know it was there. An almost full moon was coming up in the east, and if I'd left the horse close to the cabin, she might see it if she stepped outside before she went to bed.

I lifted my Winchester from the boot and eased back through the trees until I was close enough to see her door. She'd surely have sense to lock her door, and by the time Rawlins kicked it in, I'd be on top of him. I wasn't sure how I'd handle him. I couldn't shoot because I might hit Rosy. Her bed was opposite the door and she'd rear up when she heard the door getting kicked in, so she could very well stop the slug instead of Rawlins if I wasn't careful.

When I sat down with my back to a tree, my Winchester cradled across my lap, I thought I wouldn't have any trouble staying awake, but I hadn't slept much since Saturday night and all of a sudden it caught up with me. I found myself nodding and then jerking awake and wondering how long I had slept. I got up and walked around through the pines for a couple of minutes, then came back and sat down to do it all over again.

I don't know how many times that happened, but the moon was riding high above me when I heard Rosy's door being kicked open. I jumped up and headed for the cabin on the run, but I was groggy and bleary-eyed and still didn't know just what I was going to do.

It had to be Rawlins. I cursed myself for staying as far from Rosy's door as I had, but I was lucky in one regard. He took time to light a lamp, saying, "So you're Dance's girl. Well, I'm going to carve you up good and I want to see what I'm doing."

I had a crazy feeling I was running through molasses and I wouldn't get there in time to save Rosy. Rawlins pulled a knife and turned to Rosy who was sitting up in bed so terrified she couldn't even scream.

I plunged through the door before Rawlins reached Rosy's bed. I yelled "Rawlins" just to turn him away from Rosy. I aimed to shoot the instant I could get Rosy out of the line of fire, but I never did. There was a two-inch lift of the cabin floor above the ground, and as I charged through the door, my Winchester on the ready, I caught a boot toe and went sprawling. As I fell, I cracked my head on the side of the stove. Somehow that turned me half over so I lay on my side staring at Rawlins who had wheeled the instant I yelled at him.

He came at me with his knife in his hand. I saw an explosion of stars and although I wasn't knocked cold, I couldn't speak and I couldn't move. Rawlins was grinning when he came toward me, not hurrying because I guess he saw I was paralyzed.

I tried to lift a leg to kick him in the crotch, but I couldn't move a muscle. I cursed myself for my awkwardness; I expected to feel his blade in my belly the next second, but it didn't happen. A gun roared and Rawlins toppled forward on his face to lie beside me.

Then I saw that Rosy was holding a gun, smoke slowly twisting from the muzzle. She couldn't seem to move, either, or at least not for a few seconds, and then she slowly put her feet on the floor and walked toward me.

She got down on her knees and held my head in her lap, kind of crooning to me. She was pale, but she had control of herself then. I don't know how long it took me to get over that knockout fall, but the first thing I did when I could move was to reach up and pull her face down to mine and kiss her. When she lifted her head and I could move mine enough to look at Rawlins, I saw that he was dead. She was right about being able to use a gun.

After that things began to take their natural shape and size, and although my head hurt like hell and blood was dripping down the side of my face, I felt good just to be alive. I got to my feet with a little help from Rosy, swayed there for a moment as I clutched the end of the table, then I got a blanket off the bed and covered Rawlins' body.

"You can't sleep here the rest of the night," I said. "I'll take you to Paul Adams. He and Minerva will be glad to put you up. Then I'll get the sheriff out of bed and tell him what happened. He'll move the body."

She didn't argue. She didn't say anything, but she nodded as she took my hand. I blew the lamp out and we walked through the pines to town. When we reached Main Street, we turned toward the parsonage. Rosy still hadn't said a word.

I had to pound on the parsonage door three times before Paul padded across the front room and opened the door. He was wearing a robe over his nightgown and held a lamp in one hand as he peered at us.

"Rosy has had some trouble," I said. "She'll tell you about it. I've got to go fetch the sheriff. I thought you could give her a bed for the rest of the night."

He nodded and said, "Be glad to. I'll go get Minerva up."

I started to turn away, but Rosy caught my arm. "Paul," she said, her voice shaky, "I guess it's no secret that Jim has wanted me to marry him for a long time. I kept turning him down for what I thought was a good reason, but tonight I discovered it wasn't a reason at all. I want you to marry us in the morning." She turned to me and tried to smile and failed. "I discovered I'm no better than you are, Jim. Now I know how it was."

I held her in my arms and looked past her at Paul Adams who was staring at us goggle-eyed as if he thought we were both out of our minds. I said, "Early in the morning, Paul."

THE DEBT

Jeanne Williams

One of the articles agreed to by all members of the McBride Company when it was forming up in Iowa was that anyone who killed another member of the party during the trip to Oregon was to be tried and hanged. So when, a day west of Split Rock, Jed Hoffman shot Harry Drew in a card game, Jed didn't beg, though his tanned young face went pale and haggard when the other men found no way to call what he'd done anything but murder. Harry had a foul mouth, but it shouldn't have been answered with a gun.

Jed was well liked and it was a shame that his wife, Mary Ann, was big with their second child, but the articles had to be followed. Make exceptions and the fifteen interdependent families would lose all order, perhaps fatally, long before they got to Oregon. So Jed was hanged with the best rope they had to the best tree they could find along the sulky Sweetwater.

After he kissed Mary Ann and four-year-old Billy, Jed looked at his friends. "I know you got to do this. But since you're taking me, you owe it to Mary Ann to get her to Oregon."

"We'll do it," promised Tam McBride, the captain, a stocky man with a grizzled spade beard and brown eyes that were merry except when he had something like this to do.

Mary Ann didn't beg, either, but though Mrs. McBride tried to lead her away, she stood and watched Jed hang. She was thin, weathered past her twenty years by farm work and the wind and sun of the trail, but her eyes were like a mountain lake, blue-green and fathomless beneath dark brows that winged up at the sides, a strange contrast to hair the pale shade of the underleaf of a cottonwood.

She kept Billy's face buried in her skirt while the women murmured with shock and pity. When Jed's legs hung slack and his poor face was something no one should see and some of the men were sick and old Mrs. Steubens fainted, Mary Ann got a knife to cut Jed down.

Talt Braden took the knife and did it for her. Rangy, broad in the shoulder, Talt had straight black hair, a lean rock-hard face, eyes like a summer storm, and a half smile that seemed to mock the world. It was whispered that he'd been a squaw man, a trapper on the Yellowstone, till his woman died. He'd joined the company at Fort Laramie and knew a lot more about the country than the little Emigrants' Guide Tam McBride had previously relied on.

Not that there was much chance of losing the way. It was a devastated swath several miles wide in places, marked with dead oxen, horses and cattle, discarded furniture and belongings that had proved too heavy for the long ordeal, and a few graves. In order to prevent looting by Indians, most burials were made in the trail and driven over so that they were obliterated.

This was how Jed and the man he'd killed were buried, wrapped first in blankets because there was no wood for coffins. Talt helped cover the graves before he came over to Mary Ann.

"I'll drive your wagon."

She stared at him as if waking from a deep sleep. Her bewildered gaze moved over the hurrying company who were eager to get away from what they had done.

"I—I can't travel with these people."

"You can't stay here!"

"I can wait till another train comes along."

He swore. "That might be a week. Indians don't bother trains much but they're always ready for easy pickings." When she said nothing, Talt demanded roughly, "What about the kid? Think of him if you don't care about yourself."

She stroked Billy's blond head as he still clung to her. "I don't want to be beholden to anyone who had a hand in—in this."

"You won't be." Talt frowned. "It's something we owe." And without allowing her further argument, he lifted her up on the seat and put Billy beside her.

Mary Ann had always been one for keeping to herself. She had no real friends in the company and, with the reproach of Jed's death on them, people were relieved that Talt had taken on the responsibility of looking after the dead man's family. It took away the awkwardness of trying to talk to her when, no matter how friendly or matter-of-fact a body tried to be, Mary Ann just looked through you and wouldn't say anything past yes or no. She got even chillier after the children started teasing Billy.

"Your pa wet his pants when he died!" they'd taunt, when out of earshot of their elders. "His eyes booged out and his tongue was purple!"

Talt dragged a few of the boys by the scruffs of their necks over to their folks and saw they got whomped, but there's no way to stop a thing like that. Billy quit playing with the other youngsters and stuck close to his mama. Talt made him a willow flute and carved him a whole menagerie of bone animals, buffalo, horses, bear, antelope, beaver and coyotes. Billy had them march to funny little whistle tunes or made up long stories about them as he moved them around on the wagon seat or the ground. Folks began to wonder if he was touched in the head but they didn't dare talk to Mary Ann about it. When Mrs. McBride ventured a question to Talt, he just rared back on his heels and stared at her till she turned redder than a turkey gobbler's wattles.

"My God, woman!" That was all he said.

So, though Mary Ann's wagon moved along with the company, she and her little son were more like some kind of ghosts. They made everyone uneasy, squelched the jokes and laughter that helped ease such a grinding, monotonous journey. Still, it was an obligation to get Mary Ann to Oregon. No one questioned that.

For sure, if she'd had any appetite, she could have eaten better with Talt than ever she had with Jed. Talt was far and away the best hunter in the company and when Mary Ann couldn't fancy even hump or tongue of buffalo, he brought in sage grouse or caught fish to broil till they were a mouth-watering gold. After camp was made of an evening, he often took Billy to hunt for berries and wild turnips and onions. They often had a swim before they came back and if Billy's short legs were worn out, Talt brought him back on his shoulders.

"You're good to Billy," Mary Ann said one night after the boy had gone to sleep with the bone animals arranged close to him.

Talt shrugged. "Never had any folks. I know a kid can get lonesome."

She regarded him with the first real interest she'd shown in anything. "I was an orphan, too. My aunt raised me, talked on how Christian she was while she worked me like a slave. Couldn't get out of there fast enough—"

Her voice trailed off. She'd never said how she'd felt about her husband and she didn't say now. Just stared at the sunlit snow on top of the Wind Rivers to the north of where the company would cross the Continental Divide at South Pass, that broad, high plain that stretched for miles between the ranges.

At Pacific Springs, where water could for the first time be seen flowing toward the Pacific, the company found what seemed to be an abandoned wagon, amid signs of a hastily broken big encampment. Tam McBride went over to look and came back in a hurry, brown eyes wide with fright.

"Cholera!" he choked. "Woman's dead and the man's close to it." This was supposed to be the night's halting place, but he gave orders to move on. Most of the drivers were already ahead of him.

"Hold on!" called Talt. "One of you come drive Mrs. Hoffman."

"Why?" demanded McBride.

Talt was climbing down as he spoke, and his storm-colored eyes had lightning in them. "Man shouldn't die alone when there are people."

"He's out of his head," McBride argued. "And you could pick up the contagion." Talt didn't answer, just started for the death wagon. "You poke around here, man, and we don't want you rejoining the company!" McBride warned, sweat popping out on his seamed forehead. "Hell, it could take away every soul of us!"

"Don't worry," said Talt. "I'll pass you up and have my land staked before you cross the Snake."

He went on toward the wagon. McBride scowled, looked unhappily at Mary Ann, and then bellowed for one of the single men to come drive her. There was a scramble. Women were scarce out west and all the bachelors had been waiting for some hint in Mary Ann's behavior that would show she had properly decided she needed a man for herself and a father for her kids. No one had pushed. Talt had the inside track there. But at this opportunity, Mary Ann could have had her pick of the unmarried fellows.

Not even looking at them as they hustled around her wagon, she said to McBride, "I'll wait for Mr. Braden."

"You can't do that!" Tam growled.

"I will."

His eyes fell under her strange blue-green ones. "But you might catch the sickness! Little Billy might! Looky here, Mrs. Hoffman, this party owes it to you—"

She made a gesture with her hand as if she were throwing something away. "I'm sick of you and your whining about a debt! Do you think you can give back a man's life? I'm sick of being tied to you on account of your duty. Go along!"

Mrs. McBride made a helpless gesture. "Now, Mrs. Hoffman, Mary Ann—" Her voice thinned to a whisper. "You can't be wicked enough to risk your little boy! Let us take him."

"So the boys can make mock of him again?" Mary Ann hugged

her child against the swell of the one that was coming. "If he can't make it with us, he'd be better off dead than being kicked around like a stray cur! You better go fast. The wind might blow the cholera your direction!"

The McBrides paled and swung their wagon. One by one, under Mary Ann's sightless stare, the young single men, muttering, went back to their horses.

"Play with your animals," Mary Ann told Billy.

Heavily, she climbed down from the wagon. Talt, going for water, stopped in his tracks and shouted at her, "Go on with the others!"

She shook her head.

"You fool woman! Hurry up and rejoin the company."

"Reckon I owe you something."

"Is that the only word anyone knows? Owe?" He must have realized he couldn't budge her. "All right, wait if you're crazy enough! But you keep away from this wagon and me. If I don't come down with it in a week or two, I'd reckon we could travel along. Drive over to those willows and set up camp."

Talt dug a grave for the dead woman that afternoon. He brewed some herb drink for the man and got quite a lot of it down him but the sick man passed with next morning's dawn. Talt dug his grave, too, and burned the wagon and tainted possessions. He made his camp in sight of Mary Ann and the boy, but didn't go near them. For their meat, though, he managed to shoot a pronghorn a hundred yards from the wagon, which Mary Ann laboriously skinned and butchered. Talt shot another for himself and feasted.

He also kept constant watch for Indians. South Pass was a favorite spot for various tribes to skirmish with each other or just come looking for excitement. Shoshoni, Sioux, Snake and Crow. He sighed, wishing he'd told Mary Ann that. Then he reflected that if cholera wouldn't send her with the company, nothing could have. She smiled sometimes at Billy. Talt wished that she would smile at him.

Five mornings after the abandoned man had died, Mary Ann climbed off the shuck mattress in the wagon and glanced toward Talt's camp. Usually, he'd wave at her, shout a greeting. This morning, he lay in his blankets.

Fear gripped and squeezed her heart. *He's just tired,* she told herself stoutly. *Man has a right to sleep late if he's not going anywhere.* And because this just had to be the answer, she got breakfast before she'd let herself look over at Talt.

He hadn't moved.

"Talt!" she shouted. There was a panicky note in her cry. Little Billy gave a whimper and ran to her. That made her get hold of herself, force herself to think.

She'd heard that about half the people who got cholera died of it, some in a day, others taking closer to a week of terrible retching agony, fever and chills. Talt Braden, if she had anything to do with it, was going to be one of those who got well.

But Billy—

What if she got the sickness, too? Terror swirled over her but she fought it down. Surely a wagon train would be along soon, it was just a fluke that none had passed while they were camped by the springs. She had often doubted there was a God. Now she had to pray that there was and that He would take care of her son.

"Billy," she said, kneeling, swallowing to steady her voice and keep it calm and reassuring. "Talt may be sick and I have to take care of him. You've got to be a big boy and take care of your animals here at the wagon. I baked bread yesterday and there's cooked meat and that I've been smoking. You can gather berries but don't get out of sight of the wagon."

His mouth trembled and his blue eyes were bewildered. "But, Mama—"

"You can see me," she assured him. "We can wave at each other and you can play some tunes on your whistle. But you mustn't come over where you could get sick." She gave him a fierce squeeze. "Whatever happens, keep away from us till I tell you it's all right."

"Talt get well?" he pleaded, tightening his grip on her dress. Gently, she unpried the chubby brown fingers, dimpled so sweetly at the knuckles.

"Yes. He's going to get well. But you have to help. Go see if you can find some berries. If you do, put them right over there by that biggest sagebrush. Then I can give them to Talt."

"I'll get a lot of berries!" Billy promised. Clutching his whistle, he went off at a trot with a little bucket.

Mary Ann gathered up things she would need and moved across the space to Talt.

Talt's sunken eyes stared at her without recognition as she coaxed him to drink the tea she'd made from the herbs left from treating the stranger. She got a few swallows down him before he convulsed in long shuddering cramps. He threw up a thin, stinking bile, kept heaving when nothing more would come. When he collapsed, she bathed him, taking off his shirt and wondering where a white scar in the shoulder had come from.

The stomach cramps tortured him again. She heated their skillets and applied them to Talt's abdomen, wrapped in one of his shirts. His legs twitched and strained. She rubbed them, trying to work out the massed rigidity of spasmed muscles. It seemed an eternity that the cramps continued. She applied heat, rubbed his arms and legs, and talked, hoping that beneath his delirium, he could know someone was there.

Billy's whistle sounded after a time. She glanced up to see that he was cautiously depositing berries on a plate by the big sagebrush.

"For Talt!" he shouted.

Rising, she waved at him and went to get the fruit. Billy looked very small and vulnerable, standing uncertainly by the wagon. "Why don't you get some nice long grass for Midge and Sam?" she called.

The oxen were finding ample graze, but Billy would feel better if he had something to do. "Billy find good grass," he promised, and trotted off.

Mary Ann crushed the berries into water and got some of the thickened juice down Talt. She was encouraged when he didn't vomit at once, but within the hour, hideous cramps contorted the body which seemed to be shrinking before her eyes.

More heated skillets, more rubbing till her hands and shoulders ached. Sometimes his contortions and retching were so violent that she thought they must kill him, but his breath labored on. And thinking he surely needed fluid to replace all he was losing, she would wait for half an hour or so after a bout of retching and then get him to take tea or broth or the fruit drink.

Several times that long, hot day, Billy sounded his whistle. Mary Ann would walk as near the wagon as she dared and tell him how much the berries seemed to be helping Talt and make sure the boy was eating. Seeing her even for a few minutes seemed to reassure Billy and he would go back to playing with his animals, moving them up and down the wagon tongue.

As the setting sun made rose-gold of the high peaks of the Wind Rivers, Mary Ann looked down at Talt and thought he was resting easier. Or perhaps he was simply exhausted, slipping over that line between sleep and death?

Raising him against her breast, she gave him the rest of the fruit juice. At this altitude, the air cooled rapidly after sundown. She wrapped him warmly, went back to call good-night to Billy.

"Do you have your animals all ready to sleep?"

"All but bear. Bear's going to stand guard. He'll watch out for you and Talt, too, Mama."

"Thank him, honey. Now you cuddle up in the blankets and sleep sound."

"Talt sleep sound?"

"He's a lot better. Maybe you can find him some more berries tomorrow."

"I will." She heard him talking to his bear. Dear God, what if he should be left with only his toy animals for comfort? It didn't stand thinking about.

She wrapped up in her blankets, close enough to wake if Talt stirred much, and dropped instantly into slumber.

Twice that night, Talt's threshings roused her. She heated skillets, rubbed the knotting muscles, and got him to drink. He slept late next morning, face haggard and dark with whiskers that made his cheeks seem even more hollowed. But the dreadful vomiting and the worst cramping seemed to be over.

Billy brought more berries, and today Talt could relish their tart sweetness whole. Mary Ann enriched the broth with bits of meat and bread. Most of that day, Talt slept, but once when she was slipping berries into his mouth, his eyes looked full at her, no longer glazed.

"You're a stubborn woman," he mumbled.

"I pay my debts."

His eyebrows lifted but he was too weak to argue and lapsed back into a drowse.

He improved steadily after that. Within a week, he said he could travel though he wasn't yet up to a full day. They burned his bedding and clothes and what Mary Ann had worn while nursing him. Then, before going to Billy, they both scrubbed themselves thoroughly in water from the spring, using strong lye soap, and washing their hair as well.

"Want me to wash your back for you?" Talt called softly through the willows.

Mary Ann blushed in spite of the chuckle in his voice, but she was glad he felt good enough to be a little pesky. "I washed yours often enough," she retorted.

"But I couldn't enjoy it, ma'am. Why don't you be real sweet and do it again?"

"You—you *man!*"

He seemed to be coming through the bushes. She made for the wagon as fast as her condition permitted and stood behind it while she dried off and got into clean clothing. Then she rummaged his extra garments out of the wagon and deposited them on the willows.

"Now you can get decent," she called primly, and fled as she saw him approaching shamelessly through the wispy trees. His laughter followed her. Drat the man! Weak with cholera, he'd been safe, but now it seemed she was going to have to fight him off! It was purely ridiculous when she was big as a barn.

The baby kicked within her and she put her hands over it as if to soothe it. Anyhow, it seemed she'd escaped cholera and she didn't see any way Billy could have caught it. But her labor was before her. If only there was a woman around since there couldn't be a doctor! She'd have to deliver with no one to help but a man who was, after all, a stranger.

They got stuck in Big Sandy. In spite of Talt's warnings, Mary Ann helped push, and an hour after they were back on the road, her pains began. She hoped the birthing would hold off till they stopped for the day. Talt's sickness had made them late and every day counted now in getting through the mountains before the snows. But the muted pangs grew harsher, closer together, and within another hour, Mary Ann was chewing her lips and perspiring cold sweat.

"What's the matter?" Talt shot a sidelong glance at her involuntary moan, gasped, and stopped the oxen. "The baby?"

She nodded, panted and squeezed her eyes shut as a great hand seemed to grip the inside of her belly and wrench it around. Billy squealed and grabbed her.

"Listen, son," said Talt, lifting him down. "Your mama's going to be fine but we need some hot water. How's about you bringing in lots of sagebrush and any dried chips you can find? And then you go play over in that draw till I call you to see your new brother or sister."

"Billy want brother."

"I'll see what I can do," Talt promised. "But sometimes the good Lord decides we need a woman so there'll always be plenty of mamas. Scoot, now!"

Mary Ann wanted to lie down but Talt wouldn't let her. "You'll have that baby a lot faster if you keep walking around."

"How do you know?"

"That's how Indian women do."

"Damn you, I'm not an Indian!"

"Well, you're going to have this baby like you were, lady, because that's the only way I know how to help—and from what I've seen, it sure works better than the white way."

He made her walk while he built a fire and put water to boil. Then he drove two poles into the ground and tied a braided rawhide rope between them. "Kneel in the middle," he said, "and hang onto the rope. It'll help you push."

She was still skewered by dizzying surges of black-red pain but gradually she found that being able to push down and encourage the pains made her feel better than if she'd been lying prone amid a flock of anxious women, passively enduring her labor rather than urging it on.

Talt brought her hot tea frequently. When she was so exhausted that her sweating hands slipped from the rope, he gripped her wrists and supported her in a squat. She screamed, strangled the sound in her throat so Billy wouldn't be scared. She was splitting, being torn apart— She faded into soft darkness, conscious only of Talt's hands.

When she roused, she felt something at her breast. Wonderingly, she touched her stomach, found it flat. Bending her neck, she gazed down at a silk black head, a funny little squished-up visage.

"That's brother?" Billy was saying in disgust. "Mama, he's too little!"

"He'll grow," Talt promised.

"Bear won't like him much."

"He will later. Now why don't you and bear go find some berries?"

Billy loped off. Mary Ann sighed, blissful at being free from pain and the cumbering bigness, and drifted off to sleep.

She lay on the mattress next day as they traveled on. The baby was fretful and didn't suck much. By the fourth day, when real milk should have replaced the clear fluid, she realized that her right breast was hard and swollen, increasingly painful. By night, the other breast was caked, too, and she had to confess her condition to Talt before the baby starved.

"Fool woman!" he growled, something like panic leaping into his eyes. "Why didn't you tell me this morning?"

He made hot compresses applied with mullein leaves, made her drink herbal teas and eat, and insisted that she let the infant suck, agonizing as it was. "He won't get any milk to speak of but it'll help break up that abscess."

"He needs milk!"

"He'll get it from you when you get straightened out. Till then, don't you worry. I'll make him such a nice broth that he may not want milk, ever."

That didn't happen, but the baby stayed alive on broth till Talt's stern regime righted the misery in Mary Ann's breasts. As she cradled the child and relaxed to the sweetly painful tugging of his little jaws, it seemed natural enough for Talt to stand there watching them.

"Strong little guy. What you going to call him?"

Vaguely, she had planned to name a boy baby after Jed, but it seemed now that she had known the father of this child countless years ago, almost in another life. She had married Jed in the excitement of her first courtship and to escape her aunt, but had she ever loved him? He had been a habit. She was too honest to let the tragedy of his death blind her.

Looking up at Talt, she said quietly, "If—if you don't mind, I'd like to name him for you. He wouldn't be alive if you hadn't taken care of us."

"You owe it to me?"

She started to lash out at him. Then she saw a sort of hunger deep in his eyes, a look curiously like Billy's when he occasionally worried that the baby might supplant him. "I'm mighty tired of all these debts," she said levelly. "Maybe I pulled you through the cholera. You for sure saved my baby. Let's call it even."

He took a deep breath. The fire in his eyes sent a sweetness rushing through her, a sunny warmth she had never felt before. "Does that mean—well, that we're starting fresh?"

"Fresh as we can after all we've been through."

"Guess we acted like we were married—except for the best parts. Mary Ann, you reckon it's about time you got a daddy for these boys?"

She nodded. He leaned over and kissed her above the nursing baby, his kiss a promise of all they were going to share. Billy stepped out of the shadows and climbed into Talt's lap. "Bear wants someone to hold him, too!"

"Bear's come to the right place," Talt said. "And so have I."

Above the yellow head, his eyes met Mary Ann's.

THE DISGRACEFUL AFFAIR
OF
TURPENTINE JACKSON

Benjamin Capps

To the President of the Company and other officers, Dear Mister
Blackmoor:

First, they say it is a disgraceful affair, which I don't say is true,
and hope it don't reflect on the good name of the Blackmoor Land
and Cattle Company. As to giving the account, this is what I have to
respectfully say for the record and to put it in black and white. I
think Mister Jackson's name is Henry, as I found it put down H.
Jackson, but as you know he answers to the name of Turpentine. I
want to apply and say that because I paid him twice I don't think it
should be deducted from my salary. This is in the amount of sixty
dollars cash money. I was told and instructed many times when out
of contact with superior officers of the Company, to use my own
judgment, which I did to the best of my ability.

I had them put me down as Acting Foreman McWhirter, since I
did not know if I have been promoted or not. Anyway, this here's a
copy of the Agreement or contract, so as you can understand what
went on.

AGREEMENT

Whereas, it being the determination of the following various parties to settle certain serious grievances and alleged crimes and debts
and damages once and for all, we the contracting parties hereto do
agree and affirm:

That the party of the first part shall include the Honorable Mayor
of the City of Dodge City, the Chief of Police of the City of Dodge
City, the High Sheriff of Ford County, the aforesaid Sheriff also as a
representative of the State of Kansas, the Commanding Officer of

Fort Dodge, the President of the Chamber of Commerce of the City
of Dodge City, and the Secretary of the Civic Improvement League
of the City of Dodge City.

Further, that the party of the second part shall include, but not be
limited to, Elmore McWhirter, Acting Foreman of the Blackmoor
Land and Cattle Company, having authority over Turpentine Jackson, all owners and operators of said Cattle Company having authority over the employee Turpentine Jackson, and any keepers or guard-
ians having influence or control over the aforesaid Turpentine
Jackson.

Now, whereas it is agreed that herein claims do not represent final
judgments in either civil or criminal actions, the party of the first part
does nevertheless present an itemized statement of account, to wit:

One bowl of chili at Welcome Tex Café. Not paid for.	*.10*
Defamatory and libelous statement of finding dog hair in chili at Welcome Tex Café.	*$5.00*
Fee for cleaning wall, Welcome Tex Café.	*.50*
Four drinks first-class whiskey at Cowboy Oasis. Not paid for.	*.80*
Libelous and defamatory statement calling first-class whiskey at Cowboy Oasis epithet approx. "liquid mule waste." Damages.	*$2.00*
Grabbing money back improperly from Slick Hendricks, sporting man and part owner of Cowboy Oasis.	*$7.00*
Calling Slick Hendricks "crooked as rail fence" and also "crooked as dog's hind leg" at Cowboy Oasis. Damages to reputation of Slick Hendricks.	*$5.00*
Referring to occupation of Hog Nose Kate in public and making disparaging remarks about professional compe- tence. Mental anguish and damage to reputation of Hog Nose Kate.	*$1.00*
One large mirror, Cowboy Oasis. Replacement cost.	*$14.00*
Failure to halt at first order by officer of law, to wit: City Marshal Owen Sims. Fine.	*$3.00*
Resisting arrest. Fine.	*$3.00*
Court costs, if tried, above two counts, @ $1.00 per count.	*$2.00*
Damages to Marshal Sims's firearm.	*$4.00*
Sending Peewee Hawkins down in city well to retrieve firearm. Cost.	*$1.00*
Striking city marshal in eye while in performance of his duty. Fine.	*$3.00*

One pound beefsteak.	*.10*
Four yards cotton bandage.	*.20*
Five drinks first-class whiskey, Eddie's Emporium. Not paid for.	*$1.00*
Insulting and defamatory remarks about Eddie. Damages.	*$4.00*
Public statement that Mayor J. B. Krenshaw cheats at poker and is bigger crook than Slick Hendricks. Severe mental anguish and damage to reputation, also contempt of elected official.	*$7.00*
Calling New Orleans Rose epithet while she was verbally defending elected official. Also making lewd and suggestive references. Damage to reputation of New Orleans Rose.	*$1.00*
Breaking plate glass over large art picture of "Venus Bathing with Maidens," Eddie's Emporium. Cost.	*$9.00*
Drunk and disorderly, including statement that Turpentine Jackson can whip mayor and two soldiers. Fine.	*$3.00*
Making reference to mother of mayor. Damage to reputation and good name of mother of Mayor Krenshaw.	*$7.00*
Fighting on public streets, namely Front Street by Cattlemen's Hotel. Fine.	*$3.00*
One window, Cattlemen's Hotel. Cost.	*$1.00*
Assault and battery against two soldiers, to wit: one corporal and one private. Fine.	*$3.00*
Resisting arrest by Deputy Sheriff Perkins. Fine.	*$3.00*
Calling one corporal and one private "Yankee" plus epithet denying marriage of parents. Damage to reputations.	*$2.00*
Two gold teeth of Deputy Sheriff Perkins. @ $4.00 per tooth.	*$8.00*
Three stitches in nose of aforesaid Perkins, seven stitches in mouth. Doctor's fee.	*$2.00*
Miscellaneous damage to signs of retail establishments along Front Street, including one barber pole ruined.	*$1.50*
Refusing to halt at request of three duly constituted officers of the law, to wit: Chief of Police Webbington, Sheriff Trueblood, and Constable Orr. Fine.	*$3.00*
Continuing to resist arrest, after warning. Fine.	*$3.00*
False, misleading, and defamatory remarks about aforesaid officers.	*$4.50*
Sheriff Trueblood's pocket watch. Damages.	*$9.00*
Constable Orr's spectacles. Damages.	*$6.00*

Chief Webbington's coat, sleeve torn and pocket ripped out. Damages.	*$1.50*
Damage to bench in front of City Jail.	*$1.25*
Miscellaneous derogatory and malicious statements about officials, employees, and citizens of the City of Dodge City, and also the State of Kansas, including U. S. Army personnel stationed therein.	*$8.00*
Damages inside City Jail, including, but not limited to, one sprung door, one mattress, and toilet facilities.	*$24.00*
Three counts of Contempt of Court before Justice of the Peace Adcock, @ $3.00 per count.	*$9.00*
False and defamatory statement that said Turpentine Jackson can whip Justice of the Peace Adcock.	*$2.50*
One pound beefsteak.	*.10*
Six yards cotton bandage.	*.30*
Grand total of damages, fines, costs, unpaid bills	*$179.35*
Minus $4.00 credited to said Jackson for one gold tooth discovered following morning in chamber pot, Miller's Boarding House, and returned to owner.	*$4.00*
Balance	*$175.35*
Withdrawal of damage claim to reputation of Hog Nose Kate plus statement that Turpentine Jackson is a good man at heart. (Opinion only.) Also statement of Civic Improvement League that said Hog Nose Kate is not a nice person. (Opinion only.)	
Withdrawal of claim	*$1.00*
Final Balance	*$174.35*

Now, whereas, the representatives of Turpentine Jackson decline to submit an itemized account of any monies owing to him, the following statement by said Jackson is incorporated as part of the agreement herein: "I know (expletive) I had sixty dollars, two whole months pay, when I came into this (four expletives) town. I sure didn't spend it, and I got only twenty-five (expletive) cents now."

Further, in answer to the above, Justice of the Peace Adcock swears and affirms that said Jackson had only twenty-five cents on him when he was admitted to the City Jail; and said Adcock says two residents of the City Jail, namely Joe Lefors and Charles Blankenship, saw that aforesaid Turpentine Jackson had only twenty-five cents, and he can prove it by the said witnesses.

Further, whereas Acting Foreman Elmore McWhirter of the Blackmoor Land and Cattle Company says he only wants to do a good turn and make peace between the parties involved, he, the aforesaid McWhirter, affirms that the Blackmoor Land and Cattle Company takes responsibility for acts of employees only when they are doing assigned duties for the said Company. And further he swears and affirms that he did pay Turpentine Jackson sixty dollars in cash money, and does not know whether Jackson got his money's worth in recreational benefits.

Therefore, whereas no full statement and itemized account is forthcoming from the party of the second part, it is agreed as follows, to wit: The aforesaid Jackson did enter the City Limits of the City of Dodge City with the said sixty dollars; and that subsequent to his entry the money was taken from him, legally or illegally, by person or persons unknown.

Furthermore, whereas various claims are made herein, but not admitted, if one principal condition shall be met, then all debts, damages, fines, and similar charges shall be canceled and forgiven. The principal condition being thus, namely, to wit: that the party of the second part, in particular Acting Foreman McWhirter, but including the owners and operators of the Blackmoor Land and Cattle Company and all persons who may have any control, authority, or influence over the aforesaid Jackson, either now or in the future, shall immediately and forthwith remove the said Jackson from the vicinity of the City of Dodge City. Further, they, the aforesaid party of the second part, shall prevent said Jackson from entering back into said City Limits at any time in the future, either south of the tracks or north of the tracks, nor shall he be allowed to approach the military reservation of Fort Dodge or any personnel stationed thereon. Further they, the aforesaid party of the second part, shall prevent the said Jackson from entering Ford County; and further they shall prevent said Jackson from entering the State of Kansas.

And be it further agreed that Acting Foreman McWhirter and others, should Turpentine Jackson quit the employment of the Blackmoor Land and Cattle Company and thereby come out from under their control, authority, and influence, then Acting Foreman McWhirter and others, if they believe the said Jackson is heading for Kansas, shall notify the proper officials by telegram.

In witness whereof, we, the various parties of the various parts, do affix our signatures in good faith and in the presence of a Notary Public.

End of Agreement

Well, Mister Blackmoor, that's the facts as requested, and I admit I signed the agreement for the Company, as I was told and instructed many times when out of contact with my superiors in the Company to use my own judgment, which I did to the best of my ability. I was also asked to make suggestions for the profit and good name of my employers whenever I deemed I ought to, so here goes: We could ship at Denison, Texas, or go plum past Dodge and up to Ogallala, Nebraska, next spring. Sir, there is a rough and rowdy element at Dodge City, which comes from the uneducated buffalo skinners and soldiers and teamsters and such types as gamblers, as well as some that is highly placed officials, and this is a bad influence on cowhands.

I hope this gives to you the explanation in black and white as requested, and respectfully say I don't think you should dock me the sixty dollars.

Yrs. Truly,
Elmore McWhirter
Acting Foreman

ED

Frank Roderus

Like most other people he knew, Ed Firston had never named a horse in his life. Horses were tools. A way to get from here to there. More often adversaries to be fought and conquered than partners to be depended upon. Names were for play-pretties, not tools. They were likely to be attached to a horse by a woman or by one of those runaways who kept popping out of the bushes bent on the idea that he was going to "be a cowboy" and "make his mark" and carry a "six-shooter" and all that dime novel stuff. Poor little things. They just didn't know.

Well, Ed Firston knew. He'd had the best part of a lifetime—maybe even all of it—to do his learning in. And he knew.

He had never named a horse nor felt he needed any more of a weapon than his own good sense and a stout maguey rope, but he knew what it was to be a hand and a good one at that. Ask anybody that had ever worked beside him and you'd get the same answer. Old Ed was all right.

They were calling him that now. Old Ed. That still seemed hard to accept. He couldn't say that he liked it, but he never called them on it. Not worth the trouble. Besides, it wouldn't do to let them think he was sensitive about it. They'd never let him be if he did.

He grinned and ran the back of his hand across cracked, dry lips, feeling the pain and not much caring, feeling the stubble of more beard than was seemly for a man to carry. Strangers saw that, they might think he was some kind of a bum, too poor to pay for a shave. Ed Firston wasn't any bum and never had been.

And there, he'd gone and done it again. Let his mind wander off away from the subject at hand.

He knew what he was doing. He was putting it off, delaying what had to be done, as if that would change anything. It wouldn't. Not a bit of it.

He reached out to rub the horse's poll and finger it behind the ears. The horse didn't move and he wondered if it was even aware of what he was doing.

That was what had started all this shilly-shallying. Of course he remembered that. The no-name horse. Just like all the others. He could remember every one of them, from that first hardscrabble bunch when he'd had to put out a day's work with a string of exactly three green ponies to that drive all the way up to the Marias River with a mixed herd of stockers and fifteen head in each drover's string. That was the best string he'd ever rode, and he'd needed every one of them. That was the flightiest bunch of fool bovines, not a steer in the bunch to help settle them and all of them rank and spooky.

Good as those horses had been, this one was better. It wasn't the name that made a horse nor even its training, it was the heart. That's what this one had too. More heart than would fit in a hogshead cask.

He quit scratching and tilted his hat against the glare of the sun and squinted at the no-name thing.

It sure wasn't pretty. Nobody could accuse it of that. Head too big. Ears too long. Neck like an old ewe sheep. A back end that would have looked just fine on a wolfhound. If anybody'd been around Ed might have felt shamed to be seen on such a poor horse.

If anybody'd been around.

Except that wasn't true either. The no-name thing probably didn't weigh seven hundred pound now, he guessed, but five hundred of that was heart, and the two hundred that was missing since he started out riding the thing was melted off because of all that heart. It hadn't quit on him and still wouldn't quit on him and no, Ed Firston wouldn't be shamed to be seen on that scarecrow of a mount even if it didn't have a name.

He looked at it standing head down and spraddle-legged, salt-crusted and just too damn dry to sweat any more.

It had been going on nothing but heart the last seven mile or more. Longer than that probably. It had been twice that since he pulled his saddle and let it lay where it fell. About seven from where he'd started walking.

The no-name thing wouldn't go down, though. It stumbled and wallowed and went to its knees but always it shivered and floundered and somehow fought its way back onto its feet. It hadn't quit on him.

No, he wouldn't be shamed to be seen beside this old no-name.

He reached a rope-burned, work-hard hand forward and fumbled with the buckle that held the jaw strap of his patched and sweat-stained old bridle. He couldn't make his fingers work just right and eventually moved closer to use both hands on the buckle. He hadn't needed two hands on one small buckle since he was a pup so young and clumsy he couldn't roll a smoke without it falling to pieces.

He chuckled out loud and the sound provoked a twitch of one ear from the no-name horse.

That was back when he sure was a pup and just learning to roll a smoke. Back when you had to go to Kansas to find a shipping pen. They'd been on that long, nervous stretch through the Indian Territories, nervous because some civilized Indian might want them to pay a trespass fee and they hadn't the money to pay any with, none of them including the boss. That day he'd been riding that spooky yellow horse that had been wished off on him because he was the youngest and the least of the bunch and should heal the fastest if he let it booger. He'd rolled himself a smoke that forenoon and rolled it loose and didn't wet it tight enough and as soon as he'd touched a lucifer to the end the paper went up in a flash that singed his eyebrows and that burning tobacco fell down on the yellow's shoulders. And between those hot flakes and his own yelp the yellow had sure enough boogered and they just had them one wild fight that ended up with him limping for a week afterward and the butt of the camp jokes a whole lot longer than that until he finally closed the subject by whipping Horace Tolliver when they were both supposed to be on night herd.

He must really have had a mad on that time because Horace outweighed him by thirty pounds and had a rowdy disposition. Then. The last he heard Horace was running a shop in San Angelo and had got respectable. Probably didn't even remember those lean times with no sleep and poor food and gyp water.

Water. Now why'd he gone and thought about that.

So many rivers they'd swum. So many creeks and drainage runs they'd splashed across. So many hand-dug wells he'd helped dig at so many line camps. So many tails lifted and water befouled and it hadn't seemed at all important at the time. So much he would give right now for a hatful of any of it.

He looked at the no-name horse standing with its legs braced wide and its eyes glassy-dull like frosted glass in a tavern—*quit* that—window. Jesus, the thought of a beer off the tap. His throat worked involuntarily. It hurt, but the memory was almost worth it.

He looked around at the hard-baked surface, deep cracked and ugly, that was the only and the final hope for too far around.

The last sweetwater seep had been passed fourteen miles back and it was drier than this pothole, if that was possible.

He glanced up toward the sun. Back at the TY they would be . . .

No, he wasn't going to start that. There was no need for it. He didn't regret leaving. He had been right to leave, and if the breaks didn't go with him that was just his tough luck. Young Tony'd wanted him to turn in his string and take to fence-building from the back of a wagon and harness-mending in the back of the shed, and that wasn't right. When they ask for your string of horses you ask for your time, and that's just the way it is. If you are a man you do, and Ed Firston never took a charity job from anyone nor any kind of a job that couldn't be done from the back of a horse. Never had and never would.

Well, almost never. Not since he left the cotton patches of east Texas. And kid chores don't count.

He grinned at another spate of memories, and the movement cracked his lips open painfully but there was only a faint ooze of blood that came to the surface and that glazed dry quickly enough. He didn't hardly mind it even.

The no-name horse slumped abruptly at its near shoulder, caught itself and staggered for a moment before it regained its brace with all four legs. It made a very human-sounding groan.

"Sorry, old boy." There was no response from the ears this time and its eyes stared sightlessly into the distance.

Ed reached deep into the pocket of his chaps and pulled out a folding clasp knife. It annoyed him that he had to try three times before he found enough strength in his fingers to pull the blade open. It was an old knife, the blade considerably narrowed from countless stonings, and not that hard to open.

He stepped forward to stand beside the big, ugly head of the dying horse and felt of its jaw and neck with practiced fingers to find the jugular.

He had been putting this off entirely too long for the selfish sake of the animal's companionship, and he was ashamed of himself.

"You been a good ol' thing," he said aloud.

In a whisper, as if he were afraid someone might overhear even here so far from anything human or even anything animate, he added a faint, "I love you."

As best he could remember he had never spoken those words before to anything or anyone.

He made his cut, quick and clean, and stepped aside.

There was no point in going anywhere now and he didn't seem to have the strength to be walking at the moment even if there were someplace to go.

Maybe in the morning he would feel more like it.

He carefully folded his knife and replaced it in his chaps where it belonged, then sat down and leaned back against the barrel of the fallen horse.

He had quite a bit to think about. So much to remember. He tipped his shapeless, sweat-browned hat forward over his eyes and remembered. And waited.

THAT DAMN COWBOY!

Judy Alter

Each day the old man wheeled his chair out to the veranda and sat staring over the distant river and, farther, the purplish, faint mountains. Some days he sat as still as the landscape before him; others, when the wind swept across the plains and struck him forcefully, he would shift restlessly, long bony fingers stroking his white stubble of beard and pulling at his shaggy hair. But always, his eyes, intense and blue, seemed fixed on the river.

He rarely talked, and the family had grown accustomed to his silence. The grandchildren treated him dutifully, their parents a slight bit more tolerantly. Friends and neighbors, visiting the house, nearly ignored him, and everyone generally agreed that his mind was gone. "Addled with age," they called it. Still, he was the first thing newcomers to the small ranching community heard about. After all, he had been an artist—no, not exactly famous, but he had lived next door to Frederic Remington once.

But Rufus Jones wasn't really addled. It was just that in the years of his old age he had found the world less absorbing than his own interior battle. Retreating from everyday concerns, he tried, with a desperation born of old age, to puzzle out some reason for the turn of his life. He had to know why, before death closed the question forever.

Some days when the fire of anger was less strong in him, he would muse on the quirk of fate that led his son, Davey, to settle in Montana, bringing the then aged Rufus back to the land which had captivated him years ago.

I loved this country from that first trip . . . 1883, no '84, that time I came to follow the cavalry and do some field sketches. Remember thinking it was like the Scotch highlands . . . rolling hills covered with sage brush and in the distance, those great snowcapped mountains . . . only this was grander, more immense . . . so much space that the very openness could make a man feel caught. And all that light and shade on the whole thing. My first sketches were failures. But they got better, got to the point I was proud of them, thought I had found my place, the subject that was all mine. I was going to be a famous Western artist. What happened?

Other days he would think about that damn cowboy, and the flames of bitterness would rise again within him. Too often, he recalled that day when he had first felt the heat of jealousy. It was in New York where he and the great Frederic Remington were neighbors and, in those days, pretty much equals in the artistic world. Both interested in the West, they often sat late at night sharing experiences, swapping Arizona stories for Montana. They tried to joke about their failures and bragged about the successes—the sale of a painting, the signing of a contract with *Harper's Weekly*. Rufus had never thought of Remington as greater or better than he, at least never until that day. He remembered that afternoon clearly, even now, some forty years later.

Young Davey came running home to tell me that Mr. Remington had a new pony. "And a silver-studded saddle and bridle." I can still see the child's eyes, overcome with excitement and pure envy. I was working on that portrait of the old man collecting buffalo bones. The surroundings, even the pile of bones, were right but I couldn't bring the bone man himself into focus. I was frustrated and it wouldn't have done me any good to keep trying, so I told Davey I'd go see the pony.

But as we crossed the lawn, Remington called: "Rufus! Come here! I've done something splendid."

I remember thinking something about egotists, but it didn't really bother me . . . I was used to the man, his bluster and roar, it was just part of him. And I went to look—at a mass of clay and a bunch of sculptor's tools, and Remington with that stupid, proud grin on his face. He looked so superior, and all I saw at first was a lump of clay.

"What do you think, Rufus? I think this mess is the beginning of something great. In fact, I'm convinced of it. Don't you agree? I may give up oils and become a sculptor."

That was when I saw it—that mass of clay was a horse and rider, well done, too. That flash of anger that went through me, it came so suddenly, it surprised, even frightened me. I'd never been jealous before, yet this was almost an instinct . . . I remember making the effort, saying all the right things and wanting really to reach out and destroy that lump of clay. But I just stood there and watched, fascinated in spite of myself, as he added a bit of clay here, scooped some away there, and that damn cowboy took shape before my eyes.

Going home, I was almost feverish with anger and hate . . . couldn't work at all. That blasted old bone man got worse instead of better, and I even jumped at Davey when he came in for his afternoon visit. Poor kid. He wanted to talk about the new pony, and I flew in a rage, scared him out of the studio.

Wonder if Davey would remember that day now? No, he'd probably dismiss it as old age if I asked him. He doesn't know how I grew to hate Remington—no one knows, I've kept it buried all these years. Everyone assumed all along that Remington and I were the best of friends . . . probably thought it was nice of the great Remington to be so kind to a second-rate artist. Remington sure got so he acted that way, kind of condescending. Or was I touchy?

Sometimes Rufus Jones would relive his own career, the near-success of it, or was it near-failure? No, success, for he had done some important works, had been known and praised in his day. His mind would begin with that mural in the state capitol . . .

Quite an honor to be asked, and I did them a good job. Was pleased with it. And the one in the Woolworth Building . . . by that time, I was known for historical subjects, the history of this great land. Oh, I was riding high.

And then there was that business about cowboys at play . . . I was so proud of that drawing when it came out . . . "Painting the Town Red," four cowboys literally holding a town at bay with their high jinx. Everyone else was so busy painting the cowboy at work, roping cattle, riding herd and all that, but no one paid any attention to the cowboy at play. I was the first—it was my idea!

But barely two years later, Remington did a sketch with the same title, looked a lot like mine, too. Anyway, the idea was the same. It came out in that book of Roosevelt's about hunting trails or whatever. Why didn't TR ask me to illustrate it anyway? I just had that letter of praise from him saying how much he valued my Western work and hoping we could collaborate, then the next thing TR asked Remington to illustrate the book. I thought that was the final insult—using my sketch and title!

Of course, it wasn't the final insult. The worst came later in another one of those bronzes Remington did . . . they were all so popular after that first damn cowboy. This one he called

"Coming Through the Rye," but the figures were almost exactly those of my painting. And who got all the credit for capturing the cowboy as he really was—who else?

Sometimes Davey would come to stand silently beside his father, staring at the scene that so absorbed the old man each day as though by looking, he, too, could see something. But one late summer day when the wind off the river promised cold weather soon, Davey came with something on his mind.

"Dad?" The tall man in jeans and denim jacket bent almost gently over the older one who sat erect in his chair, fingering the lap robe that covered him. Davey had to speak twice before Rufus turned and looked at him, still saying nothing.

"There's someone who wants to come see you tomorrow. She's an artist, or says she is anyway. The town kind of wonders about her. But, she stopped me on the street today, said she'd heard a lot about your work and wanted to meet you. I couldn't do anything else . . . I told her to come on out in the morning."

Rufus turned away as though none of what Davey had said meant a thing to him. Davey kicked at a cigarette butt with one scuffed boot, stared at the river for help, and finally went on.

"Sir, did you hear me?"

"Ummm."

The next that he had to say made Davey uncomfortable, and he fidgeted a minute before plunging in. "Dad, you will talk to her, won't you? She says she knows your work, wants to talk to you about it. Try to be polite, won't you?"

Davey walked away abruptly, only half hearing Rufus's mumbled, "Can't you tell her I'll be at work on a new painting, can't see visitors?"

But Rufus had understood that someone had heard of his work, and he was secretly pleased. Maybe she knew "Painting the Town Red," or, perhaps, some of the Oklahoma pictures. His mind went back to reliving his achievements, and slowly he saw himself standing in the gallery at his 1899 exhibition. Somehow, though, memories of Remington's earlier, more successful exhibition, in 1893, crept in.

He looked so cocksure, so smug . . . when I congratulated him, he was almost too hearty, telling me that someday I'd have a success like this too . . . People kept coming up to shake his hand, ooze their flattery all over him, and he ate it up . . . All I could do was wonder what it would really be like to have that much attention paid to your art, have all those compliments and empty words . . . imagine myself standing there saying, "Thank you, Mrs. Vanderbilt, I'm so glad you like my pictures of the West . . . yes, it's a very exciting land . . . and Mrs. Astor, how nice of you to come . . . You like the sculpture? Well, I'm most humble . . ."

Rufus had thirsted after fame so long, he almost felt himself savoring that of his rival. Bitterly, he brought his thoughts back to the present, surprised himself at how far from reality he occasionally drifted these days.

It was midmorning the next day when Rufus, seated in his wheelchair and staring at the river, heard steps approach him from behind. Not Davey, nor any of the family. They were womanly, small steps that sounded mincing.

"Mr. Jones, it's so good of you to let me visit. I can't tell you how delighted I am to talk to another artist."

Rufus turned slowly and fixed his stare on her. She wore pink, an outfit so unsuitable it seemed to insult the landscape, and she smiled too much.

"I said, I'm glad to meet you after hearing so much about your work. I've long been an admirer of the great Rufus Jones."

No response for several seconds, then a glance, a barely uttered, "Eh?" and Rufus turned again to the river.

"Mr. Jones, I came to tell you how very much I appreciate your Western work—I've seen it in museums and I just think it's marvelous, so wonderful! Particularly that mounted horse and rider you did in bronze—your first, wasn't it?"

That damn cowboy again! Rufus stared at the river with an intensity so great it even alarmed the lady artist. Finally, long minutes later, he turned to stare at her. Then a wave seemed to sweep over his entire body. The burning look disappeared from his eyes, his face grew calm, and he actually smiled.

"Thank you very much, my dear. I'm glad you like 'The Bronco Buster'—that's what he really is. And yes, he was my first bronze. But I'm afraid you have my name wrong—I'm Frederic Remington."

A KIND OF JUSTICE
Bill Gulick

The Reverend Thomas Powell was splitting kindling in the yard in front of his mission cabin when the Indian boy, Richard, came up to him and said in the Nez Perce tongue, "A *suyapo* camps two miles up the valley. My father sent me to tell you. He thought you should know."

Coatless under the warm June sun, the sleeves of his flannel shirt rolled up above his elbows and the collar open, Thomas Powell leaned his axe against the chopping block and mopped his perspiring forehead with a handkerchief, frowning down at the stocky, square-shouldered Indian boy. The minister was a tall, rawboned man, used to hard physical labor; he had the deep-set, inward-looking eyes of a man of firm moral fiber; the straight-lined, uncompromising mouth of a man unafraid to face stern practical problems.

"A white man? Who is he? What is he doing here?"

"He does not say. He makes his camp, eats, then sits and smokes and watches the valley, his rifle across his knees."

"Does he know the mission is here?"

"Yes. My father told him. The *suyapo* says his business is not with you. My father thinks he is waiting for someone."

The news troubled Powell. One of the advantages of this valley as a mission site had been that it was well removed from trails traveled by Oregon-bound emigrants, American trappers and Hudson's Bay Company fur brigades. Here a missionary could work with his Indian flock, as the Reverend Powell and his wife had done these past five years, reasonably well isolated from the degenerating influence of nonreligious whites. Powell rolled down his sleeves, took his coat and hat off the woodpile and put them on.

"Thank you, Richard. I'll ride up and have a talk with him."

Going into the split-rail corral adjacent to the cabin, he saddled the placid gray mare on which he was accustomed to ride his errands and was leading her out the gate when his wife, Ruth, and four-year-old daughter, Mary, came along the path from the springhouse, where the family's butter and milk were stored to keep them cool. They were skipping along hand in hand, laughing at some shared game, but when Ruth saw him preparing to mount the mare her face sobered.

"Thomas! Where are you off to in the middle of the day?"

"We have a visitor camped up the valley, Ruth. A white man."

"Who is he? What does he want?"

"That's what I must find out."

"But dinner is almost ready! Can't you wait until after you eat?"

Mary, seeing the saddled horse, ran up to her father, lifted her hands and begged to be put astride the mare. Powell picked her up and gave her a hug and a kiss. Though quite aware that as his and Ruth's firstborn, as the godchild of Chief Elijah and the pet of every Indian in Elijah's band, she was already quite adequately spoiled, he proceeded without a qualm of conscience to spoil her some more, stroking her hair and calling her by the name the Indians had given her. "Not now, Little-Princess-with-the-Golden-Hair. But this afternoon, after you've had your nap, I'll take you for a long, long ride."

"Now, Daddy, now!"

"Later, my dear. I promise."

He put her down and swung into the saddle shaking his head at his wife. "Elijah is worried, else he wouldn't have sent Richard to tell me the man is here. You know how much trouble the wrong kind of white man could make for us. My dinner will have to wait."

Ruth's eyes grew concerned and he knew what she was thinking. In the beginning, back East, it had seemed a fine and noble thing to dedicate their lives to taking God's Word to the unenlightened Indians of the Oregon country. But the dream and the reality were poles apart. Five years of brutally hard physical labor, heartache, isolation from their own kind, frustration and bitter disappointment had taught them that. True, this one small band of Nez Perces, led by the good, kind, intelligent chief whom they had baptized and named Elijah, had been receptive to their mission. But Elijah's band consisted of only one hundred and fifty souls and the chief's influence did not extend beyond this sheltered valley; outside the valley, scattered through the rugged mountain country on both sides of the Salmon, Clearwater, and Snake Rivers, lived the sixteen other bands which comprised the great Nez Perce nation—and these Indians still lived as they had from time immemorial, still clung to their old heathen ways. To them, the mission was little more than a curiosity to be visited, observed, laughed at, and then ignored.

In all the years that Powell and his wife had labored here they had made only one Christian convert belonging to a band other than Elijah's. That modestly cheering event had occurred yesterday when a subchief who went by the name of Cut Face, a member of the upper Salmon River band, had come in, declared his faith, and been baptized.

What concerned Ruth, Powell knew, was the knowledge that if force had to be used to eject this white intruder from the valley, he himself must apply it. Twice before, such a thing had happened when unscrupulous white traders had come into the valley bringing whiskey which they intended to trade for Indian horses and furs. Powell had ordered the men out, and, when they refused to go, had broken their guns, poured their whiskey on the ground, and then driven them out of the valley with stern warnings never to return. Neither man had had the courage to offer physical resistance. But the next one might; so always now when a white stranger came into the valley, a shadow clouded Ruth's mind until she learned what kind of man he was.

"I'll pray for you, Thomas," she said softly. "Bring him home with you, if he'll come. I'll keep dinner warm."

Kicking the mare into motion, Powell rode up the valley, lifting his hand in greeting to Indians he met or passed along the way, waving to boys on spotted ponies, to women working in the communal vegetable garden which he had encouraged them to plant and tend, and to men lounging in the shade of their family tepees, talking importantly of hunts and wars while the women worked.

He saw his new convert, Cut Face, squatting with his relatives before their lodge, and he smiled in response to the Indian's cheerful greeting. A tall, powerfully built man with a long scar running diagonally across one cheek, Cut Face seemed to be a happy-go-lucky fellow, a born storyteller fond of exaggerating the valor of his own deeds, a bit on the lazy side where physical labor was concerned, but capable of any amount of exertion if hunting, horse racing or war were involved.

Powell was pleased to have the Indian on the church rolls, though he suspected that it had been vanity rather than any deep Christian conviction that had led the savage to ask to be baptized yesterday. Cut Face loved being the center of attention. But whatever the Indian's motives, Powell and his wife were delighted that he had professed his faith, for he was the first longhair—as the heathen Indians outside the valley were called—to become a Christian. Inevitably, when he went back to his mountain band, he would brag about what he had done. That would stir jealousy in the breasts of his fellow tribesmen, and it was Powell's hope that one by one they would drift

into the mission and demand, like sulking children, to be baptized
too.

Gazing at the soft green line of hills flanking the valley, the
minister wrestled with his conscience. Was it a compromise in principles to baptize a savage whom you suspected to be motivated by less
than sincere Christian faith? No doubt it was. But when mountains of
indifference must be moved, one used the tools available to him. Perhaps vanity and jealousy were such tools.

He found the white man sitting cross-legged in the shade of a tree,
a stubby pipe in his mouth, a long-barreled rifle balanced across his
knees. He wore stained, blackened buckskins, had a lean, tanned
face, alert gray eyes, and appeared to be in his late twenties. Something about him struck a chord in the missionary's memory; he was
sure he had seen this man before, but he could not at once place him.
Powell swung down off the mare.

"Hello. I'm Thomas Powell, a minister. I have a mission two miles
down the valley."

The man got to his feet, pocketed his pipe and let the butt of the
rifle rest upon the ground as his left hand gripped its barrel. "I
know."

"Your face is familiar. Where have I seen you?"

"Quite a piece from here," the man said, a twinkle coming into
his eyes. "Found any rattlers in your bed lately, Parson?"

Suddenly Powell remembered. Five years ago he and Ruth had
traveled from Westport to Green River rendezvous grounds in company with a brigade of American fur trappers. One frosty dawn he
had wakened to discover with horror that a rattlesnake was sharing
his bed, and his involuntary scream had brought a young trapper on
the run to snatch the cold-numbed snake away and kill it. This was
that man.

"Good heavens! You're Joe Knapp!"

"Sure am, Parson. How have you been?"

Filled with a vast sense of relief, Powell seized the trapper's hand
and pumped it enthusiastically. He remembered Joe Knapp as a
quiet, good-humored young man who had gone out of his way to be
helpful to Ruth and himself; certainly such a man would make no
trouble here.

"I'm delighted to see you, Joe! What have you been doing these
past five years?"

"Trapping, mostly."

"What brings you to this part of the country?"

Knapp's eyes were suddenly veiled. "I'm on the trail of an Indian.
A Nez Perce named Cut Face. Do you know him?"

"Yes."

"Is he at the mission?"

"Why, yes. He came in yesterday morning."

"He don't belong to this band, according to what the Nez Perces up Salmon River way told me. What's he doing here?"

"He has relatives in the valley. He came down to visit them, I suppose." Powell frowned. "Why are you interested in him?"

Knapp did not answer directly. "Did you notice the horse he was riding, Parson? Was it a big sorrel with two white forefeet?"

"It was a sorrel, yes. I didn't notice its feet."

"He stole that horse from my partner and me a week ago."

"I'll speak to him about it. If it is your horse, I'll certainly make him give it back to you." Powell smiled. "Ruth will be pleased to see you, Joe. Pack up your gear and we'll go down to the mission—"

"No, Parson," Knapp said quietly. "I can't go down to the mission with you."

"Why not? If you want your horse back—"

"There's more than a horse between me and Cut Face."

"What do you mean?"

"He killed my partner."

Powell's lips compressed. Now he knew the nature of Joe Knapp's errand. "And you intend to kill him, is that it?"

"I'll make no trouble here. But sooner or later he'll head for the mountains. When he does, I'll be on his trail."

"How did it happen?"

Briefly the trapper told his story. He and his partner, a man named George Weber, had been on their way to rendezvous when Cut Face walked into their camp one evening leading a lame horse. Recognizing him as a Nez Perce, a tribe traditionally friendly to whites, they fed him and let him spend the night with them. He tried to trade his crippled horse for one of their sound ones, but being heavily laden with their season's fur catch they had no horses to spare and turned him down. Next morning, while Knapp was fixing breakfast, George Weber and Cut Face went out to the meadow where the horses were picketed to bring them in. Knapp heard a shot. Running out to the meadow, he saw Cut Face galloping away on the stolen sorrel and found his partner lying on the ground, shot through the back and dying.

"I buried him," Knapp said in a harsh voice, "then I took to the trail of the murdering devil. It led me here." His burning eyes focused on Powell. "Why did he run to you, Parson, instead of stopping in his own village? Did he think you'd protect him?"

"Possibly."

"Will you?"

"I won't let you shoot him down in cold blood, if you call that protecting him."

"Yeah, I figured you'd see it that way," Knapp said, and his voice now was edged with contempt. "That's why I stopped here."

Anger stirred in Powell. There was both a moral and a practical problem here and he intended to solve both if he could, but he meant to do it in his own way. "I've spent five years trying to teach these people Christianity," he said sharply. "I won't stand idly by and see my work destroyed by your vengeful murder of an Indian."

"I told you I'd make no trouble here."

"Very well, we'll leave it that way. But I insist that you come down to the mission with me."

"What good would that do?"

"Ruth has dinner ready. She'll be happy to see you. All I ask is that you don't mention this matter to her. After we eat, we'll have a talk with Chief Elijah."

Knapp's eyes were puzzled. "You'd take me into your home, knowing what's on my mind?"

"I'd rather have you in my home than waiting to kill a man." Powell smiled. "Come, Joe, I want you to meet our little girl."

It had been so long since a white man other than her husband had sat down to her table, Ruth outdid herself in her efforts to make the trapper feel welcome. As for Mary, no one was a stranger to her, and she was soon confiding all sorts of childish secrets and fancies to Joe Knapp, who gradually lost his uneasiness and sat regarding her smilingly. Troubled by the problem facing him, Powell ate absent-mindedly, taking little part in the conversation.

News spread quickly through an Indian village, he knew. By now, he had no doubt, every Indian in the valley knew the white stranger was here and the nature of the errand that brought him. If Cut Face were guilty of murder, he certainly had compounded his crime by attempting to buy immunity from punishment by joining the church. Letting him get away with that would be a confession of weakness on Powell's part and do his cause irreparable harm. But if he let Knapp take personal vengeance—even outside the valley—he would be a disgrace to his calling.

Ruth was telling Joe Knapp about the many disappointments they had experienced. "We seem to accomplish so little. Not until yesterday has any Indian from outside the valley come into the church. But he's such a friendly, good-hearted man—we're sure he will have a great influence on his people when he goes back to the mountains."

She smiled at her husband. "Thomas, we must give Cut Face a new name. Can't we call him 'Matthew'? Or 'Luke'?"

Knapp shot the minister a penetrating look but said nothing. Powell pushed back his chair and rose. "We'll talk about it later, Ruth. If you've finished, Joe, we'll go see Elijah now."

Knapp got up. "It was a fine dinner, Mrs. Powell."

"We were happy to have you."

The trapper crossed the room, took his rifle down off the wall where he had hung it on pegs to keep it out of reach of childish fingers, and went out of the cabin. As Powell followed, Mary ran around the table, wrapped her arms around her father's legs and pleaded, "Will you take me for a ride now, Daddy?"

"After your nap, dear." Gently he disengaged her hands, picked her up and kissed her. Going outside, he found Knapp staring out over the sun-splashed valley, his face wooden.

"So he joined the church yesterday."

"Yes."

"He came riding in on a stolen horse with my partner's blood fresh on his hands and you took him into your church, asking no questions—"

"I ask only one question of a convert: 'Do you believe?'"

"You count him a real prize, don't you? He's the first longhair you've put your brand on. Is that why you're so anxious to protect him?"

"I'm protecting you as well as him. Nothing can justify a man's taking vengeance into his own hands."

"He killed the best friend I ever had, Parson," Knapp said in sudden bitterness. "I couldn't live with myself if I let him get away with that."

"If he's guilty of murder, he'll be punished."

"How? By who? There's no law in this country, save what each man makes for himself."

"You're wrong there. When I first came here, Joe, I realized I could make no progress in Christianizing the Nez Perces until they learned to live as civilized people do. Elijah and I worked out a code of laws. His people respect them."

"And I'm to respect them, too, is that what you're saying?"

"Yes."

"Suppose I don't?"

Powell's voice was quiet but firm. "I've dealt with that problem before. Twice white traders have come into the valley, planning to swap whiskey for Indian horses and furs. I broke their guns, poured their whiskey on the ground and drove them away. I judge you to be a better type of man than they, but if you aren't I'll be forced to give you the same treatment I gave them."

"What if I object?"

"We'll cross that bridge when we come to it." Powell smiled disarmingly. "Let's go see Elijah."

The chief's lodge was a stone's throw from the mission cabin and as they walked toward it through the still heat of the afternoon neither man spoke. Earlier, coming down the valley, Powell had sent word to Chief Elijah requesting a meeting within the hour; he had not mentioned its purpose, but the unwonted quiet of the village, the lack of cheerful greetings from the men and women who eyed them as they passed, told him that every soul in the valley knew what their meeting was to be about. Suddenly Knapp put a hand on his arm.

"Look yonder!"

Cut Face was riding toward them on the stolen sorrel. He carried a rifle balanced carelessly across the saddle before him, but he looked at ease and unconcerned as he reined in, smiled and lifted a hand in greeting to Powell.

"I go back to my village now."

"Why do you leave so soon?"

"My wife is sick. My children are sick."

"Where did you get that horse?"

"It is mine. It has been mine for a long time."

"This *suyapo* tells me you stole it from him."

"He lies."

"He also tells me you killed his friend."

"That is a bigger lie."

"Perhaps it is you who lies. We shall see. I go now to talk to Elijah. You will not leave the village. You will give me your gun and the horse—"

Something flickered in the Indian's eyes. "No. I must go to my wife and children."

As the Indian started to ride past him, Powell caught one of the sorrel's reins, stopped it, reached up and jerked the rifle out of the red man's hands. With an exclamation of anger, Cut Face leaped to the ground, started to move toward Powell, then, aware of the gun in Joe Knapp's hands and of the crowd of Nez Perce men that had gathered around, relaxed and laughed indifferently.

"I will do as you say."

Powell searched the crowd, seeking a man he could trust, and his eyes settled on Billy Bird, a short, solidly built Nez Perce whom he knew to be dependable. "Put the horse in my corral, Billy. Take Cut Face to your lodge and keep him there under guard."

Billy Bird's black eyes flicked to Cut Face, then back to the missionary. "I will watch him well, Sent One."

Silently the crowd opened up to let them through and they walked to Elijah's lodge. They found the chief sitting alone there, waiting for them. He was a man of middle years, with graying hair, large, thoughtful eyes, and a broad, intelligent face. His voice was deep and curiously gentle, and he gave the impression of being a man whose position of leadership had been well earned. After the usual courtesies had been exchanged, Powell stated the purpose of his visit.

"This *suyapo* is my friend. He is a man whose word I trust. He says that seven sleeps ago Cut Face killed his partner and stole his horse. That is why he followed Cut Face here."

"What do you wish me to do?"

"We agreed on a code of laws. The *suyapo* has accused Cut Face of horse theft and murder. He must be brought to trial before the council of elders, as the law requires."

"He is not a member of our band. He is a Salmon River Nez Perce."

"That does not matter. He and his accuser are here in your land. He has broken the law and you must try him."

"Even though he is a Christian?"

"The law is the same for all."

Elijah looked troubled. "The penalty for murder is death. If the elders find him guilty, we must hang him."

"That is the law."

Chief Elijah was silent for a time, lost in thought, then he raised his head and spoke. "Listen to me, Sent One, for I speak wisdom. Cut Face is a bad man. He is a braggart, a liar, a thief. Even among his own people, he has long been known to be a bad man. He deserves to die. But he is not a member of this band and my elders would never consent to sit in judgment upon him."

"They must."

"Wait, I have more to say. The upper Salmon River Nez Perces are Cut Face's people. If the elders of this band condemned him to death and killed him, by the old tribal laws of blood vengeance his people would become our enemies. Bad feeling would arise between us. We might even go to war. That would be a great evil."

"I agree. That must not happen."

"The murdered man was not an Indian. If he had been, his relatives would have the right to kill Cut Face and the matter would end there." The chief gestured in Knapp's direction. "The murdered man was a *suyapo,* the brother of your friend. He alone has the right to vengeance. So this is what I will do. I will order Cut Face to leave

the valley. Your friend will follow and kill him where he finds him."
The chief made a sign indicating he had finished. "That is all I have
to say."

Joe Knapp had been eying Elijah closely, listening, and now he
looked at Powell and murmured, "He talks good sense, Parson. Let's
leave it that way."

"No! I'll never consent to such a thing!"

"You've got no choice."

Powell stared down at the rifle which he had taken away from Cut
Face and brought along to the chief's lodge. The law of personal
vengeance was the oldest law of all. He recognized that. An eye for
an eye, a tooth for a tooth, a life for a life, the Old Testament said.
But people in those days had lived in bands as savage and nomadic
as the Indian bands of this day. His mission was to bring light to an
ignorant people, but before Christianity could be taught the Nez
Perces, they must learn to respect an impartial, objective kind of law.
And the white people in the country must respect it, too. It gave him
no pleasure to be put into a position where he must enforce his will
upon Elijah and Joe Knapp in direct opposition to their convictions,
but it had to be done and somehow he would find a way to do it.
Picking up the rifle, he got to his feet.

"You are not a child, Elijah; you are a chief. You are not a cow-
ard; you are a brave man. I expect you to act like one. There must be
a trial. Call the council of elders together and we will tell them what
they must do—"

The stillness of the afternoon was suddenly shattered by the shrill
sound of a woman's scream. For a moment Powell stood paralyzed,
realizing that the voice was Ruth's and that the scream had come
from the direction of the mission cabin. Joe Knapp grabbed up his
rifle, leaped to his feet and ducked out through the lodge entryway.
Powell moved then, and, once outside, a fear such as he had never
before known poured strength into his legs. In half a dozen strides,
he had passed the trapper and was running toward the corral, from
whence the scream had come.

The corral gate stood open. Within the enclosure, the sorrel was
pitching wildly, whinnying in fright, as Cut Face tried to check it
long enough to swing into the saddle. Sprawled on the churned earth
under the horse's slashing hoofs lay Mary, while Ruth, screaming
hysterically, beat at the Indian with frantic hands.

Powell saw the sorrel break away from Cut Face and shy to the
far side of the corral. He saw Cut Face strike Ruth, seize her hair
with his left hand and draw his knife with his right. He saw Ruth

drop to her knees, the Indian towering above her, the knife blade glittering in the sun.

He was perhaps twenty yards distant now. Suddenly he became aware of the weight of the rifle in his hands. Though he had hunted birds and small game in his youth, he was not an expert in the use of firearms, but he acted instinctively, without conscious thought. He stopped. He dropped to one knee, thumbed the big hammer of the percussion-cap rifle back, took aim on the Indian's breast—and pulled the trigger.

He was conscious of no recoil. But he heard an explosion, closely followed by another. He saw the knife hand drop; saw the Indian stagger backward and sag to the ground. Then, casting the rifle aside, he ran into the corral and gathered his wife and child into his arms.

Save for the fright they had suffered, they were unharmed, and presently he led them through the crowd of excited Nez Perces that had gathered in and around the corral and took them into the cabin. When Ruth had regained a measure of composure, he asked her what had happened.

"Mary and I laid down to take a nap. When I woke up, she was gone. I went outside looking for her and saw her in the corral, talking to the horse and trying to pet it. Cut Face came running into the corral and started to get on the horse. Mary wanted to get on with him. He slapped her away and she fell. I screamed and ran out—" She shivered. "Oh, Thomas, whatever came over that man?"

"We misjudged him badly, I fear. The fault is mine."

"I heard shots and saw him fall. Is he dead?"

"I don't know." He crossed the room to the door. "Stay inside, please. There are things I must do."

Going out of the cabin, he closed the door behind him and walked toward the corral, his steps heavy and slow. The weakness in his limbs was only a temporary physical reaction, he knew, a relaxing of nerves and muscles tensed to a high pitch in a time of extreme danger. It would pass presently. Then would come the soul-searching, the torment of facing his own conscience, the reckoning with his inmost being for the thing he had done.

Seeing him approach, the crowd of Indians fell silent, parting to make a lane through which he walked to the spot where the still figure lay. Joe Knapp was there; so was Elijah. Without speaking, they watched him draw near. Squatting on his heels beside the body, his black eyes unblinking, was Billy Bird. He was naked from the waist up and across his chest was a long, raking wound, oozing blood. Powell looked inquiringly at Elijah.

"He's dead?"

"Yes. He is dead."

"I told you to guard him, Billy."

The Indian avoided his eyes. "The day was warm. He laid down on the floor of my lodge and pretended to sleep. I sat between him and the entryway, watching him for a time. Then I grew sleepy too. I closed my eyes for a moment. When I opened them, he was trying to creep past me. We fought. He got away. I got my rifle and followed. When I saw him strike your wife, I shot him."

Powell recalled having heard a second shot, just after he himself had fired. "So it was you—"

"And me," Joe Knapp said quietly.

The missionary stared uncomprehendingly at the trapper. "There were only two shots, Joe, I'm positive of that."

"Yes. One was Billy's, the other mine." A sympathetic gleam touched the trapper's eyes. "If it's worrying you any, Parson, you didn't kill him. Your rifle never fired. You pulled the trigger, all right, but nothing happened. The firing nipple had no cap on it."

Unable to speak, Powell looked away. Despite what Joe Knapp had said, his soul-searching began in earnest now. When was it right to take a life? In vengeance? In anger? In protecting one's loved ones? Or only after the cold, dispassionate trial of a man by a jury of his peers—as he had tried to teach these people? He found he could not honestly answer that question now, but this much he knew: he had shot with intent to kill and would do so again under the same circumstances. The mere fact that his rifle had not fired did not matter. He would take his share of the blame for the fact that an Indian not of this band had been killed on mission grounds. His eyes sought Elijah's.

"What will his people think of this?"

"They will say justice has been done. They will say a bad man is dead. That is all. Nothing evil will happen."

"Will his relatives take revenge on your people or the whites?"

Elijah shook his head. "Who can say whose bullet killed him? Perhaps it was the bullet from the *suyapo's* gun. Perhaps the bullet came from the gun of Billy Bird, who was blood brother to Cut Face. It does not matter. He was a bad man. He tried to harm the wife of the Sent One, so both the *suyapo* God and the Nez Perce Great Spirit agreed that he must die."

Long ago, Powell had learned that an Indian's use of the word "brother" was very loose and apt to be applied where there was only the faintest of kinship. But there was something in the way Billy Bird was staring at the dead man, something deep and brooding in his eyes, that made him wonder. Gently he put a hand on Billy Bird's shoulder.

"He *was* your brother, Billy?"

"Yes. His mother and mine were the same."

"I'm sorry."

Billy Bird stood up. He was so short he had to crane his head back to look directly at the missionary, and as he did so there was a simple, childlike faith in his eyes, a sincere belief that he had done what a man must do, that touched Powell deeply.

"He was not all bad, Sent One. He told fine stories, though most of them were lies. He was brave in hunting and in war. But he was like a child—when he wanted a thing, he took it, and he grew angry at anyone who got in his way. It was as if he were two men, one good, one bad. I loved the good man in him. I hated the bad man. It was the bad man who had to die. I am not sorry I killed that man. But I am sorry the good man in him had to die too."

The Reverend Powell made no answer. There was no need to say anything more. For he realized that Billy Bird had expressed better than he himself ever could the dilemma that men had faced since time began—and must grapple with until the stars in the heavens grew cold.

It was a satisfaction to Powell to know that from this day on he would not have to face it alone.

HOW CALVIN MULLINS
BECAME THE CABALLERO
OF COWBOY FLAT

Bill Burchardt

Cowboy Flat lies out a league or so west of the Chisholm Trail in the middle of the Indian Territory. Expansive and beautiful, encircled on three sides by the big bend of the Cimarron River, it is the drover's dream of Kingdom Come. W. Hazlitt found it by accident. He was grazing his Texas trail herd off to the side of the Chisholm, looking for green grass.

It was late on in the summer trailing season, moving into fall, and the trail grass along the Chisholm was brown, dry and grazed down to dusty roots. So old man Hazlitt had kept on drifting his cows west, hunting for graze, and come out in this little bit of longhorn lagniappe.

Buffalo grass curing out saddle horn high, mixed with bunches of curly grama getting ready to turn autumn red. Blackjack oak timber for shade on the warm Indian summer days, and tall cedars the birds had sowed. The cedars would be green all winter. The river bent around it, wide and easy, hardly more than wading deep, with a broad sandbar pointing toward the precipice that fenced off its northern perimeter.

Out on the sandbar the spring floods had heaped up enough driftwood to last all winter alongside a brown sand dune maybe twelve foot high and thirty foot across. The tall sandstone bluffs that arose across the river to the north would be a natural barrier against any blue norther that might come bearing down, and prevent winter drift. W. Hazlitt knew the hallelujah land when he found it.

"Boys," he said, "we're going to winter here."

The "boys" were the Rollins brothers, Dick, Wyatt, and George, and young Calvin Mullins who had come along on the drive as drag rider and general swamper. It wasn't a big drive, around five thousand odds-and-ends head W. Hazlitt had cleaned out of west Texas—canners and cookers, heifers with late calves, a summer gaunt bunch to start out with. Hazlitt reasoned, "If we was lucky enough to graze these critters through a mild winter in this tall grass, we could haze them on into Hunnewell next spring fat an' sassy. Be one of the first herds in, while the market was still strong. A bigger dollar share for all our pockets."

George Rollins voted against it, but his two brothers voted aye, and young Calvin abstained. He figured he should go along with the boss, which got him in on the first trouble they ran into. Hazlitt set the Rollins boys to work splitting cedar to build a dugout in the big sand dune, and took young Cal along with him for a ride to survey their winter range.

Mr. Hazlitt and Calvin had not got out of sight of camp when it became apparent that another outfit had already preempted their range. The strange outfit was grazing a bunch of big steers in the willow breaks to the north and west of where Hazlitt had decided to build his headquarters. As soon as Hazlitt saw them he pulled up at the crest of a rise where the country sloped off a little down toward the river's edge.

Hazlitt motioned for Calvin to set tight, and they just stopped, skylined there, waiting for the other outfit, sure to be their adversaries, to see them. It took a while. Calvin could make out three riders yonder, holding their cattle in the edge of the willows. The three got together for a powwow then and Calvin figured they had been seen. Presently one rider broke off from the other two and came cantering back toward Calvin and Mr. Hazlitt.

The approaching stranger rode a tall roan gelding and looked like a man of authority. The closer he got the harder he looked. Mr. Hazlitt stepped down off his horse, planting his boot heels in the sandy soil like the stubborn man Calvin knew him to be. So Calvin got down, too, and stood holding his reins with his left hand, maybe ten feet away from Mr. Hazlitt. The Rollins brothers' axes were ringing out loud and clear in the morning air, felling cedar for poles up the grade from the round-topped dune.

The authoritative man identified himself as he pulled up his roan gelding. "Good morning," he said. "I'm Phillip Hoffer, field foreman for the Wyeth Wholesale Shoe Company out of Kansas City."

Calvin Mullins did not move a muscle. He watched Mr. Hazlitt nod and say nothing. The Wyeth man tried again. "We aim to winter our cattle here," he said stiffly.

"Well, you can't do it," Hazlitt said. He was a mean-looking codger, scowling over a wide handlebar mustache. He loosened his gun in the holster. The Wyeth man, even from horseback, could see that Hazlitt's gun had two deep notches cut in its protruding walnut butt. He made no inquiries about what their significance might be, but looked off toward the Rollins brothers, then asked, "Is this your range?"

Hazlitt nodded, once.

"How did you acquire it?" the Wyeth man asked thinly.

"I leased it when I took range delivery on the cattle I'm driving."

Hoffer, the Wyeth Company foreman, could see the Hazlitt herd, well spread out to the south. He could see the Rollins brothers, quiet now, with their axes leaning against their pants legs. He could see them put aside their axes, secure their rifles, and stand wide apart, clearly silhouetted in the morning light, not with their rifles leaning against their trouser legs as their axes had been, but held at ready, across their chests. To Calvin, the Rollinses looked as if they would like to shoot somebody. To hear the sound of bullets hitting human flesh would be their meat and drink. Even at this distance, Calvin could make out Wyatt Rollins' wolfish grin of eagerness.

The Wyeth man did not ask to see Hazlitt's leasing paper. Calvin had seen no more than the two Wyeth cowboys yonder in the willows. Foreman Phillip Hoffer apparently figured that Hazlitt's force was greater than his own. Five against three. He said, "Very well. We'll ride on farther."

As he rode away, Calvin burst out, "But Mr. Hazlitt, this is the Indian Territory. We're on Indian land. It isn't yours or his either. It belongs to the Indians!"

Mr. Hazlitt grinned infernally beneath his handlebars. "It's like old Rob Roy said, boy. 'They should take who have the power; and they should keep who can.'"

They rode on around the big bend, surveying the terrain, and Mr. Hazlitt opined, "This is good country. It is bound to be opened for settlement someday soon, and if a man is tired of Texas he couldn't hardly do better than this."

That afternoon he told the Rollins brothers and Calvin, "I'm going to ride on up to Hunnewell. I'll get myself in a poker game and win some dollars, buy our winter supplies and be back here in a couple weeks."

Dick and Wyatt kept busy building the dugout. Though they were hard workers, Calvin had heard gossip. There were rumors that these brothers occasionally indulged in irresponsible enterprises, like holding up the Katy Flyer at Caddo Switch in east Texas a few months ago, but one was better off not knowing the details of such engagements. Calvin joined them in splitting out cedar poles, digging into the heaped dune of sand and river dirt, lining the walls with cedar as they dug, until they had a cozy room eight foot square and seven foot high with a low, narrow entryway that could be covered with a green hide.

Calvin and George got the green hide by butchering out a yearling for veal, with Calvin doing most of the work while George complained. George was redheaded, gruff, discontented, different from his brothers. Wyatt, the oldest, was sandy-haired and quiet. Dick, the youngest, was blond, boyishly handsome and good-natured. All three brothers were restless, but George was vociferously restless, bellyaching steadily about their preparations to winter out here in the boondocks.

It seemed to Calvin like a good place for wintering. The dugout was fragrant from the split cedar logs that walled and roofed it. With a couple more days of hard work they built a lean-to off its east side to shelter the horses and the camp wagon. None too soon, Calvin thought, as they covered the floor of the dugout with prairie hay and prepared to spend their third night in it. That afternoon, it had turned overcast and cloudy, looking like the first cold snap of the season was ready to blow in. Toward evening, Dick filled their kerosene lantern from a five-gallon can and set the coal-oil can outside the dugout door.

As darkness came on they spread out their blankets for warm sleeping on the hay-covered floor, played poker 'til midnight, then turned in. Calvin felt mighty comfortable, burrowed in among the deep hay, with a cold fall wind whistling outside. About two o'clock he woke up. Flames of fire were spreading through the hay, flickering on the cedar walls and ceiling.

Calvin yelled. Apparently Dick had spilled a little kerosene around the lantern while filling it, and a spark from the embers of the fire had leaped into the coal-oil-soaked hay. By the time the three Rollinses were awake and they all managed to get outside both hay and blankets were afire. The cedar logs and ceiling caught quickly as they stood in the cold wind outside watching their cozy dugout become an inferno. The can of kerosene Dick had left outside the door exploded, setting the lean-to and hooligan wagon afire.

While they hurried to lead the horses and carry their saddles from the flaming shed, spare rifle and revolver cartridges began popping and banging inside the dugout. When the fireworks were over, sweaty from the work of saving their horses and tack from the consuming heat of the fire, they stood huddling in the cold considering what to do next.

Dick Rollins, usually cheerful and outgoing, was downcast. "What are we going to live on?"

"Beef," Wyatt said practically. "If we get tired of that, we've still got the ca'tridges left in our guns. There's squirrel, rabbits, ducks, geese, even wild turkeys around here. We'll live off the land."

George Rollins rebelled. "You all can stay out here in the boondocks if you want to. I've got close to five hundred dollars saved up." He did not say from what. "Ol' man Hazlitt gets to gambling good he might not come back here for a month. I'm going back down to Red River Crossing, hunt up that pretty little widow Nettie Wheeler we met there, and take her to Dallas and marry her."

He saddled up and took out—and was back in less than a week.

Calvin, Dick, and Wyatt had been busy trying to contrive some kind of living out of the scanty remains rescued from the fire. They were downright discouraged, and George's experiences brightened their aspect.

George related, "She was ready and willing. We went down to Dallas, I kept out enough to buy myself a new suit to get married in and gave her the rest to go get a marriage license and open us a joint bank account. I never saw her again!"

Dick Rollins jigged, and deviled his pompous brother mercilessly.

"I followed her as far as Denison," George lamented, "then she just disappeared off the face of the earth. But it put me onto something else." His sonorous voice became secretive. "That sleepy little town," he said, and shook his head in disbelief.

They waited.

"It's got three places of business," George confided. "The Butterworth Stage office, the Drovers' Rest hotel, and a mercantile store. That's all there is in town. An' they're right next door to each other."

Calvin had no idea where George was heading, and Wyatt and Dick seemed willing to keep on waiting.

"Don't you see it?" George demanded in impatient disdain. "We could take all three places—I could get the mercantile, Dick the hotel, Wyatt the stage office, while Calvin holds the horses. We could clean out that little town and be back here before Hazlitt rides in from Hunnewell."

It was the first self-admission from his companions that they had a predilection for the owlhoot trail. Calvin was momentarily shocked. But he was tired of grubbing salvage out of the charred remains of the dugout and eating unsalted meat. The more he thought about it the more sensible it sounded. As Mr. Hazlitt had counseled, "They should take who have the power; and they should keep who can."

"What about the cattle?" Calvin asked.

"They're fenced in on three sides by the river," Dick pointed out pleasantly. "The only way they can drift is south. If they scatter a little, we can chouse them back in here when we ride back up from Denison."

Wyatt was brief, and also more avid. "Let's do it."

They saddled up and headed south.

The three Rollins brothers made good company. They were as different as three cards thrown heterogeneously out of a deck, no two belonging to the same suit. George was pretentious, a blocky-built man inclined toward pomposity who liked to swagger a lot. But trim and handsome Dick seemed easygoing, the kind the girls might call "cute." Calvin felt flattered to be in Dick's personable company.

Wyatt was more mature than his brothers, stood a little taller, and had a generous share of self-pride, but he carried it well. Calvin could sense Wyatt's sure arrogance but the senior Rollins brother was not oppressive or imperious. He seemed most qualified to be the leader, but neither Dick nor George appeared to think of him in that light.

As they rode south over the next couple of days they argued a good deal. Not petty bickering or in bitter contention, but it was disagreement nevertheless.

"What we ought to do," Dick urged impulsively, "is to hang onto the money we get until we get to Hunnewell, or maybe even Wichita. Then we ought to rent us a house, and throw ourselves a play party. Lay in plenty of grub and liquor, hire us some music, then bring in the girls. Why, we could keep it going in high style for quite a while—a week—a month." He skeezicked his tongue in anticipatory ardor.

"Prodigally wasteful," George contradicted grandiloquently. "These kacks we're riding are wore out and creaky. Think how nice it would be to have hand-tooled saddles and braided horsehair reins. New duds from the skin out. Shirts with mother-of-pearl snap-on buttons. Stiff new ducking britches and leather coats—"

Wyatt interrupted, drawling, "We could take the same money you boys just blew on wine, women, and wearing apparel for horse and man. We could buy us a herd of pure blood heifers and a couple good herd bulls. We could ease back down to that same Cowboy Flat country we just left. Hazlitt has already run the shoe people off for us and he won't use it more than just this winter. Once those bone racks he hired us to drive are fat enough to sell he'll be off after a new scheme. With the protection that wide river provides from scrub range bulls, another year and we'd have purebred Hereford whiteface calves to sell at a real profit!"

Calvin listened patiently to all three ideas, then suggested in innocence, "Maybe the best way," he said naively, "would be to split the money four equal ways. Then everybody could do what he wants."

George jumped on that idea with cold feet. "There wouldn't be no fair way to split the money equally. This is my idea. I found the marks. I get a bigger cut!"

"Huh uh," disagreed Wyatt. "We can't go jumping in there helter-skelter. You all know we're going to have to have some plan and it will finally come down to me to figure out that plan just like it did at Caddo Switch. I'll be stepping out in front when we pull this off and I'll be due a bonus for my brainwork. Don't count your chickens before they're hatched."

"Or your calf crop before it's dropped," Dick grinned. "I'll vote with Calvin. Share and share alike. That makes us a majority of two."

Calvin kept listening and riding, and thinking. In his mind's eye, he carefully picked up a corner of his hole card and peered at it. I ain't supposed to do nothing but hold the horses, he thought. That don't seem like much. What if Wyatt gets together with George and votes that my share ought to be not much? Would Dick hold steady? Holding the horses will make me look just as guilty to the law as anybody. What if I wind up, not only holding the horses, but holding the sack? What if I wind up in jail? What am I going to do now? I need time to think—now! He reached into his saddlebag and brought out his fence-steepling pliers.

Calvin dismounted, hoisted his horse's off hind hoof and inspected it. All right here. Putting it down, he went to lift the other hind hoof. The Rollins boys drew rein. He felt of the shoe. "Getting a little loose," Calvin fibbed tentatively. He brought the steepling pliers to bear on the inside horseshoe nail just above the caulk. Instead of pinching the nail to tighten it, he clipped the nail's clinched end clean off. He climbed back in the saddle, dropped the pliers in the saddlebag, and they rode on.

By the time they were approaching Colbert's Ferry that near hind shoe was visibly slipping up and down, and Calvin dismounted again. With a worried frown, he wiggled the shoe. "Boys," he said. "My horse is going to throw this shoe. I'm going to have to hold up in Colbert's Ferry long enough to find a blacksmith."

"Be a hell of a note if you threw a shoe while we were hightailing it out of Denison," Wyatt agreed. "We'll ease on. You can catch up before we get there."

Calvin dropped off in Colbert's Ferry and rode around the little frontier settlement asking for a blacksmith. One of the whittle-and-spit old-timers loafing in front of the hickory-log post office told him,

"Juve Frontera's place is right at the west edge of town. He does the smithing here. I expect he can fix you up."

Without any trouble, Calvin found the place, with its crudely hand-lettered sign attached to a white picket fence. *Juvenal Frontera—welding—plowshares pointed.* An exceedingly pretty girl was feeding a flock of rust-colored Dominicker chickens in the front yard.

Calvin doffed his hat and asked politely, "Your husband at home, ma'am?"

"Señor Frontera is my father," she replied. "He is working in his shop—*detrás de la casa.*" She motioned to the rear with a gesture of her pretty dark hair and Calvin said, "*Gracias.*" He reached down to lift the front gate's latchstring, and rode around toward the sound of the anvil that was just beginning to tune up.

The anvil was ringing in earnest by the time Calvin stepped down beneath the towering hickory tree that sheltered the forge. The sound of the girl's gently pleasant voice was still amiable in his ears as he watched the bright red coals in the forge turn dull and smoky. Calvin went over to the bellows, pumped them, and the coals flared bright again as the husky Spanish smith tonged the plowpoint he had been shaping back into the odorous coal-smoky nest of heat.

In moments the point was red-hot again and with swelling biceps the broad-chested Spanish blacksmith heaved it onto the anvil, tapering it to spear sharpness, then tossed it with a hiss of live steam into the wooden tub of water at his elbow.

"Thank you," he said, as his forearm swept the sweat from his forehead. He offered his hand. "Juvenal Frontera, *a sus órdenes,* at your orders."

Calvin's hand, rope callused from work at the branding fire, iron-gripped from a boyhood of cow milking, had to react quickly to keep itself from being crushed in Frontera's vise grip.

Calvin felt a desire to try his own cowpen Spanish in reply, but it was very bad, and he was not always sure what he was saying, so he satisfied himself with English. "Glad to meet you, señor. My horse is about to throw a shoe."

"If you will permit me to look." Frontera leaned to pick up Calvin's gelding's near hind hoof. He pushed the shoe up against the hoof, wiggled the loose nail, reached for his tongs and pulled it out. "This nail has been cut," he said. "How unusual!"

He selected a square, handmade nail from the hotchpot box beside the huge hickory stump on which the anvil rested, drove the nail home, and clinched it neatly.

Calvin had been surveying Juvenal Frontera's husky body, his nut-brown countenance, the horseshoe-shaped scar on his sweaty fore-

head where some previous equine client had left a distinguishable
mark and wondered, perhaps irreverently, how such a *macho* of a
man could have sired the tender slip of pulchritude and lovely femi-
ninity he had seen in the front yard.

"Your horse is ready," said the blacksmith.

Calvin wasn't. He shifted his weight from one boot to the other
and, standing hipshot, asked, "How much do I owe you?"

Frontera shrugged. "*Ni un centavo.* That is to say, it is nothing. A
return of the favor of your heating my forge."

"Well, thank you." Calvin shifted again, and stood, studying. "Do
you know where a fellow could buy something to eat around here?"
He jingled the silver in his pocket to signify his willingness to pay,
and Frontera comprehended with a friendly grin.

"You are at your own house, señor," the blacksmith said.
"*Háganos el favor de compartir nuestras comidas pobres.*"

Calvin knew that he had just been asked to supper, and the
thought of missing a chance to dine with the pretty girl out front was
disagreeable, but the thought of delaying the Rollins brothers in their
project was giving him more trouble. Whatever the risks of holding
the horses in Denison, the risks of *not* doing so suddenly seemed
greater. If I was to double-cross them, he thought, there is a chance
they would be almighty sore at me. I ought to just ask for something
I could eat on the road, but he thought once more of the girl, and it
was a little more than he could bear.

He accepted Frontera's direction to the washstand on the back
porch, poured water from pitcher into basin, washed his hands and
face, combed his hair in the piece of looking glass that hung up
above and, after the smith had done the same, followed Juvenal
Frontera into the kitchen.

"*Permítame presentarle a usted—*" The blacksmith looked embarrassed and apologized. "I slip too easily into the Spanish. Permit me
to present my daughter, Constancia."

Calvin grew bold. "Would it hurt your feelings if I was to call you
Connie?" he asked.

"Certainly not." She smiled. "If you are polite in saying it."

Her complexion was persimmons and cream, her teeth Choctaw
hominy white, her lips holly berries in autumn, and though he could
not eat her, he surely ate his share of the delicious supper she had
prepared. Toward its end, there was a knock on the front door.

The Rollins brothers, he thought, in sudden alarm.

But she went and returned to report, "Our cattle have broken
down the fence in the pasture across the river, *Papá.* Mr. Weill, who
brings the report, says they are straying across the plantation fields

there, eating the cotton bolls as they go. He saw them as he was driving his wagon this morning on the way to the ferry."

The blacksmith replaced his white napkin in its silver ring and stood up at once. "I must go and drive them back."

Calvin stood up, too. "I'll go and help you," he said, feeling that there was no other course of action open to him.

Frontera protested, but beneath the protest Calvin sensed a sincere appreciation of his offer, and they left the house together. It was farther than Calvin had anticipated. The pasture was on the Texas side of the river. They had to ride the ferry, which took more than an hour, and by the time they had galloped up the river to the pasture, darkness was setting in—a darkness accelerated by the fact that it was clouding up and looked like rain.

The loose cattle had worked their way across the cotton field, down into the breaks beyond the river, and scattered. Hunting them out took time. Driving them out, in singles and small bunches, took more time, and as the darkness became stygian the fine mist that had started to fall turned into driving rain. Calvin was soon soaked to the skin, wandering up and down the broken coulees and draws in the pitch-dark night, and lost.

He tried yelling but his shouts were lost too, swallowed up in the soggy wet timber and the rough, eroded terrain of the tangled canyons. The rain was pouring down. He huddled in a gully beneath the sprawling roots of a washed-out burr oak, holding onto the reins of his horse, and spent a long night.

The day dawned fresh and autumn bright, with wheeling crows overhead, cawing in repartee about this sodden, miserable human critter that had invaded their domain. Calvin, his teeth chattering from the night's chill, mounted a spongy wet saddle, ferreted out another covey of Frontera's loose cattle and choused them up and out on the flat.

The blacksmith, now with the help of a couple of mounted Walullu Plantation hands, was holding together a considerable herd, moving them back toward the Red River, and hurriedly rode to meet Calvin, greeting him with a flood of friendly Spanish.

"*Señor Mullins, pienso que ahora los tenemos todos. ¡Tú éres muy amable! Te aseguro que es cosa de pocas horas la reparación de la red, entonces regresaremos a la casa.*"

Calvin accepted the statement that they had recaptured all the cattle, that it would take only a few hours to repair the fence, and they would return to the Frontera house in Colbert's Ferry, not only as evidence that he was very amiable, but as assurance that he had been fully accepted by Juvenal Frontera as a friend, countryman and companion.

Returning to the house carried an unanticipated bonus. "Connie" left him alone in the kitchen only after his assurance that he would strip to the buff and bathe himself in the tub of steaming hot water she had drawn. He then relaxed in the luxury of a soft blanket while she washed, dried, and ironed his clothes. He did this dozing peacefully on the living room couch and drowsily listening to the conversation between Constancia and her father as she insisted that, this afternoon, she must go up to Fort Washita to visit her friend, the commanding officer's wife, and take her a gift of sand plum preserves she had canned. Juvenal was urging her not to go until he had time to accompany her. She might encounter soldiers of the fort en route, and some of them were rough and dangerous men.

"You know that you should not travel alone," Juvenal insisted. "*Pues,* the old men who gossip in front of the post office tell me they saw three *desperados,* train robbers, the Rollins gang, ride through town yesterday morning. You never know who you may encounter in this wild and untamed country."

Calvin saw no reason that he himself could not accompany her now. It was probably too late to join Dick, Wyatt, and George in their Denison enterprise anyway. But by the time he went to Fort Washita the Rollins brothers would be back here, waiting for him, and he forced himself to confront the possibility that they might try to kill him for his desertion and for his guilty knowledge of what they had been up to in Texas. He remembered how threatening those three had looked, standing with their rifles at ready for a shoot-out with the Wyeth crew.

But the temptation was too great. He got dressed, offered his services, and Constancia accepted them pleasantly, almost of custom, as if that is what she had expected all along. They went by buckboard, with Calvin driving, the vehicle being hitched to the Fronteras' light team of dappled mules, a spanking and lively pair, fleet and sure of foot. If Calvin had let them out they would have traveled the easy trail north to Fort Washita in a couple of hours, but he was in no hurry.

He dallied. The deciduous timber of this well-watered country was in full autumn glory—red hickory, purple gum, towering bright yellow cottonwoods, pin oaks incandescent, flamelike in hue. It was delightful. The soft beauty of the petite girl beside him, with her delicate heart-shaped face, again was almost more than Calvin could bear. She elicited considerable information from him about his growing-up years.

She said, "When we had *posole* for supper last night I noticed that you called it *pashofa*."

"Yes'm. I'm a quarter Choctaw. Born not far east of here in fact, over near Bokchito. I had a kind of a dogie boyhood, working for cow outfits, mostly in Texas."

"My father is *mejicano*," she said. "Equally Spanish and *Zapoteca*. So I am myself one-fourth Indian."

It gave him an excuse to stare. "You sure look altogether Spanish," he said, drinking in the vision of her loveliness as a parched man slakes his thirst.

She stared back, her eyes sparkling and eager. "And you look wholly—"

"Gringo," he supplied. "Yes'm. The way we meander around nowadays, most folks have a mixed-up heredity."

"There is a story of a young girl engaged to a soldier of the fort to which we are going," she related. "He had been ordered here and arrived in the fall—at this time of year. It was planned that she would travel here in the spring and they would marry. Instead, he sickened and died. When his *novia*, the girl to whom he was engaged, learned of his death, she, too, sickened and died, only a month later, and far away. It is said that on a certain night in the fall of the year his ghost appears outside the gates of the fort, beckoning toward the river where we are about to cross. Exactly a month later her ghost appears at the river crossing, beckoning him to come from the fort."

"Then if we go back late tonight," Calvin augured, "we better watch out for ghosts."

They forded the river crossing, rode into the fort, and were presently in the office of Major Logan Goddard, commanding officer, and promptly escorted to the cottage where Calvin met Dolores Goddard, the commanding officer's wife. Like Constancia, though somewhat older, she was Spanish. Their friendship based itself on a mutual desire for occasional conversation in the language of their birth, and when Calvin was introduced, Señora Dolores Goddard said to Constancia, "*Tu joven es muy guapo*."

Calvin thought that he would blush at this secretive comment that he was very handsome, but if he did it went unnoticed in his general discomfiture at being here in the high society of an upper-echelon army officer and his obviously cultured wife.

Calvin was impressed at the ease Constancia revealed in this rarefied social atmosphere. He was glad that, due to Constancia, his clothes were at least clean, his ducking pants and homespun shirt neatly pressed and, due to his own efforts while waiting for the pressing, his boots were polished.

Constancia delivered her gift of sand plum preserves, and the major showed Calvin around the fort with all the courtesy he would have extended a visiting inspector general. They dined that evening amid silver service and crystal—the kind Calvin had seen in Dallas store windows, but never before on a table at which he was himself an honored guest.

On the insistence of Major and Señora Goddard they spent the night. Again Calvin had the feeling Constancia had known beforehand that it would be that way. He would readily have accepted a cot in a barn or with the enlistees, but was awed to find himself installed in one of the big house's elegant bedrooms. About midmorning the next day, after a late and hearty breakfast, they started the return drive to Colbert's Ferry.

It being broad daylight they encountered no ghosts at the gates or in crossing the river. The ghosts Calvin was fighting were in his head. How would it be when they got back to Colbert's Ferry and he met the Rollinses head on?

The three outlaws would separate themselves wide apart, Wyatt in the middle taking the lead as usual. It would probably happen right there in Connie's front yard. She and her father would be forced to watch in horror as Wyatt would say, "Fill your hand, kid."

Calvin would try to draw his gun but he would be too late and .45 slugs fired by all three of the Rollinses would jerk and twist his body, driving him down. Calvin anticipated that he would die a sudden death, leaking blood on the ground right at Constancia Frontera's pretty feet. *O beat the drum slowly, and play the fife lowly.* They would sound the dead march as they carried him away.

Having been riding in silence, Constancia sought to break into his funereal introspection by speaking. "I am so grateful to you," she said, "for helping *Papá* gather his stock when they got out. The pasture in which he must keep them is too small. We have been unable to find any more good land for leasing. I am sorry you had to remain out in the rain all that night."

Being shocked out of his gloomy reverie and feeling forced to say something, before he could stop himself a phrase of the dreaded, untrustworthy cowpen Spanish that he had been avoiding slipped out. *"No vale un grillo,"* he said.

Then it came to him in horror that he did not know what *grillo* meant. He had heard the expression many times while working with Mexican *vaqueros* south in Texas—*it is not worth a ????*—but it had never occurred to him until this moment that he did not know what a *grillo* was. Maybe it was a dirty word!

She did look surprised. "Oh!" she said, startled. "You speak Spanish?"

Calvin was deeply embarrassed. "Cow country lingo," he admitted. "It's pretty crude, and a good deal of the time I don't really know what I'm saying—"

"It is a common saying you have used," she said.

Common, he thought with sinking heart. Mighty common, probably. You might even say vulgar! "I'm sorry, ma'am," he said miserably. "My grandma used to wash my mouth out with soap for using dirty words I'd heard without knowing what they meant before I said them. If it wouldn't shame you too much to tell me, what does *grillo* mean?"

"*Grillo* means cricket," she replied in mystification.

His relief that he had not committed an incredibly obscene indiscretion turned into joy that bordered on euphoria. Here he was on a lovely autumn morning, riding through the tinted countryside with the prettiest girl he had ever seen. The whole world suddenly seemed a rosy place where troubles had their own way of working themselves out. It emboldened him to the point of almost certain indiscretion.

"Señorita Frontera—Connie—Constancia—" He braved himself. "Would you consider marrying me?"

"I have been considering it," she said sedately, "for the past two days. *Y pienso que sí.* I have been thinking that the answer is yes."

The euphoria took hold in earnest. Calvin reached across the buggy and took hold of her hand. She scooted over so that the reach would not be so far, and he drove the rest of the way back to Colbert's Ferry completely forgetful of the Rollins brothers. Until they pulled up at the Fronteras' front gate.

The front yard was empty.

They disembarked from the buggy and he swung the front gate open. As they ascended the porch steps he took her arm to assist her. His heart was pounding. Partly from the excitement of touching her. Partly from an unnamed dread of the unknown but anticipated scene of violence to be encountered when they entered the house.

Juvenal Frontera came from the kitchen to meet them. He was eating a sandwich of thick homemade bread, roast beef, and drinking a bottle of beer.

"*Papá,*" said Constancia, "I should have mentioned that we might remain overnight with Dolores and Major Goddard."

Her father shrugged. "I expected you to stay. We always remain overnight when I accompany you. I have just been for the mail. Those lazy ones who loaf at the post office may have been right in thinking they saw the Rollins gang pass through town the day before yesterday. The Dallas newspaper has gotten out a special issue."

It lay on the dining room table. Calvin glanced at the headline: ROLLINS OUTLAWS KILLED ATTEMPTING MULTIPLE HOLDUP IN DENISON. He leaned on the table, his blood pumping, as farther down the column he read, "—town marshal recognized the famed bandits as they were simultaneously entering the Butterworth Stage office, the Drovers' Rest, and the Compton Mercantile. He opened fire and other townsmen quickly followed suit. All three outlaws were slaughtered—"

"Mr. Frontera," Calvin said, trying to speak calmly, as if he had never heard of, and had no interest in, outlaws or holdups. "Connie was saying you need more pasture. There's a place up in the middle of the Indian Territory where I'm wintering a bunch of cattle. Some friends of mine built a cedar-lined dugout there. Then we got careless and burned it out. We had started rebuilding it. There is an oodle of pasture, and I intend to claim it when it's opened for settlement. I could move your cattle up there, and finish that dugout." He glanced at Connie. "It sure would make a cozy place for a winter honeymoon."

A FAREWELL TO
MISS LOTTIE

John R. Erickson

While the preacher was saying his words, I couldn't help looking off to the south where Buffalo Canyon joins the Canadian River. The sun was bright and the wind was soft, the wild flowers were starting to bloom in the draws and the air hung blue and deep and mysterious down along the Canadian brakes. And there for a little while I just couldn't help letting my mind go back to *that* day, so many years ago.

If old man Patterson had thought that I had the slightest interest in his daughter, he would've kicked me off the ranch in record time. In the first place, he didn't believe that *any* cowboy was good enough for Miss Lottie. In the second place, he probably considered me a worse choice than most. "Cowboys and ladies just don't mix," is what he always said. And they didn't, not until that hot weekend in May 1895.

Henry, Lottie's older brother, had gone to Higgins to look at some cattle. We'd just had a big rain that Thursday and Mr. Patterson had felt so good about it that he'd taken his wife on a three-day shopping trip to Dodge City. I figured Lottie had gone too.

I was supposed to be putting in water gaps. On the Patterson place that meant two days of riding and camping in the brakes. I'd ridden south from the house that Friday morning and found the first large draw full up with water. The gap had washed out, all right, but there wasn't a chance of putting it back until the water went down. So I rode back to the place, figuring I'd catch up on my sleep, or since I was going to be the boss for three days, maybe I'd shout a few orders to the hogs, just to stay in practice.

I left old Dollar in the lot and was going to the saddlehouse to get a brush when I noticed that the door was standing open. That was funny. I was sure I'd closed it. Then I heard someone talking inside and I thought, well, I've cornered me up a thief here. I got the Winchester from the saddle and crept up to the door. The thief's voice was real high-pitched, almost like a woman's, only from the way he was cussing and using vulgar language I knew it *couldn't* be a woman. Well, I thought, he must really be a bad man, so I better give him a good scare. I cocked the Winchester, threw open the door with a bang, and hollered, "Put up your hands, son of a gun, 'fore I blow you away!"

Now, Miss Lottie, you understand, was a grown woman with a serious mind. Why, she'd just gotten back from two years at the convent in Stanton, where she'd studied Latin, and literature, and manners, and all kinds of stuff. Anyway, she was every inch a lady. She read poetry and could quote Shakespeare and knew which fork to use on what and ordered her dresses out of St. Louis.

So, when I busted in the saddlehouse door, what did I see? There sits Miss Lottie on a keg of tenpenny nails. Her skirts are hiked up to her thighs and she's puffing on one of her daddy's five-cent cigars. Boy, was I shocked. When she saw me, she screamed, throwed the cigar at me, jerked down her skirts, stamped her feet, and burst into tears. I was so surprised, I just dropped the Winchester and ran. But I couldn't run fast enough to forget what I'd seen—Miss Lottie Patterson smoking a cigar and swearing like a nester—and halfway between the saddlehouse and Dollar it hit me. That was the funniest sight I'd ever seen in my life, and I started laughing and couldn't stop. Couldn't stop, that is, till I heard the crack of a rifle and the zing of a .44 slug right above my ear. That sobered me up pretty fast.

"Shut your vulgar mouth!" she yelled. Then she cocked and fired again, and I shut my vulgar mouth. "You come back here, Zack Morris, or so help me I'll . . ."

"Yes ma'am! Here I come!" I put up my hands and lit a shuck for the saddlehouse. I didn't know but what she really would shoot me.

When I got inside, she was still crying. "I don't know whether to shoot you or not," she said with a wild look in her eye.

"Your daddy wouldn't like that."

"Well, I *will* unless you promise never to tell what you saw. *NEVER!*"

Boy, don't think I didn't promise when she showed me the hole in the end of that rifle!

"Oh, I could just *die!*" she bawled, throwing the rifle on the floor and blowing a hole in the north wall. I said a quick prayer that she'd run out of ammo before she got around to me. "I could just *die!* Where did you come from, Zack Morris? You're supposed to be riding fence." I tried to explain but she wouldn't listen. "I'll never live down this humiliation. I could never look another man in the eye again. I might as well kill myself right now, and don't you try to stop me, Zack Morris! If you so much as *touch* me, I'll tell Daddy and you know what he'll do."

Sure, I knew all about Mr. Patterson and his spoilt little daughter, but I also had a pretty good idea of what he'd do if I let his spoilt little daughter commit suicide. So I took a step toward her, and she showed me that rifle bore again.

"Don't you come near me, you vulgar nasty boy! I know about your kind. You peek through windows and try to look up girls' dresses. I intend to tell Daddy everything when he gets home."

Now, I can't say that it made me mad, what she said about me, mostly because she was pretty right. I *was* a peeker and a dress-looker-upper. I'd never looked up *her* dress, mainly because she'd never got that close to me, but I had watched her through a crack in the saddlehouse wall a couple of evenings in the summer. She'd swung in the glider on the porch and read poetry and looked off at the blue hills along the Canadian River and sighed, and that's when I first knew that Miss Lottie was lonely.

But anyway, what she said about me being a vulgar nasty boy didn't make me mad, but it did hurt my pride, and all of a sudden her suicide began to sound like the best idea I'd heard all day long.

"Yes ma'am," I said, "well, if you'll scuse me I'd better get back to them water gaps." And I swaggered right out the door and started hitching up Dollar.

"I'm going to kill myself, Zack," she called to me. "Would you explain it to my parents?"

"Yes ma'am, sure will."

"On second thought," she said, a little burnt that I was taking it so easy, "I'll leave a note. I'm going to tell them everything. Do you hear me, Zack? I'm going to tell them that it was all *your* fault." I led old Dollar to the gate, and that really burned her up. "You don't even care, do you? You're too crude! You don't have the manners of a sheep raiser, Zack Morris!"

I swung up into the saddle. "Just hang the Winchester on the wall when you get through. And if you need more shells . . ."

The heifer actually shot at me! I gave Dollar the spurs and we split the wind. I heard one more shot and one more shout and then we dropped off into the brakes, and everything was quiet and I was glad to be away from the spiteful little thing. Who did she think she was, anyway?

The draw was still running like a river when I got there, so I laid down under a cottonwood tree to wait. I watched the clouds for a while and dropped off to sleep. I woke up hearing horse hooves and thinking, "Son of a gun, she's gonna kill me yet!" I jumped on Dollar's bare back and would have made tracks for Buffalo Canyon if she hadn't called out.

"Zack, don't go! Please wait!" And like a fool, I waited. But as she came closer, I could see that she'd had a change of heart. We said hello. "I'm sorry, Zack," she said, looking at the ground. "I'm sorry I shot at you."

Well, now, that was something to be sorry about, all right. But I couldn't stay mad at her for very long. "Oh, that's all right," I said, trying to look taller and older than I really was. "They say that gettin' shot at builds character."

"I'm really sorry, Zack. Really." Then she looked at me through those deep pools of blue and smiled, kind of sad. "I brought you a basket lunch. Would that help any?"

Fried chicken, potato salad, okra pickles, fresh bread, wild plum butter . . . uh huh, it sure did help.

"What's that?" I asked. She'd just pulled a dark bottle out of the basket.

"*WINE!*" she gleamed.

I was shocked. Lottie was a good Baptist lady! Or so I thought. "Wine! I didn't know you were a drinker."

"Oh, I'm not, silly boy. One bottle doesn't make you a drinker. The Catholics drink wine all the time. Here." She handed me a glass and we took a drink.

"That's real good," I said, lying like fifteen dogs. I thought it tasted awful but I didn't want her calling me a sheep raiser again, so I acted like it was real good.

"I brought it back from school. I've been saving it for a special occasion." We drank another glass and I began to feel flies buzzing around in my head. "Well," says Miss Lottie, "are you going to forgive me?"

"Oh sure. But tell me somethin', Miss Lottie. What in the world were you doin' in the saddlehouse?"

She turned red in the face. "I wish you wouldn't talk about it, ever. I could have just died!"

"Oh, I won't tell. Cross my heart and hope to die, stick a hunnerd pins in my eye. Now tell me what you were doin' in there."

She thought it over a minute. "Oh, all right. I know it looked silly and immoral, but everyone was gone, Zack, and I just felt . . . wild. All at once I was the only person left in the whole world and I could do anything I wanted. Haven't you ever felt that way? Wanted to do all the things your mother told you never to do?"

"Oh yow, I've felt that way before."

"Have you really? Do you feel that way now?"

"Well, yow, I guess so." And it was true. The wine was warming me up.

"Well, I do too," she whispered, "and do you know what I want to do?"

"No ma'am."

"I want to go swimming."

Something in her eyes made me squirm. "Well, it's a good day for that, all right, if a person just had a swimmin' hole." She pointed to the draw. "Oh, you wouldn't wanta go swimmin' in that. It's rainwater, real cold, and the current's pretty swift. You don't wanta end up in the Canadian River, do you?" Her shrug said she wasn't going to worry much about it. "Well, I guess you can swim if you want."

"Can I?" She smiled, and right then I knew how come she was so spoilt.

"Sure," I says, "you're the boss's daughter. Me, I'm just an ordinary cowboy."

She took ahold of my hand. "Yes, but you're a nice cowboy. You didn't even get mad when I shot at you."

"Uh huh, I reckon." I was on my guard by this time because I could see that something was going on in her eyes.

"Zacky," she said, "I want to go swimming, and I want *you* to go with me."

"Uh. Well, that'ud be all right, Miss Lottie . . ."

"Call me Lottie."

"Sure will. That'ud be all right, Lottie, but, see, I wouldn't be able to go back to the house for dry clothes, see, 'cause I gotta fix them water gaps before your daddy gets back, and I gotta fix them water gaps . . ."

"I see," she said, picking a piece of grass off my shirt. "So we better not get our clothes wet. Is that right?"

"I think so, ma'am, I really do."

"Well," she said, running her tongue over her lip, "can you think of any way we could swim without getting our clothes wet?"

It looked like the devil himself had drawed that smile on her pretty little face. I didn't have to *think*. That smile said it all.

"No no," said I.

"Yes yes," said she.

"No, I'm sorry, Miss Lottie."

"Oh, don't be sorry, Zacky."

I tried to laugh. "You, you don't really mean . . . *that*, do you?"

"Oh-h-h-h yea-yus, I do."

"No no no, no ma'am, I'm sorry, but, why, if I did your daddy, why, he'd . . ."

"But if you don't I'll tell Daddy you did anyway."

I have to admit that I was glad she'd won the argument, even though I figured I'd end up getting killed by somebody. That wild feeling was starting to burn inside me. And yet, at the same time, it was humiliating to be forced to do things, even nice things, by such a strong-willed young lady.

But I didn't think of that until a week later. Right then I wasn't complaining.

"Well," I said after a minute, "what do we do now?"

"I'll undress in that thicket around the bend and you undress here. We'll meet in the water. Only I want you to give me your Gentle-man's Word that you won't peek on me. Let me hear you promise."

"I promise."

"No, say that you give your *Solemn Word as a Gentleman*."

"I give my Solemn Word as a Gentleman."

Hell, she'd never thought I was a gentleman anyway, so after she'd gone, I climbed up the cottonwood and watched the whole show. She went through her slips and stuff one by one, hanging each on the plum thicket. When she got down to the last bit of lace between her and the great outdoors, she unbuttoned it down the front, glanced over both shoulders, then tore it off, ran to the edge of the water, and jumped in. The flash of her nakedness left me trembling and dizzy, and I had to be mighty careful climbing down the tree.

As I'd predicted, the water was cold as ice, and if I hadn't been scared of exposing myself to the young lady, I might've stayed on the bank all day. But while I was testing the water with my toe, Lottie sang out that she was coming, ready or not, tee hee. Tee hee hell, I said, and jumped in, just as she came floating around the bend.

I couldn't see anything but her head, of course, but what I *thought* I saw more than made up for what I missed. As she drew closer, carried by the current, I reached out and tried to grab her arm. When she saw what I was doing, she laughed and paddled away, and before we knew it, we were playing tease and chase. Then I finally grabbed one of her arms, grabbed it, you know, thinking that it was all part of the game. Well, Miss Lottie set me straight about that. She rared back and busted me across the face, and I'm not lying, I saw red checkers for a whole minute.

"Don't you *ever* try that again, Zack Morris! Do you hear me? Don't you *ever!*"

I don't know what it was came over me. Maybe it was the wine.

Maybe it was the wild feeling we'd talked about. Maybe it was something I'd never even heard of before. I don't know. But all at once I busted out laughing, and the madder she got the harder I laughed, because I knew right then that Miss Lottie Patterson had gone too far.

I turned around and waded ashore. When she saw my butt rising out of the water, she gasped and hid her eyes. "Zack Morris! What on earth are you doing!"

"You'll find out."

"Zack, you come back here! Zack, if you don't get back in this water immediately I'm going to tell Daddy!"

"Do that, will you?"

I gathered up her clothes and tied them into a bundle on the back of her horse. Lottie was stealing glances one minute and sparing her poor eyes from my flesh the next. When I came back to the tree, she was still sputtering out threats.

"Zack," she whooped, "I'm going home! I don't know what you're doing, but I demand that you stop it right now!"

"Miss Lottie," I said, "look here for a minute, would you please?"

"Are you decent?"

"Decent as you are, which ain't sayin' much. Now lookie here. I want you to come out. Now."

"You must be crazy!"

Then there was a long silence as the truth began to chew at the edges of her brain. It was just like she'd said: We were a-l-l-l-l-l-l-l alone, no one was around to tell us what to do, and we were both feeling kind of wild. And the rest of it was that she'd started something and I intended to finish it, and right then I didn't give a hoot about the consequences.

"Zack, what are you doing!" She uncovered her eyes and we looked at each other for a long time.

"Lottie, you have summoned up the devil and now the devil must have his due." I hoped she'd think I was quoting Scripture. "I'll give you ten minutes to come out."

"I'd die first!" she bellowed.

"And if you don't come out, I'm gonna send your horse and clothes back to the house."

"YOU WOULDN'T!!"

"Uh huh, yes I would, I sure would, and then I'm gonna ride off and leave you to the coyotes and rattlesnakes. Now, I don't know whether they'd eat a Patterson or not, but . . ."

At the mention of rattlesnakes, she went into a fit of crying that I couldn't have resisted for very long on another day. But it wasn't an-

other day and I resisted it just fine. Five minutes passed. "Five minutes, Lottie. How are you at fightin' wolves with your bare hands?"
This brought on another change in character.

"You nasty filthy man! Animal! I hate you! I hope you burn in ev-
erlasting hellfire! Daddy's going to string you up to the nearest tree
when he gets home!" And so on.

I stood up and started putting on my shirt. "One minute, Lottie.
In one more minute I'm goin'." She glared as I pulled on my jeans
and boots and saddled Dollar. "Well, what do you say, Lottie?"

"You're an animal and I hate you!"

I drew back my arm to slap her horse across the rump.

"Wait!"

I waited. "You comin' out?"

With her head bowed, her voice seemed very small. "Yes, I'm
coming out."

We spent the afternoon beneath the cottonwood tree. We watched
time pass in the iceberg clouds that sailed across the sea of prairie
sky, in a buzzard that hung like a kite in the air above us, in the
muddy water of our own little river. A red ball of sun rolled down
the hill of sky, and all at once we noticed our growing shadows.

"Zack," Lottie said, breaking the long silence, "you won't talk
about me, will you? I know that cowboys do that sometimes."

"No, Lottie, I got a little bit of sense."

"You really do, Zack. You amaze me. You know a lot of things."

"Not much, but I know you're beautiful."

"And you're sweet," she said, and to this day I believe she meant
it.

I bent down and kissed her on the nose. "Lottie, you want me to
ride back to the house with you? It's gettin' dark."

"Oh, Zack!" she cried. "I don't want to go back to that big old
lonesome house. Let me stay with you. I can help you put in the
water gaps."

I laughed. "Can you handle bob wire?"

"Well, no."

"Can you drive a steeple?"

"No."

"You know which side of the post the wire goes on?"

"No, I guess I don't know anything."

I laughed again. "You'll do just fine, honey." She tried to hug me
but I stopped her. "But you gotta understand that we're gonna be
sleepin' on the hard ground. No featherbeds out here."

"That's all right."

"And you may have to eat roast rabbit for dinner."

"I can do it."

"And you won't have no outhouse to go to."

"Zack, don't be vulgar!" She gathered up her clothes and scampered off into the thicket. I just sat there, looking at myself in the water and wondering if it was really true that Lottie cared for me.

The next morning we rose with the sun. The water had fallen during the night and we went right to work. I stripped down to my jeans and worked in the creek, while Lottie stood on the bank and handed me my tools. It was hot and we were both sweating. It came as a real shock to me to find out that Lottie could sweat. That sounds pretty dumb, but that's how much I knew about ladies in those days.

For two days we forgot the rest of the world. We galloped our horses over the greening plains, picked wild flowers in Buffalo Canyon, and were as happy as two people could be. On Saturday night I asked Lottie if maybe she'd marry me someday, and she said maybe she would. And to this day I believe she meant it.

But Sunday came and we had to ride back to the ranch, back to the world where I was a cowboy and she was a lady. I kept hoping that maybe things could stay the same, but as we rode I could see the changes coming over her face. She grew nervous and wouldn't talk. I could see her stealing glances at me when I wasn't supposed to be looking. Her eyes were filled with doubt. Then, as we rode into the lot, the doubt left her face and I knew that it was all over.

"Unsaddle my horse. I have to get cleaned up." Then she stopped and said, as cold as though I'd never looked into her soul, "I hope you'll keep your word. If you spread stories, I'll just deny them. Who are people going to believe, you or me?"

It was over, all right, and six months later Miss Lottie got married to a rancher named Sims.

I've often wondered if Miss Lottie ever realized how those words crushed her bowlegged cowboy, or if she ever suspected that Zack Morris stumbled into the saddlehouse, tore the Winchester from the wall, and for a minute of heartbeats considered shooting her dead, or if she heard him crying as he jumped on Dollar and rode out on the prairie.

And there I stood, fifty years later, looking off in the distance toward Buffalo Canyon and the blue Canadian River. I was still wondering about those things and still thinking back to that weekend in May—the clouds, the smells of flowers and new grass, the way the wind kissed you on the face. And I remembered the smile on her lips and her long brown hair spilling over her shoulders as we rode across the prairie.

When the preacher had finished his prayer, I walked to the grave and gave Miss Lottie my flower. I wanted to say something, but nothing came and I went home.

THE EASY WAY
Wayne C. Lee

Dan York finished his morning chores at the livery barn and headed up the street to the sheriff's office. Sheriff Ivan Boggs owned the livery stable but he seldom came down there.

Dan, twenty years old, was four inches taller and twenty pounds heavier than the sheriff but he figured that the sheriff had the answers to all the problems of the little town of Serene. This morning, however, Ivan Boggs was glaring at a telegram on his desk.

"Something wrong?" Dan asked.

Boggs snapped the paper with his fingers. "This telegram from the sheriff over in Butler County says the Tovar gang is working this area. That's all we need just when we're set for our big cattle sale."

Dan caught his breath. Not the Tovar gang! He had thought that by putting two states and eight hundred miles between him and them they'd never find him.

"Does that poster describe them?" Dan asked shakily.

Boggs nodded. "The leader is a big man about forty-five. The two men with him are also big but in their early twenties. That could fit a lot of men around Serene."

Dan nodded weakly. "I reckon so. I came to tell you we're running low on oats at the barn. We have a lot of horses there."

"Just feed a little less," Boggs said. "Taking care of the horses ain't my big worry right now. With all the cowboys and buyers here, how am I supposed to pick out members of this Tovar gang if they do show up?"

"Maybe they won't come," Dan said and turned to the door.

The sheriff had a problem, he admitted, as he headed back to the livery barn. But Dan had a problem, too, one of the biggest he'd ever faced.

Orphaned at twelve, Dan had been sent to live with his aunt, who was a widow. A year later she married Lem Tovar who brought along his two sons, Ozzie and Al. Ozzie was five years older than

Dan, and Al three. Lem Tovar and his sons often disappeared for a week at a time but it was more than a year before Dan and his aunt discovered that they already had a reputation for robbing banks and holding up stages.

The shock was too much for Dan's aunt who died within a few months. Dan tried to get away but Lem Tovar stopped him. He knew too much about the Tovars so he made him one of the gang. Dan was watched like a prisoner and became the flunky for the others. It wasn't until about a year ago that they took him on a job. They held up a bank and killed the teller. Lem Tovar drove home the point that Dan was now one of the gang, just as guilty of murder as any of them.

Six months ago, Dan slipped away on their return from a stage holdup and he kept riding. He considered it his lucky day when he arrived in Serene just as Ivan Boggs had decided that he couldn't do justice to both his livery barn and his newly assumed job of sheriff. Dan was hired to run the barn. He was sure he was far enough away from Tovar territory that they would never find him.

Now this telegram said the gang was in the next county. Had Lem Tovar discovered where Dan was? Or had he heard of the big cattle sale and knew there would be a lot of money here? Either way, Dan was in dire trouble. If Lem Tovar saw him, he'd surely kill him.

Before stepping back into the barn, he looked out on the prairies. There were three big herds, gathered on local ranches, grazing on the hills west and south of town. The local hotel was full of cowboys from Wyoming, Montana and western Nebraska. Their bosses would be coming in on the train tomorrow, the day advertised for the competitive bidding.

Serene wasn't a cattle town. This was just the town's way of getting the best price for the mixed herds the ranchers of the area wanted to sell. These herds were mostly heifers and young cows with a few bulls. They'd go to stock new ranges.

There would be few bank drafts here. Most transactions would be made in cash. An ideal setup for the Tovar gang. Dan was guessing they had seen the advertisements meant to lure ranchers wanting to increase their herds to Serene. But every trap set for a mink ran the risk of catching a skunk.

Dan had just gone into the barn when a shadow darkened the door. He looked up to see Jennie McWilliams. Jennie was the daughter of the banker, Hubert McWilliams, and was the main reason Dan liked Serene. Jennie was small, her black hair barely coming to his shoulder. But there was a light in her sparkling black eyes that lit a fire in Dan that he didn't try to put out.

"Will you take care of Nugget for me, Dan?" she asked, coming down the alley, leading her chestnut.

"Sure," Dan said, deliberately touching her hand as he took the reins. "Have a nice ride?"

"Fine. There are thousands of cattle out there. Pa says they could bring over a hundred thousand dollars."

A chill ran through Dan. That much money would draw the Tovars from a dozen states away.

"You look worried, Dan," Jennie said. "Were you afraid I'd fall for some cowboy out there?"

She laughed lightly and he tried to grin. He did worry often that Jennie would find some glamorous man who would cut him out. He didn't know how he could rate so high with Jennie. She was the most beautiful girl he'd ever seen and she was the banker's daughter. He was at the bottom of the employment ladder, working in a livery barn. But she made no effort to hide the fact that she liked him. For his part, he didn't just like Jennie, he loved her. But what did he have to offer her?

But even overshadowing his feelings for Jennie was the thought of what would happen if the Tovars came to Serene. Jennie waited while he put the horse in a stall and unsaddled him. Then, as he stepped out of the stall, Jennie pointed to the door.

"Looks like you have more customers. I'll see you around."

"You sure will," Dan promised.

He went to the front of the barn as Jennie went through the office and cut across the street toward the bank. He stepped out into the sunlight and stopped dead in his tracks.

Lem Tovar stared at Dan, his two-hundred-and-thirty-pound body slouched in the saddle, his face camouflaged by a three-day beard stubble. "Well, well," he muttered as he got over his surprise. "Never thought I'd see you again, especially in a barn. At least, that's fitting work for you."

"What are you doing here?" Dan demanded, although he knew as well as Tovar did.

"Heard there was to be a cattle sale here for people figuring on starting up ranching or increasing their herds. Thought we might get into the action. Right, boys?"

Dan switched his eyes to the other two riders. Both were big. Ozzie Tovar was a little bigger than his younger brother, Al. But both were larger than most men. They grinned now, watching Dan with wicked amusement.

"Picking up a good start for a ranch may be a little easier than we thought," Lem Tovar said. "Always easier when we've got inside help."

"I'm not helping you," Dan said with more force than he'd ever used before in opposing Lem.

Lem Tovar's mouth formed a big circle in the center of his sprouting beard. "Oh? Now think it over a minute. We might need help to round up all this floating cash in town. When it gets right down to the nubbin of things, you'll help us, all right. You always did take the easy way out."

Dan frowned, trying to squelch his fear of the big man. Lem was right. Dan always had taken the easy way out. That's why he had taken part in their robberies. Instead of making a clean break with the Tovars, he'd waited for his chance and then sneaked away. He'd likely look for the easy way out of this, too. But right now he didn't see any easy way.

"Put our horses up and feed them well, Dan," Lem said. "We'll just saunter around and look the town over."

Dan took the reins of the horses as the three men dismounted. As they headed off toward the main part of town, he stood and watched them. What could he do? The people of Serene were his friends. The Tovars would rob the town and kill anybody who opposed them. Certainly they'd kill Dan if he didn't do what they said. He'd thought they would kill him on sight. But Lem saw a way he could help them. They wouldn't kill him till he'd done that.

Dan took the horses inside and found a place for them. The barn was almost full of horses belonging to the cowboys from the northern ranches. They had come prepared to drive home any cattle their bosses bought. The cowboys were likely up in Kathka's saloon now.

Dan's thoughts returned to his problem. Who could he tell about the Tovars? Suddenly he realized he couldn't tell anyone. People here thought he was an upstanding young fellow. If he told what he knew about the Tovars, he'd paint his own name almost as black as theirs. What would Jennie think of him then?

Besides, who in Serene would be brave enough to face up to the gang? Thinking over the men in town, he realized there weren't any. Ivan Boggs, the sheriff, was the bravest of the lot but Dan had never seen him tested. Hubert McWilliams was a banker, not a fighter. Tom Cole, who ran the general store, was a little mild man who would find it hard to kill a fly that was bothering him.

Frank Bleckenstaff, who owned the hardware store, and Wolf Kathka, who ran the saloon, were good friends. They had come here together from Pennsylvania. But neither were fighters. Both were in their fifties. John Garber, the preacher, could hardly be expected to take part in a fight against the Tovar gang.

Dan realized that this whole town was like him. Everyone here looked for the easy way out when things got rough. Maybe that was why they called the town Serene and why Dan liked it so well here. But it didn't look to Dan like there would be an easy way out of this situation. Dan had reached no decision when the three big men came back to the barn.

"Quite a town here," Lem said. "But it's not a fighting town. The only man I saw who looked like he might give trouble is the sheriff. Now I want you to keep him out of our hair."

"How am I to do that?" Dan demanded.

"That's for you to figure out. I'll tell you when to do it. I saw a girl leaving the barn when we rode into town. You picked a pretty one, Dan. But she won't be so pretty if you try to double-cross us."

A chill ran down Dan's back. If he had an extremely vulnerable spot, Jennie was it. Lem Tovar had a knack for ferreting out a man's soft spot. Tovar spun on his heel and left the barn, followed by his two shadows.

Dan could take his chances facing the Tovars or he could take the easy way out and follow instructions. But even that wouldn't be easy this time. He'd have to leave town when this was over. He had what he wanted right here in Serene. The best girl in the world, a good job, and a town full of friends. He'd betray every friend and give up Jennie and his job if he listened to Lem Tovar. If he didn't listen, Jennie would likely get hurt. Maybe her father and the sheriff would be killed.

Dan scowled as he weighed the outcome of any decision he made. He was no stranger to a gun. Tovar had seen to that when he'd been training him to take his place with the Tovar gang. He didn't wear his gun here in Serene. Nobody but the sheriff did. There had been no need for it up to now.

Leaving the barn, he went by Sheriff Boggs's place where he boarded. He got his gun belt and strapped it around his waist. He didn't plan to use the gun but he felt more prepared for whatever happened now.

From the house, he went to the sheriff's office. Boggs was standing at the window looking out.

"Train will be coming soon," he said when Dan stepped in. "Then with all the buyers here, they'll ride out to look over the herds."

"When will the money change hands?" Dan asked.

"After the deals are made. They'll come to town and the ranchers will be paid off."

"With cash?" Dan asked.

Boggs nodded. "How else? I told them there was a bank here so they'll put their money in the bank while they're talking with the cattlemen."

"Have you taken a good look at those three new men?" Dan asked. "They look like they might be outlaws."

Boggs turned to look squarely at Dan. "Did they do something to make you suspicious?" he asked.

Dan shrugged. "Maybe I'm just suspicious of everyone," he said lamely. He was taking the easy way out again, trying to get the sheriff to do something about the Tovars without implicating himself. "Will Mr. McWilliams put the money in the safe or just leave it in the drawer till it's called for?"

Boggs rubbed his chin. "I'm not sure. Let's go over and talk to him. With this many strangers in town, we'd better take some precautions. We've never had a robbery in Serene. But we've never invited so many strangers into town, either."

Dan and the sheriff walked across the street to the bank and went inside. Dan almost swallowed his tongue when he saw Lem Tovar leaning at the teller's window, visiting amiably.

Boggs moved over to the back of the bank where Hubert McWilliams had a desk. He didn't have an office. The only space in the bank not included in the one big room was the vault.

"With all the strangers in town, we thought it might be well to put the cattle buyers' money in the vault," Boggs said.

McWilliams nodded. "That's just what Mr. Tennyson was saying," the banker said, indicating Tovar. "He just left two thousand dollars here till after he looks at the herds. He's a cattle buyer from Wyoming."

Dan shot a glance at Tovar who was grinning at them. Dan could see the fury behind that grin. Lem was surely guessing what Dan and the sheriff were doing here. Dan knew why Tovar had suggested to the banker that he put the money in the safe. If it was all concentrated in one place, it would be easier to get in a hurry. Being in a bank vault was no worry to Tovar. He had ways of making people open vaults.

As Dan left the bank with the sheriff, after McWilliams had agreed that he'd put the money in the vault, Dan had the feeling that he was in deeper trouble than ever. Lem Tovar would suspect that Dan had told the sheriff about the gang. Would Tovar strike at him or Jennie? Dan knew that nothing was too extreme for Lem Tovar.

The train came in just before noon and more than a dozen potential buyers got off. Some riders came in from the herds, apparently the owners or the foremen who would negotiate the sale of the cattle.

Dan kept busy at the barn, feeding and currying the horses. In spite of the furious pace of his work, Dan made special note that the buyers, after talking to the sheriff or McWilliams, went to the bank. They'd be leaving their money in the bank vault until they made a deal. Dan knew that Lem Tovar would be taking note of this, too.

After dinner at the hotel dining room or cheese and crackers at Tom Cole's store, the ranchers, buyers and their cowboys made a rush for horses at the livery stable. Dan put out every horse in the barn except his own and the three Tovar horses.

The town seemed deserted when they were gone. But Lem Tovar came in the back door of the barn.

"I told you to get the sheriff out of town," Tovar snapped when he saw Dan. "You could have said something that would have sent him out to the herds with those men."

"Those cattle deals mean nothing to him," Dan said. "His job is here in town."

Tovar's eyes ran down the stalls to the three horses he and his boys had ridden in. "At least, you didn't rent out our horses. The way they were going out, I wasn't sure."

Dan frowned. He had thought of it. But he knew what the consequences would be so he'd taken the easy way out.

"I see you've got one extra horse back there," Tovar said. "Get our horses ready and tie them over in front of the store. Saddle that other one for yourself."

"I'm not riding with you," Dan said.

Tovar glared at him. "You ain't got much choice, boy. If you think you're fast enough with that gun to beat me, just try it. I should kill you, anyway. You know too much about us to be allowed to run loose." He paused and stared at Dan for a long minute. "I thought you'd take the easy way," he said at last. "Now then, you listen and listen good. You get those horses out to the hitchrack at the store. Then you tell the sheriff something to get him out of town. We're hitting the bank just thirty minutes from now. If you ain't got things ready, we're going to hit the bank, anyway, and we'll take that girl with us when we leave."

Dan's mind had been racing, trying to find a way out. But that threat to take Jennie as a hostage was too much.

"I'll have things ready," Dan said.

Tovar went out the back door of the barn. Dan stared after him. He'd been a boy when he'd been sent to live with his aunt. He wasn't grown when his aunt died. Lem Tovar had dominated Dan since that day. The only time Dan had rebelled against his orders, Ozzie and Al had thrashed him until he was sure he was going to be killed. He hadn't attempted to stand up to them since.

He knew he'd have no chance against the three of them now. They were all faster with guns than he was. They were all bigger and used to rough fights. Reason told him he couldn't lick any one of them, much less all three. There was no one in town who could. He had no choice but to follow orders as he had always done. But the thought made him sick.

Angrily, he saddled Lem Tovar's horse and led him out to the hitchrack in front of Cole's store. Sheriff Boggs's office was next door. Instead of going back to the barn, he stormed into the office.

"What's wrong with you?" the sheriff demanded.

Dan wheeled to look into the street. It was empty. The Tovars were in town but they were keeping out of sight. Dan turned back, knowing that he could no longer take the easy way out.

"That fellow who claims to be a cattle buyer from Wyoming is really Lem Tovar," he blurted.

Boggs's feet came off the desk and hit the floor with a thud. "How do you know?"

"He's my uncle by marriage," Dan said, seeing his vision of living a peaceful life here in Serene disappearing like a bird in a fog. "He made me ride with him until I sneaked away six months ago. I didn't think he'd ever find me here."

"Why didn't you tell me and Hubert this morning?"

"I'm no hero," Dan said. "I can't match Lem with a gun and he was right there in the bank. He'd have killed me on the spot. Still, that might have been better than what I'm facing now."

"We've got to do something," Boggs said.

"What?" Dan demanded. "The Tovars are all very good with guns and they love to kill. There's nobody in this town who can face them."

The sheriff nodded. "Probably not. Did he tell you what he's going to do?"

"He ordered me to get their horses saddled and tied in front of Cole's store. They're aiming to rob the bank before the men get back from looking at the cattle."

The sheriff's lips were a thin line across his face. "You do what he told you to. Don't give him any reason to think you're not obeying his orders. I'm going to talk to people."

"He told me to get you out of town," Dan said.

Boggs frowned. "After I see some people, I'll ride out. But I won't go far."

Dan didn't know what Boggs was planning but if there was anyone in town who would try to stand up to the Tovars, he was the one. He went back to the barn and saddled Ozzie's and Al's horses. He stared at the horses. The easy way was to follow Lem's instructions exactly. But he'd already stepped over the boundary when he'd told the sheriff who the Tovars were.

Digging a knife out of his pocket, he carefully cut the cinches on the saddles almost in two. He wished he'd thought of that before he took Lem's horse out to the hitchrack. He'd do it when he got back there if he had the chance.

He led the two horses out to the hitchrack and tied them. He was going around to Lem's horse when he saw Jennie coming toward him from the bank. He also saw Lem Tovar back in the alley beside the bank watching him. He couldn't meddle with Lem's saddle now.

Jennie was obviously upset when she reached Dan. "The sheriff was just in the bank. He was telling Pa that the Tovar gang is in town. Pa doesn't believe him. Do you?"

Dan nodded. "He'd better believe it because they are here."

"We've never had any trouble in this town. If you really believe we might be facing a bank robbery, go over and talk to Pa. Maybe you can convince him."

Dan thought of Tovar's threat to take Jennie as a guarantee of safe passage out of town. "Where are you going?"

"To the church. The women are making toys for the orphanage in Denver. I'm going to make doll clothes." She laughed softly, suggesting to Dan that she didn't really believe that the Tovar gang was here, either. "I don't think the Tovars will rob the church."

Jennie went on to the church at the south end of town. Dan looked around. Lem was still where he could see Dan so he couldn't tinker with the cinch on his saddle. He turned toward the bank. Somehow he'd convince Hubert McWilliams that the Tovars were here. It might make a difference if the banker was expecting his bank to be robbed. Maybe he could lock the bank door. That would keep the gang from getting to the vault.

But he had barely reached the desk where the banker was sitting when somebody in the street yelled, "Fire!"

Dan beat the banker to the door. The back of the livery barn was blazing. With wings on his feet, Dan flew down the street, grabbing a bucket in front of the bar and filling it from the tank at the corner. By the time he had thrown the water on the fire and come back for more, other men were pouring into the street.

Frank Bleckenstaff came from his hardware store with three buckets in each hand. Wolf Kathka dashed out of the saloon and grabbed two of the buckets from Frank. The sheriff and the preacher, John Garber, arrived at the same time. Boggs had apparently been talking to the minister when the alarm had been sounded.

With that many men and all the buckets that Bleckenstaff had brought, they soon got the fire under control. As the blaze began to die down, it suddenly hit Dan what had started this fire. His eyes shot up the street. He saw a head peeking out of the doorway of the bank.

"The Tovars!" he yelled, running to Boggs. "They set this fire to get us all down here while they robbed the bank."

"Where's Hubert?" Boggs demanded.

Dan hadn't noticed that the banker hadn't followed him outside when he'd dashed out to fight the fire. "He's probably opening the vault with Lem Tovar's gun in his back," Dan said.

Dan and the sheriff started up the street while the rest of the men smothered the last of the fire with water. Suddenly Lem Tovar came out of the bank, carrying a white sack in his hand. His two boys were just a step behind him.

Sheriff Boggs dropped his hand to his gun but Dan reached over and stopped him. "They can kill every one of us before we can do a thing," he said softly. "You and I are the only ones here with guns."

"We can't let them get away."

"They won't," Dan said. "At least, not all of them."

The three men started across the street on the run. Both Ozzie and Al had sacks, too. Lem reached his horse first and swung into the saddle, starting down the street at a gallop. He swung his gun toward the sheriff and fired once but the shot was high.

Ozzie and Al grabbed their horses and swung into their saddles. Ozzie's saddle went right under his horse when he threw his weight into the stirrup. The horse kicked once then went galloping down the street without saddle or rider.

Al swung up on his horse all right but then the cinch gave way and he went sailing over the horse, thudding into the street with the saddle on top of him.

Dan ran forward. The sheriff was right with him and Dan heard the pound of feet directly behind as the other men who'd been at the fire followed them. Before the two stunned outlaws could recover, the men of town swarmed over them, pinning them to the ground while they took their guns and sacks.

Lem Tovar was half a block away before he realized he was alone. He wheeled to look at the confusion. Dan expected Lem to come back shooting. He dug his gun out of the holster. But Lem spun back and kicked his horse into a gallop, leaning far over the saddle.

"He's getting away!" someone screamed.

Lem Tovar swerved his horse in beside the church, out of sight of the men in the street. Dan had thought he was going to get away with what money he had, abandoning his boys. But that wouldn't have been like the Lem Tovar Dan knew. He would do anything for those two boys. Dan couldn't imagine that he would abandon them now.

Leading the dash down the street toward the church, Dan wondered what to expect if they cornered Lem Tovar. Only two men, Bleckenstaff and Kathka, stayed behind to hold the two captured outlaws under their own guns.

Then suddenly the church door burst open and Jennie came out on the step. Lem Tovar was with her, his hand gripping her arm until she winced. In his other hand, he held a gun.

"Turn Ozzie and Al loose or this girl gets hurt real bad," he shouted.

Sheriff Boggs stopped in his tracks, then turned back toward the spot where Bleckenstaff and Kathka were holding the two robbers and motioned to let them go. Dan wasn't surprised. Jennie McWilliams wasn't just Dan's favorite; she was the favorite of the whole town. Lem Tovar had found the way to control every man here.

Ozzie and Al Tovar came swaggering up the street, carrying their sacks and the guns they had taken back from the two townsmen. They were livid with rage. Right at this moment, Dan feared Ozzie and Al more than he did Lem.

The two went up the steps to stand beside Lem, their guns swinging back and forth over the men in front of them.

"Dan," Lem yelled, "you catch the boys' horses and find some saddles. Then you bring that other horse from the barn for this girl."

"You ain't taking Jennie with you!" Dan shouted, starting forward.

"And just who is going to stop me?" Lem demanded, his gun centered now on Dan. "Get those horses!"

"Better do it," the sheriff said softly. "If you haven't got any more saddles in the livery barn, I've got an extra in my barn."

It took some time and a little help from Tom Cole to catch the horses. Then he got saddles from the livery barn. Lem Tovar waited impatiently, glancing now and then out on the prairie. There was no sign of the cattlemen returning to town. Dan knew that if anything was done, the people right here were going to have to do it.

"Get that horse for the girl!" Tovar snapped when Dan brought Ozzie's and Al's horses. "And make it fast. If you don't, she ain't going to need a horse."

The implication was clear and Dan didn't question Lem Tovar's capacity to kill or cripple Jennie if he became highly irritated. Only one corner of the barn had been damaged in the fire. Dan found a sidesaddle and saddled his own horse. He saw a rifle in the corner and considered trying to pick off Lem from the barn. But he knew that he might hit Jennie. Even if his aim was true, Ozzie or Al would kill her. His only hope was to follow orders now and watch for a chance to free Jennie.

Bringing the horse to the church, he stopped and looked up at Lem. "What now?" he asked.

"Help the girl into her saddle," Lem said. "Just one false move, boy, and you and the girl will both be dead."

Dan was desperate enough to try almost anything. But he knew that either he or Jennie would die if he did. She reached a hand to him as she came down the steps. He took her hand and flinched when sharp prongs dug into his palm. Her eyes were on him and he smothered his surprise. After he had helped her onto the sidesaddle, he glanced at his hand. There were two bent pins there. He remembered Jennie saying she was making doll dresses today. She must have had these pins in her hand when Lem grabbed her.

While the preacher was sent around the church to bring Lem's horse, Dan nudged one of the other horses and it shied away. He moved over to quiet it and slipped one of the pins under the back of the saddle, making sure the bent point was aimed down.

The preacher brought Lem's horse around the corner. While Lem was stepping down from the porch, Dan slipped the other pin under the saddle of the other horse.

"You boys watch them while I get on my horse," Lem said. "Then I'll watch while you two mount up."

Since they all had their sacks of money, they'd be leaving with everything they had come for plus Jennie McWilliams.

With Lem in the saddle, Ozzie and Al came down to their horses. Dan was still standing between Lem's horse and Jennie's. The two boys hit the saddles at the same time. The moment their weights came down on those pins, both horses erupted like wild broncos being ridden for the first time.

Dan gouged Lem's horse in the flank and he willingly joined his comrades in the wild melee. Grabbing the reins of Jennie's horse, he turned him to the north and slapped him into a gallop past the startled people who were watching the impromptu bucking exhibition.

Dan wheeled back to the Tovars. Ozzie was on the ground, unseated by the unexpected bucking. Al had gotten a better grip before his horse erupted but he was clinging now by the saddle horn and both stirrups were flapping free. With his next jump, the horse shook Al loose and he sailed free, landing like a dropped sack of wheat.

The men were swarming forward to pin the two thrown robbers to the ground as they had done when the cinches broke only a few minutes before. Dan pivoted his attention to Lem. His horse had no pins under his saddle and Lem was rapidly calming him. Lem was clawing for his gun even as he fought to quiet the horse.

Dan's hand dived for his gun. Lem was swinging around toward Dan, recognizing the real source of danger to him. Lem fired first but his crowhopping horse threw him off target. That crowhopping gave Dan a shifting target, too, but his feet were on the ground and his bullet hit Lem in the shoulder. Lem's gun fell and he clutched his shoulder with his good hand.

Running forward, Dan ordered him off the horse which was finally settling down. Others came running to help. Hubert McWilliams began gathering up the sacks of money taken from his bank. Jennie had turned her horse around and was riding back.

Sheriff Boggs came over to take charge of the three prisoners. "Thanks, Dan," he said. "We've got them under control now. But it wasn't easy."

Dan grinned. The sheriff was right. It hadn't been easy. For the first time that Dan could remember, he hadn't taken the easy way out. And he had fared much better than when he had taken the easy way.

Jennie slid off her horse and ran to Dan. Only when she threw her arms around his neck and kissed him did he realize how much better he had fared.

THE RACE
Natlee Kenoyer

The story of Nana Mae is one of those things that happens once in a lifetime. I never get tired of telling it. In fact, every time I do, I still run hot and cold and wonder if anyone else ever came so close to winning such a jackpot. I was a young man, freshly married and still trying to impress my bride. Sarah said she married me because I was stable, didn't drink or gamble. I had saved up a pretty good stake and that was what convinced Sarah in the final decision. Then we came to Sandler and I got right on at the blacksmith shop and had been good enough that old Jack Abbors practically let me run it. I had dreams of him making me a partner some day. Things were going along fine until I made three mistakes.

First mistake I made was taking Sarah to the Saturday races. She liked to pet the horses and was always talking to them. Herb Sandler had donated the land and we had a right nice track. Sarah got a look at Mrs. Sandler and her group of stylish ladies in their large hats with the ostrich plumes. Actually, they were the wives of all the big ranchers thereabouts and had formed sort of a club and went every-where together. That's when Sarah wanted one of them corsets she'd seen in the catalog. Started savin' for it. Wasn't nothin' wrong with Sarah's figger but she wanted one of them shapes you got by stuffin' yourself inside a lot of whalebone. I told her she wouldn't be comfortable sittin' on the bench-board bleachers but she said if them high-fashion ladies could do it, then she guessed she could. Only difference, Herb Sandler built a covered platform for his wife and her ladies and they had chairs to sit on. Second mistake I made was get-tin' interested in a danged horse.

I'm not naturally a gamblin' man and why I got interested, I don't know. I guess it was hope. I don't even know where the mare came from. Actually, it ain't important. I wondered why she was named Nana Mae until Bill Bancroft said it was his wife's name. Said she'd been about as unpredictable. Whatever that meant. I guess Bill could

have told you where she came from. Bill could quote you bloodlines
as far back as you wanted to go. But I never got around to askin'
him. Wouldn't have meant anything to me anyhow. And, after what
happened I never felt like discussin' details. Besides, what was done
was done, I couldn't change it.

Sarah and I liked the little town of Sandler. In fact, the whole
town was located on the Sandler ranch. Herb owned land as far as
you could see on a hazy day. The town actually started when Herb
hired a steady blacksmith who was so good he found he could handle
more than Herb had to keep him busy. The other ranchers started
bringing their horses for Jack Abbors to shoe and then he was so
busy he needed a helper. The blacksmith shop was a handy place to
drop supplies so a store was needed. Freighters started coming by,
then the stagecoach made it one of their stops. One thing called for
another until there was the makings of a town. About that time Herb
Sandler put in a racetrack so his men and those of other ranchers
would have some place to go on Saturdays. Well, everything else followed. As long as Herb was there to keep an eye on things it was a
nice place to live.

We had a nice little house built next to a group of others that was
made up of the other families who had a business in the town. But
the biggest thing was the racing. The hands at the various ranches
had match races and even some of the ranchers groomed their best
horses for the regular racing that was becoming the common enter-
tainment on Saturdays and Sunday afternoons. This brought in
strangers with fast horses looking for a chance to pick up good
money. It was surprising how much money exchanged hands.

It was in the days of the three-dollar option, a long time ago, and I
ain't telling you how old I am. Pari-mutuel betting wasn't heard of.
Of course, the race I'm telling you about was somethin' else. In all
my borned days I can't remember such a pot of money upsettin' so
many people, all except the two who had a ticket on the mare.

To begin with, Bill Bancroft said she could run. He had a reputation for knowing when a horse was ready. He sure had enough of 'em
pass through his hands. He got to Sandler about twice a year. We all
felt he was honest enough for a horse trader. He'd pick up a smart
amount of change match-racing against any cowboy who thought he
had a fast horse. This time Bill decided he had a mare that was good
enough to run against any of the fast horses offered by the ranchers
themselves. I guess he figured he might as well clean up big. He always said that any runnin' horse has one good race in him. To be
sure, any cowboy comin' into town would rather bet on a good horse
than anything else. There was one little hitch, however. The way

Nana Mae acted whenever she was on the track made you wonder if she'd ever straighten out so you could depend on her. Actually, the mare wasn't much to look at. A slim muzzle came in front of heavy jowls, and her ears came out of the top of her head, standing straight up, and, I swear her poll came to a point between them. She was narrow-chested and deep-barreled and the only thing in her favor was them back legs. Big hams with definite pusher muscles. Just plain brown with no markings. A whole lack of conformation. But, as I mentioned before, Bill knew horses and if he said a horse could run, it would. That was my third mistake, listenin' to him.

"When she's got her spirits up, I'll let you know," he nodded sagely. "Then get all the money together you can dig up because the odds will be good. When she's set to go she'll lead the field."

The Fourth of July was comin' up and everyone who could would be there. Bill was as broke as any of us so we knew he was bankin' on Nana Mae to get him well. I admit I was gettin' excited. Who doesn't dream of makin' a killin' on a race. Maybe this was the time for me. Maybe this was the horse. And, if I did win, maybe Jack would let me partner his smithy.

I'd always been a cautious sort. I think that was another reason Sarah married me. I even got up early to watch the mare work out. I told Sarah I was cleaning the forge. She knew I didn't like gettin' up early. But I was out to watch Nana Mae train for the big killing on the Fourth. It was cool in the mornings. The seats of the bleachers stood bare and cheerless, like a cupboard with empty shelves, so different from the crowds of screaming folk that made Saturdays exciting. It was fun to watch the races and some of them cowboys had tough, fast horses. I could see where it was fascinatin' and how a person could get caught up in it, but when I got my stake I'd quit. I sure was waitin' for Nana Mae to give some sign that she would send me on the road to riches. Even Sarah began to watch the races but she wouldn't bet, she just liked horses. Bill always followed Nana Mae and her rider out onto the track. I couldn't hear what he said but I think he was instructin' the boy on her back.

One mornin' Bill started back to the rail with his short, steppin' walk. His cheroot traveled from one side of his mouth to the other and he wore a thoughtful expression. He stood a little straighter and hitched his trousers up over his ample waistline with a confident pull. We watched as the mare danced sideways and her slim legs worked in a chopping motion.

"She's gettin' her spirits up," Bill said, nodding his head. Suddenly, she reared high and fell over backward. The boy sprawled in the dirt where he had thrown himself, off and away from her. I sent an exasperated glance toward Bill. He shrugged his shoulders and started toward the boy. "Spirits a little too high," he threw at me over his shoulder. Bill walked back out and gave the boy a leg up. The boy didn't say anything, just gathered the reins and settled himself into the light saddle again. He headed the mare out to the middle of the track and let her go. Without wastin' time she struck out into a gallop. She looked good. She had a good way of going, a stride that stretched out like a greyhound, smooth and even. She could run, there was no question about it.

"That's the way she'll run in a race," Bill said, taking the cheroot out of his mouth. "When she's got her spirits up," he finished. I had to agree she looked good.

For the next few days I was hanging on the rail to watch Nana Mae work out. I could watch her gallop before it was time to open the blacksmith shop. I was always late getting the forge hot but I was too excited to care.

"The mare can't be that good," Jack said one day when I got there late. "Maybe when the day comes I'll put an option on her." Jack went to the races but he never bet that I know of. "I just like to watch them run." Anyways, there got to be a little bunch of us. We all began talking about how much we could raise to put down on Nana Mae's nose. We were gettin' anxious. I knew, besides the corset money, Sarah had a little more stashed away for new curtains and some other housey frills. I finally found the corset money. I was determined to use it too when the day came. We kept after Bill to give us the word. To name the day.

"I'm puttin' her in a race Saturday to see what she'll do in company," Bill told us. "You can put some money on her if you want to. This is more like a trial run. Her spirits ain't really up yet."

All good racing days are clear and bright and the track is always fast. This seemed to be one of them. We hightailed it to the track early. Sarah insisted on going too. We watched the jockeys mount up as the owners got their horses ready. Quite a few of the ranchers came too. Bill said they were checking the competition. No one said much but I guess each one of us slipped over to the betting booth and got a small option on Nana Mae. Bill wouldn't admit she was ready. But, she was going to run. That was encouragement enough.

"My, but she's a sweet little thing," Sarah said. She insisted on petting the mare but I finally dragged her away.

Nana Mae was in rare form. She did all the usual tricks. She balked, but good, when Bill tried to ease her up even with the tape. The second they were all even they broke the tape and the mass of churning legs leaped forward . . . all . . . except Nana Mae! She took one good stride, then whirled, and ran the wrong way of the track. She was an eighth of the way before the boy got her stopped and brought her back. She herded the rest of the horses all in for a safe, far rear vantage, like a spaniel pushing a covey of quail. Well, that was great! If this was a sample . . . !

"When you said she wasn't ready, you sure were right," I says to Bill. "How you gonna know when she's ready?"

"I'll know," Bill muttered and chewed hard on his cheroot.

"Oh, the poor thing!" Sarah murmured. "Something must have bothered her." What did Sarah know about horses. I was just glad I only had a small option on her.

I didn't go out and watch any more of Nana Mae's workouts. The cream was sort of off the top. In fact, I didn't mention the mare except with a chuckle. I kidded Bill about askin' Nana Mae to let him know when she wanted to run. Sarah's corset money was safe as far as I was concerned. Bill's shoulders would just hunch and he didn't have anything to say. Then the talk died down and no one hardly mentioned the mare.

"You're not giving up on the horse, are you?" Jack said to me. "If she can run, she will when she's ready." I just looked at him and sort of hoped. You can't give up, I guess, if there's a bare chance.

Bill kept putting Nana Mae in a race now and then just to keep her in form but even I could see that the boy wasn't pushing her. I figured Bill was saving her and letting the odds build up. Sarah would ask me when the mare was runnin' and she'd go down and watch.

"I think she really tried today," was her usual comment.

"Mare doin' any better?" Jack would ask me. He never did watch her run that I know of. I couldn't figure if he was pulling my leg or if he was really interested.

The Fourth of July was on Sunday but it was surprising how many folks turned out for the Saturday race. Maybe it was the idea of celebratin' two days instead of one. There were buggies lined up everywhere and all the hitchracks were full of horses. I was wishing Bill would give me the word now, if he was ever goin' to. Jack asked me if the mare was goin' to run and I told him I guessed Bill didn't think this was the right day because he didn't seem excited like he would if the time was right. But he did make a remark that made me wonder.

"She seems to be gettin' her spirits up," he said, when he led her past me. But he didn't say for sure. I knew he was gonna run her again. I thought briefly of Sarah's corset money. Sarah insisted on going along, and she did like Nana Mae.

"Just likin' a horse isn't going to make her win," I told her.

"But she has such beautiful, sad eyes," Sarah insisted. All I could see was that pointed head. What do women know about horses anyways, I thought. If she likes the mare, I reasoned, she'll have something to feel sorry for. I just stayed to one side while Sarah went to sit in the bleachers. I leaned on the rail. I didn't put an option on a single horse.

Came time for the mare's race. She didn't act any different today than she had many times before. Even the crowd was usual. There was the usual excitement, and hope, that comes before any race. I kept hearing the odds changing. Nana Mae's odds were way long. I guess no one was betting on her. The minutes ticked off. I had a brief thought that maybe, for fun, I oughta go get an option on the mare. I even had Sarah's corset money in my pocket. I even got as far as the betting booth, then I hesitated with the money in my fist. And that's when Sarah caught me.

I turned around and came face to face with her, my fist still in the air, closed around the money. Wasn't any use tryin' to hide it.

"Where did you get that money?" Sarah could be stern and she stared square at me. I never could lie to her anyways. I opened my mouth to tell her but she already knew. "You've got my corset money!" All I could do was nod. She held out her hand and I dropped the money into her palm. "And you know I don't hold with betting." Wasn't any use tryin' to explain why I wanted a quick stake. Sarah had always said that Jack would make me a partner when he was ready.

I mumbled something about being sorry but I was kinda angry 'cause she caught me. I turned around and started to walk back to the smithy, then I decided I might as well see the start of the race anyways. Maybe Nana Mae would run backward again and I'd be glad I was only tempted. Besides the mare had lost four times. If she was ever going to win a race it was turning into a mighty long wait.

The horses jumped out in a bunch as they left the start and were on their way. It was a clean start, no bumping. You couldn't tell one horse from another for the dust. Around the first turn they crowded together like ants at a conference. At the backstretch they were beginning to trail out and the faster horses moved out in front. I glanced to my left and saw Jack move in beside me. There was a slight smile on his face but he just watched without opening his mouth. I saw Bill shade his eyes and quit chewing on his cheroot. I squinted too and through the dust I thought I could see four legs striding in a familiar pattern of movement. There was no mistaking that stride. The horses were coming around the turn, four horses close together. I stared hard. I couldn't exactly make 'em out, then

. . . by God! . . . one was pullin' away . . . I knew I was seeing that stride for sure. I was! There was no mistakin' it! Suddenly, as if hit with a slingshot Nana Mae made her bid! She kept coming on! Running smoothly, swiftly, pounding down the stretch as if she did this every day. The crowd rose to their feet. The shouting grew louder. Everyone was yelling like mad for their favorites. I turned and pounded Bill on the back in my excitement, but he just stood there quiet, staring. I glanced at Jack. He was still smiling but not making a sound. On the mare came. One, two, three, on, on, four lengths ahead. She crossed the line and the crowd relaxed like a pricked balloon. I felt empty and weak. I stared at Bill. His face was pale and the lines about his mouth were tight.

"She fooled me! She fooled me!" was all he could say. I looked at Jack. He still had that grin.

"Every horse has one race in him," he winked and turned away. Then it hit me too! Nothing! This was the day I'd been waiting for and I didn't have a red cent on her. I started to walk away. I saw Sarah walking quickly toward me. She smiled at me but I wasn't in the mood for her greeting.

I grasped her firmly by the arm. I guess I shook her a little, I don't remember. "Well, your sweet little mare won, didn't she!" I said angrily. "If you had left me alone I might have had a ticket on her." I just stood there and stared at her. I guess I was hoping she'd cry and I'd feel better. But she stood there looking at me, her eyes bright and that smile on her face. "It ain't funny!" I snapped. "You just lost us some money!"

"Now, you know you wouldn't have bet my corset money." She even said this in a nice voice.

"Well, maybe I wouldn't have," I admitted. "But we shoulda had a ticket on her!"

"We did!" Sarah's face really broke out in a smile. "I thought about it when you walked away. You looked so hurt. And, I could just see Nana Mae's sad eyes. I felt sorry for both of you so I went back and bought an option!"

Only two people had options on Nana Mae. Sarah, of course. The other one . . . you guessed it . . . Jack! Three hundred and one dollars for a dollar. A three-dollar option, nine hundred and nine dollars! Just two options. Both Sarah and Jack were celebrities!

I don't remember what became of Nana Mae. She didn't go on to greater glory because I would have remembered. More like a star that flickers brightly across the sky, then snuffs out and is gone. Bill sort of eased quietly out of town, don't know where he went either. Jack did make me a partner and he let me hire an apprentice. He maintained that since he was a man of means he was goin' courtin'. I had to run the smithy by myself. And, Sarah? She wouldn't let me have a dime of them winnin's. Said she was gonna have a new house and everything that went with it. She thought it might not be long before she would be sittin' on that platform with the rancher ladies in a hat with ostrich plumes. Just one thing remains clear in my mind, however. That crazy mare paid nine hundred dollars for a three-dollar option and I didn't have a dime on her!

MARKERS

Bill Pronzini

Jack Bohannon and I had been best friends for close to a year, ever since he'd hired on at the Two Bar Cross, but if it hadn't been for a summer squall that came up while the two of us were riding fence, I'd never have found out about who and what he was. Or about the markers.

We'd been out two weeks, working the range southeast of Eagle Mountain. The fences down along there were in middling fair shape, considering the winter we'd had; Bohannon and I sported calluses from the wire cutters and stretchers, but truth to tell, we hadn't been exactly overworking ourselves. Just kind of moving along at an easy pace. The weather had been fine—cool crisp mornings, warm afternoons, sky scrubbed clean of clouds on most days—and it made you feel good just to be there in all that sweet-smelling open space.

As it happened, we were about two miles east of the Eagle Mountain line shack when the squall came up. Came up fast, too, along about three o'clock in the afternoon, the way a summer storm does sometimes in Wyoming Territory. We'd been planning to spend a night at the line shack anyway, to replenish our supplies, so as soon as the sky turned cloudy dark we lit a shuck straight for it. The rain started before we were halfway there, and by the time we raised the shack, the downpour was such that you couldn't see a dozen rods in front of you. We were both soaked in spite of our slickers; rain like that has a way of slanting in under any slicker that was ever made.

The shack was just a one-room sod building with walls coated in ashes-and-clay and a whipsawed wood floor. All that was in it was a pair of bunks, a table and two chairs, a larder, and a big stone fireplace. First things we did when we came inside, after sheltering the horses for the night in the lean-to out back, were to build a fire on the hearth and raid the larder. Then, while we dried off, we brewed up some coffee and cooked a pot of beans and salt pork. It was full dark by then and that storm was kicking up a hell of a fuss; you could see lightning blazes outside the single window, and hear thunder grumbling in the distance and the wind moaning in the chimney flue.

When we finished supper Bohannon pulled a chair over in front of the fire, and I sat on one of the bunks, and we took out the makings. Neither of us said much at first. We didn't have to talk to enjoy each other's company; we'd spent a fair lot of time together in the past year—working the ranch, fishing and hunting, a little mild carousing in Saddle River—and we had an easy kind of friendship. Bohannon had never spoken much about himself, his background, his people, but that was all right by me. Way I figured it, every man was entitled to as much privacy as he wanted.

But that storm made us both restless; it was the kind of night a man sooner or later feels like talking. And puts him in a mood to share confidences, too. Inside a half hour we were swapping stories, mostly about places we'd been and things we'd done and seen.

That was how we came to the subject of markers—grave markers, first off—with me the one who brought it up. I was telling about the time I'd spent a year prospecting for gold in the California Mother Lode, before I came back home to Wyoming Territory and turned to ranch work, and I recollected the grave I'd happened on one afternoon in a rocky meadow south of Sonora. A mound of rocks, it was, with a wooden marker anchored at the north end. And on the marker was an epitaph scratched out with a knife.

"I don't know who done it," I said, "or how come that grave was out where it was, but that marker sure did make me curious. Still does. What it said was, 'Last resting place of D. R. Lyon. Lived and died according to his name.'"

I'd told that story a time or two before and it had always brought a chuckle, if not a horse laugh. But Bohannon didn't chuckle. Didn't say anything, either. He just sat looking into the fire, not moving, a quirly drifting smoke from one corner of his mouth. He appeared to be studying on something inside his head.

I said, "Well, *I* thought it was a mighty unusual marker, anyhow."

Bohannon still didn't say anything. Another ten seconds or so passed before he stirred—took a last drag off his quirly and tossed it into the fire.

"I saw an unusual marker myself once," he said then, quiet. His voice sounded different than I'd ever heard it.

"Where was that?"

"Nevada. Graveyard in Virginia City, about five years ago."

"What'd it say?"

"Said 'Here lies Adam Bricker. Died of hunger in Virginia City, August 1882.'"

"Hell. How could a man die of hunger in a town?"

"That's what I wanted to know. So I asked around to find out."

"Did you?

"I did," Bohannon said. "According to the local law, Adam Bricker'd been killed in a fight over a woman. Stabbed by the woman's husband, man named Greenbaugh. Supposed to've been self-defense."

"If Bricker was stabbed, how could he have died of hunger?"

"Greenbaugh put that marker on Bricker's grave. His idea of humor, I reckon. Hunger Bricker died of wasn't hunger for food, it was hunger for the woman. Or so Greenbaugh claimed."

"Wasn't it the truth?"

"Folks I talked to didn't think so," Bohannon said. "Story was, Bricker admired Greenbaugh's wife and courted her some; she and Greenbaugh weren't living together and there was talk of a divorce. Nobody thought he trifled with her, though. That wasn't Bricker's way. Folks said the real reason Greenbaugh killed him was because of money Bricker owed him. Bricker's claim was that he'd been cheated out of it, so he refused to pay when Greenbaugh called in his marker. They had an argument, there was pushing and shoving, and when Bricker drew a gun and tried to shoot him, Greenbaugh used his knife. That was his story, at least. Only witness just happened to be a friend of his."

"Who was this Greenbaugh?"

"Gambler," Bohannon said. "Fancy man. Word was he'd cheated other men at cards, and debauched a woman or two—that was why his wife left him—but nobody ever accused him to his face except Adam Bricker. Town left him pretty much alone."

"Sounds like a prize son of a bitch," I said.

"He was."

"Men like that never get what's coming to them, seems like."

"This one did."

"You mean somebody cashed in his chips for him?"

"That's right," Bohannon said. "Me."

I leaned forward a little. He was looking into the fire, with his head cocked to one side, like he was listening for another rumble of thunder. It seemed too quiet in there, of a sudden, so I cleared my throat and smacked a hand against my thigh.

I said, "How'd it happen? He cheat you at cards?"

"He didn't have the chance."

"Then how . . . ?"

Bohannon was silent again. One of the burning logs slid off the grate and made a sharp cracking sound; the noise seemed to jerk him into talking again. He said, "There was a vacant lot a few doors down from the saloon where he spent most of his time. I waited in there one night, late, and when he came along, on his way to his room at one of the hotels, I stepped out and put my gun up to his head. And I shot him."

"My God," I said. "You mean you *murdered* him?"

"You could call it that."

"But damn it, man, why?"

"He owed me a debt. So I called in his marker."

"What debt?"

"Adam Bricker's life."

"I don't see—"

"I didn't tell you how I happened to be in Virginia City. Or how I happened to visit the graveyard. The reason was Adam Bricker. Word reached me that he was dead, but not how it happened, and I went there to find out."

"Why? What was Bricker to you?"

"My brother," he said. "My real name is Jack Bricker."

I got up off the bunk and went to the table and turned the lamp up a little. Then I got out my sack of Bull Durham, commenced to build another smoke. Bohannon didn't look at me; he was still staring into the fire.

When I had my quirly lit I said, "What'd you do after you shot Greenbaugh?"

"Got on my horse and rode out of there."

"You figure the law knows you did it?"

"Maybe. But the law doesn't worry me much."

"Then how come you changed your name? How come you traveled all the way up here from Nevada?"

"Greenbaugh had a brother, too," he said. "Just like Adam had me. He was living in Virginia City at the time and he knows I shot Greenbaugh. I've heard more than once that he's looking for me— been looking ever since it happened."

"So he can shoot you like you shot his brother?"

"That's right. I owe him a debt, Harv, same as Greenbaugh owed me one. One of these days he's going to find me, and when he does he'll call in his marker, same as I did."

"Maybe he won't find you," I said. "Maybe he's stopped looking by this time."

"He hasn't stopped looking. He'll never stop looking. He's a hardcase like his brother was."

"That don't mean he'll ever cross your trail—"

"No. But he will. It's just a matter of time."

"What makes you so all-fired sure?"

"A feeling I got," he said. "Had it ever since I heard he was after me."

"Guilt," I said, quiet.

"Maybe. I'm not a killer, not truly, and I've had some bad nights over Greenbaugh. But it's more than that. It's something I know is going to happen, like knowing the rain will stop tonight or tomorrow and we'll have clear weather again. Maybe because there are too many markers involved, if you take my meaning—the grave kind and the debt kind. One of these days I'll be dead because I owe a marker."

Neither of us had anything more to say that night. Bohannon—I couldn't seem to think of him as Bricker—got up from in front of the fire and climbed into his bunk, and when I finished my smoke I did the same. What he'd told me kept rattling around inside my head. It was some while before I finally got to sleep.

I woke up right after dawn, like I always do—and there was Bohannon, with his saddlebags packed and his bedroll under one arm, halfway to the door. Beyond him, through the window, I could see pale gray light and enough of the sky to make out broken clouds; the storm had passed.

"What the hell, Bohannon?"

"Time for me to move on," he said.

"Just like that? Without notice to anybody?"

"I reckon it's best that way," he said. "A year in one place is long enough—maybe too long. I was fixing to leave anyway, after you and me finished riding fence. That's why I went ahead and told you about my brother and Greenbaugh and the markers. Wouldn't have if I'd been thinking on staying."

I swung my feet off the bunk and reached for my Levi's. "It don't make any difference to me," I said. "Knowing what you done, I mean."

"Sure it does, Harv. Hell, why lie to each other about it?"

"All right. But where'll you go?"

He shrugged. "Don't know. Somewhere. Best if you don't know, best if I don't myself."

"Listen, Bohannon—"

"Nothing to listen to." He came over and put out his hand, and I took it, and there was the kind of feeling inside me I'd had as a button when a friend died of the whooping cough. "Been good knowing you, Harv," he said. "I hope you don't come across a marker someday with my name on it." And he was gone before I finished buttoning up my pants.

From the window I watched him saddle his horse. I didn't go outside to say a final word to him—there wasn't anything more to say; he'd been right about that—and he didn't look back when he rode out. I never saw him again.

But that's not the whole story, not by any means.

Two years went by without me hearing anything at all about Bohannon. Then Curly Polk, who'd worked with the two of us on the Two Bar Cross and then gone down to Texas for a while, drifted back our way for the spring roundup, and he brought word that Bohannon was dead. Shot six weeks earlier, in the Pecos River town of Santa Rosa, New Mexico.

But it hadn't been anybody named Greenbaugh who pulled the trigger on him. It had been a local cowpuncher, liquored up, spoiling for trouble; and it had happened over a spilled drink that Bohannon had refused to pay for. The only reason Curly found out about it was that he happened to pass through Santa Rosa on the very day they hung the puncher for his crime.

It shook me some when Curly told about it. Not because Bohannon was dead—too much time had passed for that—but because of the circumstances of his death. He'd believed, and believed hard, that someday he'd pay for killing Greenbaugh; that there were too many markers in his life and someday he'd die on account of one he owed. Well, he'd been wrong. And yet the strange thing, the pure crazy thing, was that he'd also been right.

The name of the puncher who'd shot him was Sam Marker.

THE WAIT
BY THE RIVER

Wayne Barton

If Sarah and Lucy Cameron had done as they were told, they would probably have been killed.

"Stay close to the wagons," old Ben Turner, the scout, had warned everyone the night before. "This is Sioux country, and we'll likely meet some young bucks looking for trouble."

And, "Don't wander off, now," Dr. Cameron said when he sent the girls back to the rear of the train with a tonic for Mrs. Peabody in the last wagon.

Sarah was sixteen, and one of her chores was to look after her restless nine-year-old sister. Usually, she was good at it. But this time, while Sarah talked with the Peabodys, Lucy followed a bright butterfly out across the prairie. She had almost reached the willow breaks along the banks of the Sweetwater, fifty yards from the train, when Sarah swung down from the wagon and saw her.

"Lucy! Come back."

Sarah ran after her, away from the slowly moving wagons. She caught up and seized Lucy's hand just as the Indians came.

One moment, everything was peaceful. The wagons swayed over the deeply rutted trail, just the way they had done every day since the train left Missouri. Men walked alongside, swinging long poles to goad the oxen. A cow, pulled along by a rope tied to one of the wagons, lowed in protest.

Then there was a shrill yell, and the prairie beyond the train was suddenly alive with Indian warriors on painted ponies. They turned, and swept down at a gallop on the two rear wagons. Sarah heard shots and the frenzied bellowing of oxen, and she suddenly realized that she and Lucy were alone in the open.

"Indians," she gasped. "We have to hide."

She dragged Lucy down into the willows along the river. Through a tangle of branches, she saw one of the wagons burning. Two or three Sioux had clambered inside the other wagon, and a big warrior was leaning over the tailboard, throwing armloads of clothes and bedding out onto the ground. A moment later, flames sprang up and began licking at the wagon's canvas top.

One of the mounted Indians shouted something and pointed toward the rest of the train. Following his gesture, Sarah saw a group of men, Ben Turner at their head, charging back toward the wagons.

"Help is coming, Lucy," Sarah whispered. "But they don't know we're out here. Can you run back with me, and not be afraid?"

Lucy picked herself up and looked at Sarah. Tears glimmered in her eyes, but her lips were clamped firmly shut. She nodded.

"As soon as they're a little closer," Sarah said. "Get ready."

Some of the Indians were firing at the approaching men, while others scrambled to mount their ponies. One warrior threw up his hands and fell, and two others leaned to haul him up across one of the horses. Then the party scattered. With horror, Sarah saw three of the Sioux galloping straight for the spot where she and Lucy crouched.

"Hurry, Lucy. This way."

There was a sort of cave in the riverbank, little more than a hollow gouged out by the spring floods. It was shallow, and light seeped through the tangle of willow roots overhead, but it was the only hiding place the girls had time to reach. Sarah pushed Lucy all the way to the back and huddled over her, shielding the girl with her own body.

The Indians passed so close that Sarah could hear the splash and clunk of hooves as their horses came down into the stream. They seemed to pause in the shelter of the bank, perhaps watching for pursuit. One of them laughed and muttered something in a strange, guttural language.

Sarah pressed Lucy tightly against her, clenching her jaws to keep her own teeth from chattering. Minutes crawled by. Lucy whimpered softly once, and Sarah held her breath, but apparently the Indians didn't hear. Finally, the sounds moved slowly away.

"They'll wait for us, won't they?" Lucy's voice was a tiny whisper. "Papa and Mr. Turner and the others, I mean. They'll find us?"

"Yes, baby," Sarah said. "They'll come as soon as they miss us."

Inside herself, she wasn't so sure. There was no sound now except for the chuckling rush of the river. Finally, Sarah crawled to the mouth of the cave.

"I'm going to look outside," she said. "Wait for me."

She crept along the bank until she could peer through the screen of willows. Smoke rose slowly from the remains of the two wagons. Except for the wreckage, the trail in both directions was empty. The train was gone.

"They left us!" Lucy's voice, behind her, was shockingly loud. The smaller girl jumped up. "They can't be far away. If we run, we can catch them."

Sarah snatched at Lucy's arm and pulled her down.

"No, Lucy. Remember what Mr. Turner said. The Indians might be following the train."

Desperately, Sarah tried to remember everything the scout had said the night before, while she listened from the safety of her father's wagon.

"The Sioux might hang on for days, watching for stragglers," he'd cautioned. "Like wolves, following a buffalo herd."

Then one of the older men had spoken up: "And anyone they capture could well wish himself dead."

Ben Turner frowned. "I don't know as that's so. Sometimes the Sioux adopt prisoners—women and youngsters, mostly—into the tribe."

"To live like Indians?" the other man demanded loudly. "I say they're better off dead."

The thoughts ran through Sarah's mind in an instant. Then, seeing Lucy near tears, she forced a smile.

"The wagon master must have decided to go on to the fort. They'll send out soldiers to find us. We may have to stay here tonight, but it'll be all right."

"But what if the Indians come back first?"

"We'll hide." Sarah scanned the low hills for signs of movement. She'd had a moment to think, and she knew what she needed to do. It took all her strength to keep her voice calm. "But first, I want to look where the wagons were and see if there's anything we can use. You wait by the cave, honey."

Lucy nodded, wide-eyed, and slipped away. Sarah took a deep breath and, before she could change her mind, scrambled up the bank and ran through the tall grass.

There wasn't much to find. One wheel, almost undamaged, leaned crazily upon a smoldering axle in the middle of a burned and blackened circle. The ground was still hot, and Sarah didn't try to get closer. Instead, she turned to the bundles that had been thrown from the second wagon before it burned.

She found clothing, a box containing papers, a few other odds and ends. There was one old patchwork quilt, and she gathered it in her arms. Lying in the grass a few yards away was a larger bundle, and she walked toward it. Not until she was almost there did she realize it was a man.

He lay facedown, and there was blood around his head. Sarah knew that he was dead. She had helped her father once or twice, and she wasn't frightened, but she couldn't bring herself to touch the still form. She started to turn away. Then she saw the gun, shining in the grass by his outflung hand.

Gingerly, Sarah picked it up. It was a revolver, new and gleaming with polished brass, the kind her father had called a Navy Colt. The cylinder was loaded, the tiny percussion caps fitted in place. Sarah had never fired a gun, but she had seen the men shoot, and she was confident she could fire this one if she had to. With new assurance, she took a last look around, and ran for the river.

"Lucy?" she called as she reached the cave. There was no answer, and Sarah's heart seemed to stop. Then Lucy answered from downstream.

"Here I am. Look."

Lucy held out her apron, full of some kind of red fruit. With quick concern, Sarah saw the girl's mouth was stained with the red juice.

"Oh, Lucy, you didn't eat those?"

"They're chokecherries," Lucy said. "Papa told me I could eat them." She looked up at Sarah, and her mouth trembled. "I just wanted to help. I'm sorry."

Sarah let out a long breath, reached to rumple the pig-tailed hair. "It's all right, honey. You just worried me, that's all. We'd better go back to our cave now."

The evening shadows were lengthening, and the cave was cool and shady. Sarah spread her quilt on the sandy floor for them to sit on, then tasted the cherries. Their tartness puckered her mouth, but they did help to quiet her gnawing hunger. Later, she sat with Lucy nestled close against her while the hard bright stars came out and strange noises began out in the night.

"I'm glad you found the gun, Sarah," Lucy said once. "If the Indians come back, you can scare them away."

"I will, honey."

Sarah turned the pistol in her hands, knowing she was lying to Lucy. She could hardly drive off a war party with six shots, even if she could manage to hit anything. There was no way the gun could help.

But now Sarah realized she was lying to herself. There was one way she could use the gun, if it came to that. She had heard stories— terrible stories—of white women captured by the Indians. She didn't know if they were true, and she didn't know what might happen to

Lucy, but in the back of her mind, she heard the old settler's words: *Better off dead.*

"Sarah?" Lucy's quiet voice startled her. "Sarah, I'm scared."

"Me too, honey."

Lucy raised her head, and Sarah could see the pale oval of her face in the darkness.

"Sarah, could you sing to me? The way Mama used to when I was afraid at night?"

Sarah hesitated. Then, so softly that no sound could carry outside the cave, she began one of the old songs her mother had known.

> *"In Scarlet Town, where I was born,*
> *There was a fair maid dwelling.*
> *Made every lad cry, 'Welladay.'*
> *Her name was Barbara Allen."*

The words brought back her home in Pennsylvania and the days before her mother had died and Dr. Cameron had decided to come west. She was homesick, and her voice sounded so lost and plaintive in the prairie night that it frightened her. But she waited until the song was finished and she was sure Lucy was asleep before she let the tears come.

She awoke cramped and sore. The sun shone brightly outside, and a bird was singing on a limb above the cave. Lucy was already awake, peering outside.

"I don't see anything," she said. "Do you think Papa and the soldiers will come today?"

"I hope so," Sarah said. Lucy looked quickly around, and Sarah smiled. "They'll come. But they won't know you, with your frock all muddy and cherry juice around your mouth."

Lucy straightened and sniffed disdainfully.

"Well, that Pritchard boy wouldn't know you. Just look at your hair."

Sarah combed her fingers through her tangled brown mane. In spite of herself, she laughed. It seemed a year since her only worries had been hair and the freckles brought on by the relentless sunshine. Gaily, she smoothed down her skirt.

"Oh, don't you think I'm fit to dance with the prince?"

Lucy laughed, too, and came across to throw thin arms around her neck. All the fear and sleepless weariness they had felt welled up into laughter, and they giggled until their sides hurt. Then Sarah, pausing for breath, heard the distant neigh of a horse above the sound of the stream.

"Shh. Be quiet, Lucy."

A cold fear clamped down on her. She pressed her hand over Lucy's mouth until the girl was silent, then released her.

"Maybe it's them," Lucy whispered. "Papa and Mr. Turner and the soldiers."

"I hope so." Sarah closed her fingers on the revolver, gripping it tightly to keep her hands from trembling. "I hope so, honey."

Something heavy slid down the bank a little way upstream and splashed in the water. A man's deep voice muttered something Sarah couldn't hear and, almost overhead, another man laughed. A trickle of dirt fell from the roof of the cave. Through a narrow opening between two roots, Sarah saw a moccasined foot and part of a leg. The Indian stood there a few moments, then slowly moved downstream.

They know we're here, Sarah thought. They were searching, and they were certain to find the cave. Almost without thinking, Sarah cocked the pistol. *Better off dead.*

"Get back, Lucy," Sarah whispered. "Close your eyes."

"Are you going to—?" Lucy didn't finish. She stared at Sarah gravely for a moment. "I'm not afraid," she said, and put her hands over her face.

Footsteps came along below the bank. Sarah saw herself dragged from the cave, separated from Lucy, Lucy reared as an Indian. Maybe the settler had been right. Maybe death would be better.

Slowly, Sarah raised the pistol until it almost touched Lucy's forehead. She thought of the man from the train, dead in the grass along the trail. It would be easy to pull the trigger. Two shots, and she and Lucy would be safe from the Indians.

Safe. The word jarred Sarah. She realized suddenly that the Sioux didn't frighten her, any more than the night just past had frightened her. She was not afraid of what the Indians might do, but of the unknown, of the waiting and the uncertainty. And being afraid to face that, she had almost given up.

Outside, one of the Indians called out. A shadow fell across the mouth of the cave. Sarah turned. She couldn't tell what might happen, but she knew that nothing could ever be quite as bad again as that moment she had just lived through. Steadying the heavy Colt in both hands, she trained it on the opening.

An Indian appeared there, stooped to look inside. With a strange clarity, Sarah saw his braided hair, long and shot with gray, his sharp hawk nose, his black eyes staring in surprise at the pistol. He froze. Another warrior came up beside him, and then a third. All three stood looking at her. Then one began to laugh.

It wasn't fair, Sarah thought. They could kill her, but they had no right to laugh at her. She raised the gun, but the first Indian held up his hands and backed away. A moment later, another man slid down the bank. In astonishment, Sarah recognized the bearded face of Ben Turner.

"Reckon you can put that down, missy," he said gently. "These are Crows, scouts for the Army. They found you."

Relief almost swept away Sarah's senses. She managed to hand the Colt to Turner, but her legs were weak as he and one of the Crow scouts helped her from the cave. Out by the trail, a detachment of soldiers stood guard by the burned wagons.

"Is my father all right?" Sarah asked.

"Just fine, missy, but he was right worried about you." Ben Turned smiled at her. "You did mighty well here by yourselves. You're brave girls."

Sarah put her arm around Lucy. Standing straight and tall, she returned the old scout's smile.

"It wasn't so bad," she said. "Come on, Lucy. We're going home."

WAY OF THE STAR

Gerald Keenan

Dan Keogh flipped the lifeless, half-smoked cigar out into the street, his sense of frustration overpowering the usual enjoyment of his mid-morning smoke. The feeling had clung to him like a shadow for nearly a week, since the day Breck Wilson arrived in Twin Springs on the same morning stage that was just now braking to a halt across the way.

Helen St. Clair had been on that stage too, returning home after a year in St. Louis, and it was her growing acquaintance with Wilson that was the source of Dan's concern.

If there was one thing he had learned in fifteen years as a dedicated peace officer, it was a realization that the laws he enforced and believed in were designed to act after, not before, the fact. Accordingly, he could not arrest Breck Wilson, or interfere with his rights in any way because of a suspicion based on nothing more than personal feelings. Nevertheless, knowing this did not relieve him of feeling a certain sense of responsibility.

He stiffened slightly as he saw Helen St. Clair emerge from the livery stable and ride out of town, in the same direction Breck Wilson had gone but a short time before. Dan watched until the girl had disappeared over the rise at the far end of town, then stepped out across the street, returning the stage driver's greeting with a perfunctory wave.

Most of the morning trade was gone as he entered the café and took a table in the far corner, plopping his hat down on a vacant chair.

"Coffee, Beth," he ordered soberly, as an auburn-haired woman approached the table, drying her hands on a worn, white apron.

"I know," she replied, "strong and black."

In a country that usually etched the lines of age on a feminine face all too quickly, Beth Romain had somehow managed to retain an aura of youthfulness that belied her thirty-four years. At an age when most women have long since been in the process of rearing a family, her sole interest in life seemed to be this small café. The profits were not great, but it did provide her with a means of support and a reason for existing.

She set the coffee in front of him and eased down into the chair across the table, watching him finger the cup thoughtfully.

"What's bothering you, Dan?"

"Just tired, I guess," he replied.

"It's that gambler, isn't it?"

He had not confided his suspicions to anyone and was caught short by her remark.

"I didn't think it showed."

"I've known you long enough to realize when something's eating at your insides," Beth observed. "You haven't been the same since he hit town."

"Neither has Helen St. Clair," Dan added dryly.

Beth Romain shrugged. "Helen's a big girl, Dan."

"Not where Wilson's concerned," he countered sharply. "You don't realize you've been cheated until it's too late."

"There's bad blood between you, isn't there?" Beth ventured softly, breaking the brief silence.

He nodded.

"Want to talk about it?"

For a moment he considered her offer, then concluded it was pointless.

"Maybe some day, Beth, but not now."

She smiled wryly and got to her feet. "You men are all alike," she remarked with a sigh. "Stubborn. You want to be coaxed like a little boy."

Dan grinned at this show of feminine logic. "You're a good woman, Beth."

"Men!" she snorted, and, gesturing helplessly, turned and walked back to the kitchen.

The sun rose higher, baking the land, its stifling heat penetrating to the very core of the town, sapping the energy of man and beast alike. At length, having completed its daily ritual of searing the land, the sun began to sink behind the jagged somber brown peaks to the west, slowly expiring in a rush of crimson and gold. Then presently the town was bathed in deepening purple shadows and the blessed coolness of evening.

Dan stood outside the office, his after-dinner cigar glowing orange-red in the darkness. It had been a long way since Abilene, he reflected. A long fifteen years, with nothing to show for his efforts but a tin star and a lot of memories. The job provided few rewards: an after-dinner cigar, an occasional drink, and the satisfaction that comes from a job well done.

Abruptly, he cast the cigar out into the street and turned to walk through the town on his nightly round. Up ahead, the soft glow of lamplight and the peacefulness from the town's small, solid-citizenry section was in marked contrast to the throaty laugh of a dance hall girl, mingled with the sound of a tinny piano, that floated up behind him.

The contrast reminded Dan that he really belonged to neither faction. He was a man alone, living by a hardened set of principles, and with a badge of office that required he administer the same justice to all, whether it be a drunken cowboy or the mayor himself.

He had always been content to accept these conditions, finding that the satisfaction of the job itself was compensation enough. Yet there had been moments, particularly in recent weeks, when he found himself thinking about a quiet niche in that peaceful section of town. Times were changing, and anyone who failed to heed those signs became the dregs of the past. Maybe it was time?

The cool of the evening was refreshing as he turned onto Front Street. Easing through the batwing doors of the Silver Dollar, he made his way slowly through the smoke-filled interior. At the end of the bar he leaned back, elbows hooked over the bar, letting his gaze sweep across the room.

In the far corner, a piano rang with the refrain of a lively tune. Two poker games were in progress, and he noted Breck Wilson sitting in on one of them. From the stack of chips in front of him, it was obvious the man was enjoying a profitable evening.

The barkeep approached. "What'll it be, Marshal?"

Dan waved him off. The barkeep shrugged and walked back to the other end of the bar.

Dan watched with interest for the next half hour, as Wilson won pot after pot. You had to give the devil his due. A man would have to look a long way to find anyone slicker across the felt green of a poker table, or for that matter, with women.

Presently, two of the four players decided they'd had enough for the evening and pulled out of the game. Young Dave Lynch staggered a bit as he arose from his chair and confronted Wilson.

"I say it ain't possible for a man to be that lucky," he declared in a whiskey-slurred voice.

Wilson, counting his chips, did not bother to look up. "Some are good. Some are lucky, and some are poor losers," he replied softly.

"I'm sayin' there's more to it than that," Lynch countered, his voice growing ugly.

Wilson looked up slowly, composure unruffled. He was no stranger to this situation.

"That's not very careful talk, sonny, but I'll do you a favor and forget I heard it."

Lynch flushed and made a sudden move for the holstered gun on his hip. The force of Dan's grip on his arm caught and suspended the movement at midpoint.

"Go on home, Dave."

Lynch swung around savagely. "You're supposed to be the law in this town. Whatta ya gonna do about him . . . ?"

Dan glanced over at the other two players, who'd elected to stay around long enough to witness the upshot of young Lynch's accusation.

"You gents feel the same way?"

"He's won plenty, Marshal," one of them volunteered, "but we got no complaints."

The second man nodded in agreement.

"Looks like you called the wrong turn, Dave. Better go home and sleep it off."

"This tinhorn ain't heard the last of it!" Lynch declared. "You won't always be around, Marshal."

"I can get here real quick, Dave. See that you remember it," Dan said.

Lynch glared viciously at Dan for a long moment, then heeling angrily about, strode unsteadily from the saloon.

"I'm obliged, Keogh," Wilson said, "but you should have let me handle him. Sooner or later I will have to, and we both know that."

"I get paid for keeping the peace in this town, Wilson, and I intend to do just that. What I said to him applies to you."

Breck Wilson smiled. "I should remember that from Abilene, shouldn't I?"

Dan glared at the man for a long moment, then eased down into a chair.

"Let's talk."

Wilson shrugged. "What's your pleasure?"

"I want you to leave Helen St. Clair alone."

Wilson laughed. "There a law in this town against being sociable?"

"No law," Dan replied. "But just remember, step out of line with her and I'll personally break you in half." He said it flat and ugly, with no mistake about the implication.

Wilson leaned forward. "I don't like to be threatened, Keogh."

"Think of it as an official warning," Dan replied, getting slowly to his feet. "Anything happens to that girl, you'll wish you'd never seen Twin Springs." He turned and walked back through the room, into the coolness of the night.

Back at the office he poured coffee into a stained mug and eased tiredly into the worn chair behind his desk, the anger and frustration inside him building. To Breck Wilson, Helen St. Clair was an object that had to be achieved, regardless of the cost. That's the way it was with his kind. And when the prize was won he'd drop her and move on to someone new. Unless someone intervened, that was precisely how it would go, just as surely as tomorrow's sunrise would come from the east.

As marshal, his hands were tied. Until Wilson broke the law, or someone lodged a formal complaint, there was nothing he could legally do.

He thought of talking with Helen's father. Old Doc St. Clair was no fool. He knew full well what it meant to have an attractive daughter in a town like Twin Springs. His own wife had died twenty years earlier, leaving Doc with a small girl to raise. And, all things considered, he'd done a pretty fair job, too, even managing to send her back East to a decent finishing school. But, like most young people, Helen would resent parental interference. Maybe he ought to have a straightforward talk with Helen? They were good friends and there was a fair chance she'd listen to him. He walked over to the cot and eased down. Stretching out, he continued to ponder the problem, before finally falling into a restless sleep.

The first rays of the sun played across his face, waking him immediately. He rose quickly, washed, shaved, and headed across the street to Beth's.

After breakfast, he stood outside the café smoking a cigar. Across the way Helen St. Clair was just emerging from her father's office. Crossing the street, Dan hailed her.

"Morning, Helen."

"Good morning, Dan," she replied pleasantly.

"Wonder if I might have a word with you, Helen?"

"Why I suppose so, Dan," she said, half surprised and glancing toward the livery stable. "Won't take long will it . . . ?"

"Just a few moments, Helen."

Taking her arm he escorted her back to the office. Inside, he offered her a chair, seating himself on the edge of the desk.

"Now, Dan," she said, smiling. "What's this all about?"

Dan studied her thoughtfully, still uncertain as to whether or not he really had the right to invade her private life. He decided the stakes were high enough to make it worthwhile.

"You've been seeing a lot of Breck Wilson lately, haven't you?"

She flushed slightly. "Why . . . yes, as a matter of fact, but I really don't see where that's . . ."

"Helen, do you mind a little advice?"

"What are you getting at, Dan?"

"Stay away from him, Helen. He's no good."

She stood up quickly, her face colored with anger and embarrassment. "Don't you think that's being a bit too personal, Dan?"

He watched the rebellion mounting in her finely chiseled features and knew he'd failed.

"Maybe so," he replied softly, "but I hoped you'd try and understand."

"Well, I don't," she said heatedly, her tone of voice matching the indignation that flamed up out of the blackness of her eyes.

"I happen to be perfectly capable of choosing my own friends, and for your information I include Breck Wilson in that group whether you approve or not. And just for the record, Marshal, a lot of men in this town could learn a thing or two from him about how a lady should be treated!"

Heeling sharply about, she stalked to the door, wheeling about to confront him one last time. "It may interest you to know that Breck Wilson has asked me to go to San Francisco with him."

"I hope you'll give that a lot of thought, Helen. I'm sure your father wouldn't approve."

"I have my own life to live," she replied coldly, and walked out slamming the door behind her.

Dan watched her go, feeling the futility of his effort. Why is it, he wondered, that they must always learn the hard way? Presently he put on his hat and walked outside, pulling the brim of the Stetson a little lower against the glare of the climbing sun.

Inside the café, Beth set a cup of coffee in front of him without being asked.

"I just had a talk with Helen," he ventured.

"And . . . ?"

"She advised me to mind my own business."

"Did you really expect anything else, Dan?"

He shook his head. "No, I guess not. Just hoping, Beth."

"Is it really as bad as all that, Dan?"

She saw the answer flame up in his eyes; saw all the anger and hurt of that other time erupt into a present-day reality.

"It's like watching the past come to life," he observed slowly. "It's like knowing what will happen and being powerless to stop it."

He rose and walked to the window, staring out into the morning, remembering a long way back, longer than a man cared to, but couldn't help sometimes. Beth followed and stood at his side, saying nothing, but ready to listen should he choose to talk.

"Fifteen years ago I was a young deputy in Abilene," he announced at length. "There was a girl. We were to be married . . ." He paused, feeling the hurt that came with the memory, then continued. "Then Wilson hit town. He had charm and a way with women. When he left she went with him. I heard later she died in a cheap Kansas City hotel."

"I'm sorry, Dan," she said softly.

He shrugged. "It doesn't matter anymore, Beth. I was young then and I've learned a lot since Abilene."

"You're bitter, Dan, and I can understand that, but don't judge the world by the actions of two people."

"You know better than that, Beth."

She sighed. "Maybe, but I also know how easy it is to go sour on everything."

He looked at her curiously. She sensed his interest and continued.

"I've never spoken of it before, but after Jim died I was at a complete loss. He drank too much, and then one day when life got to be more than he could face, even through a bottle, he killed himself. I was in a corner for a long time before I began to realize that I had been clinging to something that never existed."

"I'm sorry, Beth. I never knew."

"I know," she said. "Until now, there didn't seem to be any reason to make mention of it. Maybe it'll help some."

"Guess that makes us two of a kind," he observed. "And maybe you're right. Maybe I have been hanging on to something that never existed, but right now Breck Wilson exists and so does Helen St. Clair.

"Thanks for the coffee, Beth." He put on his hat and stepped outside. For a time she remained at the window, watching him move up the street, until he disappeared from view.

The late afternoon sun was no longer visible on the horizon, only the bloodred splash of its dying effort lay clinging to the quickly darkening land.

From Front Street came the brawling yells of the miners and ranch hands, in to celebrate Saturday night, anxious to rinse the dust and grime of a hard land from their throats.

The early part of the evening passed with little in the way of unusual excitement. Other than two cowboys sleeping it off in the confines of the cellblock, things were going smoothly for a Saturday night.

With midnight approaching, Dan prepared to make his final round of the night. Halfway up Front Street, the muffled report of a gunshot filled the air.

He was sure the shot had come from the Silver Dollar, and as he walked through the door found his suspicion confirmed. Dave Lynch was lying on the floor, blood welling from a gunshot wound high in the left chest. He didn't need a second look to know that Lynch was in a bad way.

"Get Doc," he ordered, letting his gaze sweep around the circle of onlookers to settle on Breck Wilson, who was seated at the table, calmly smoking a cigar. A small ivory-handled derringer lay on the table in front of him.

"How'd it happen?" Dan asked.

"The kid was drunk, Marshal," one man volunteered. "He figured Wilson, here, was a little too lucky, and went for his gun."

Dan glanced around, seeing the nods of agreement.

"Come to think of it, Marshal, maybe the kid did see somethin' we missed. This fella has been awful lucky since he hit town . . ."

There were mutterings of approval as the man voiced his opinion.

"All right, that's enough," Dan said. "I'll take it from here. Go on home . . . all of you. Show's over for tonight."

Doc St. Clair arrived and pushed his way through the crowd. After a quick examination, he ordered Lynch removed to his office. Doc took a long look at Breck Wilson, then turned to Dan. "I'll do what I can, but that's a bad wound. Anyone tell the old man?"

"I'll send someone," Dan said.

Doc St. Clair looked again at Wilson, then turned and followed Lynch's body out of the saloon.

Wilson was completely composed as Dan reached out and picked up the derringer.

"On your feet," Dan ordered sharply.

"Now hold on, Keogh. You heard the story."

"I said, on your feet, Wilson."

Wilson got slowly to his feet. "What are you trying to prove, Keogh? It was self-defense and you know it."

Dan looked at him steadily. "Maybe, but for now you've got ten seconds to get moving, or I'll bend the barrel of this Colt across your skull and have the boys drag you out."

Above all, Breck Wilson was a gambler, and knew from the iron-hard stare in Dan's eyes that the deck was stacked against him. Shrugging, he carefully donned his hat and walked out of the Silver Dollar, with Dan following.

Dan sat at his desk, smoking a cigar, staring out the window into the dull, gray, predawn light that was just beginning to erase the vestiges of night. He glanced over at Wilson, resting quietly in his cell. It galled him to see the man so perfectly composed.

The door opened, admitting Beth Romain with a pot of coffee. A shawl was draped around her shoulders, against the chill.

"News gets around fast," he remarked, coming around the desk to greet her.

"That it does," she replied. "How's the boy?"

Dan poured two cups of coffee and handed one to her. "No word yet."

"Does his father know?"

"I sent someone out to tell him and I expect that by now he's riding hard to sit in judgment."

"That'll mean trouble, Dan. You know what he thinks of that boy."

"If he had cared enough, that boy wouldn't be where he is now."

"What about him?" Beth asked, motioning toward Breck Wilson.

Helen St. Clair's breathless appearance interrupted them as she rushed into the office. "Dave Lynch is dead," Helen cried, shock registering on her face. "He's dead!"

Beth saw the slight sag in Dan's shoulders as he took the news; watched as he walked slowly to the window and stared out into the newly forming day.

Helen stepped quickly over to Wilson's cell. "I got here as quickly as I could, Breck. Dad told me it was self-defense. You've got nothing to worry about."

She turned to Dan. "Considering the circumstances, is it necessary to keep this man in jail?"

"I'm afraid it is, Helen. The territorial judge will be here next week. I'll have to hold him for trial."

"You can't hold me on a trumped-up charge like that," Breck Wilson called out. "A dozen witnesses will say it was self-defense!"

Dan walked over to face Wilson. "Maybe. Tell you what, though, Wilson. I'll make a deal with you."

"You never made a deal with anyone in your life, Keogh."

Dan waved off the remark. "Whatever you've cleared across the poker table since you hit town is a fair amount. Make a pretty good stake in San Francisco . . ."

"Get to the point, Keogh."

Dan nodded. "All right. Leave town and you can keep your stake. Stay, and I'll see it gets returned. What's more, you can count on facing a jury that's bound to be sympathetic toward young Lynch. The way I see it, they're going to figure that maybe Lynch was right, that maybe you were a shade too lucky."

"He's trying to trick you, Breck," Helen cried.

"Shut up!" Wilson said, glaring at Dan.

Helen St. Clair stared at Wilson in slack-jawed surprise, totally taken aback by a side of the man's personality she would have never guessed existed.

"But, Breck, I . . ."

"Will you shut up!" he thundered, pacing the cell, obviously weighing the odds of Dan's offer.

"Forget the girl," Dan said, "and you can take the money and walk out of here. On the other hand, if she means anything to you, the money won't matter. Choice is yours."

He had played his hole card, and he watched as Helen looked at Wilson, waiting to hear the words that Dan knew would never be uttered by the man in the cell.

"All right, Keogh," Wilson declared at length. "You've got a deal."

Breck Wilson looked at Helen as Dan unlocked the door. "That's the way it is, kid," he said. "I need the money worse'n you."

Helen St. Clair turned and rushed from the room. Beth Romain followed.

Dan handed Wilson his derringer and the money. "It's been a long time," he said, "but at least part of the debt's been repaid."

Wilson straightened his clothes and shook his head slowly. "All over a woman so far in the past I don't even recall her name . . ."

"Your kind wouldn't, Wilson, because people mean nothing to you. One day it'll destroy you."

"You don't forget, do you, Keogh?"

"Not often," Dan said.

Wilson walked to the door, stopped as if to say something, then changed his mind and walked out.

Watching him leave, Dan felt a sense of relief and accomplishment such as he hadn't known in a long time.

Presently, Beth returned. "It may take a while, but she'll be fine, Dan."

Dan nodded. "She'll be a better woman for it, too, Beth."

"How will you explain to the judge?"

"About what?"

She looked at him curiously. "But you said . . ."

"I know," Dan said, smiling easily.

"Dan, are you saying Dave Lynch is alive, that Wilson didn't kill him?"

"That's it, Beth. After the shooting, I got to thinking. Talked to Doc, and he agreed to go along with the idea. I had to make sure that Wilson left town without Helen, but I wanted it to be his idea. Maybe you could call it the way of the star."

"I hope Wilson never finds out," she said, laughing.

"You recall what we were discussing the other morning, Beth?"

She nodded.

"Well I thought maybe we could pick up where we left off. How about breakfast?"

She smiled and took his arm. "I'd love it," she said.

They walked out of the office, feeling the freshness of the early morning, and it seemed to Dan that this was going to be the best day he'd had in a long time.

THE TAMING OF JIM SHANNON

Ray Gaulden

Jim Shannon knew that trouble was waiting for him in the Gold Nugget Saloon; he felt it in the sudden silence the minute he stepped through the doorway. Men stopped talking and moved quickly away from the bar. In the cleared space stood Ed Burke, big and ugly. When he saw who had entered, Burke banged his glass down and put his broad back to the bar.

Jim Shannon walked across the room, his bootheels loud in the stillness, a flat-crowned hat shoved back so that some of his red hair showed. He was as big as Burke, but moved with the grace of a mountain cat.

"Hello, Ed," Jim said. "Heard that you were waiting for me, that you've been here most of the day, drinking and making your brag."

Ed Burke glared at him. "Did you think you could call me down in front of everybody, fire me and get away with it?"

"I caught you high-grading, Ed, what you'd been doing ever since you went to work at the Red Bird. Most of the boys carry off a little in their lunch buckets, but you had to be a hog."

"You're a liar," Burke said, his voice louder now that he had the attention of everyone in the room. "You've got the rest of those miners buffaloed, but I figure to show them you're more wind than anything else."

"Anytime you're ready," Jim said.

Burke rushed in and the fight was on, the crowd moving back to give them room. Bets had already been placed and the stakes were being held by Pat Robbins, the bartender. Pat had his brown derby tipped on the side of his head and was talking to Nora Lurton, the girl who sang sad songs to the customers.

"You'd think Jim would get tired of it after a while," Pat said, wiping his hands on his apron. "He's licked about everybody in Central City."

Nora Lurton got out of the way as Ed Burke, driven by a blow from Jim Shannon, slammed into the bar close to where the saloon girl was standing.

"That big Irishman won't ever be any different," Nora said, smiling. "He's tough as a Texas Longhorn."

"Toughest man that ever hit the Rocky Mountains," Pat Robbins said, watching Burke get to his feet. "Jim would walk down Virginia Canyon's winding road in a blinding snowstorm if there was a chance of a good brawl when he got to Idaho Springs."

The bartender winced as Ed Burke landed with a right that staggered Shannon and sent him crashing into one of the tables. Wood splintered and the table legs gave way. But Jim was able to flash a reckless grin as he pulled himself up from the wreckage.

They came together again with a jar that shook the room, and the crowd cheered as the pair stood close, slugging away at each other. Ed Burke should have known better, but by the time he found out, the miner was down on the floor with a smashed nose, unable to continue.

Men crowded around the bar, collecting their bets and slapping the winner on the back, while Jim rubbed his skinned knuckles and grinned.

"Just look at you," Nora Lurton said, moving up beside him. "If Beth Richmond could see you now, she might not think you're such a wonderful bunch of muscles."

Mention of Beth caused Jim to sober. He realized he was stepping way out of his class, but he had never met a girl like Beth before. Besides being beautiful, she was a real lady and also the banker's daughter.

"Hey," Nora said, nudging him with her elbow. "Remember me? I'm the one that picks up the pieces, mends the cuts, and patches the lumps you get on your head."

Jim's grin came back. "Sure, I know, you're the best, and I'm going to buy you a glass of your favorite drink. Pat, a bottle of strawberry soda pop for the queen."

Shannon picked the girl up lightly in his powerful arms, and set her on the bar. Nora was laughing and swinging her shapely legs when Porter Hobson, the gambler, got up from his table and walked over.

"You were lucky again," Hobson said.

Jim looked at the gambler, aware of the resentment in the tall man's eyes. Somehow, Porter Hobson had never been able to see that Jim and Nora were just good friends, nothing more.

On his way out of the saloon, Jim could feel Hobson's eyes following him, but Jim didn't stop or even glance around. That tinhorn was the least of his worries. Right now he had to get over to the hotel, change his torn clothes, and wash up. The fight had left him looking awful.

Crossing the crowded street of the mining town, Jim ducked around a freight wagon and was looking the other way when he crashed into a parked buggy, hitting it with such force that the rig rocked crazily and caused the occupant to lose her balance.

"Beth!" Jim cried.

The girl seemed about to fall out of the buggy along with her packages, so Jim caught her and swept her up in his arms. She didn't weigh much, he could tell, but what there was of her was soft, warm and round.

Jim held her, unmindful of the traffic and the amused stares of the townspeople.

"Maybe you'd better put me down now," Beth said shyly. "I see Papa watching from the doorway of the bank."

Jim placed her back on the buggy seat and Beth sat there, her hair like gold in the sunlight, while Jim quickly gathered up her scattered packages.

"Clumsy of me to run into you that way," Jim said.

He forgot his disheveled appearance until Beth scolded him. "You've been fighting again, Jim Shannon, and I can smell whiskey on your breath."

"I only had one drink," Jim said. "And the fight didn't amount to nothing."

Her blue eyes were serious. "If you would only try harder to stay out of trouble, I'm sure Papa would be more approving of our relationship. Why, we might become very good friends."

The promise in her eyes caused Jim's pulse to race. Before he could find words, Beth lifted the reins in her gloved hands and drove off. But the buggy had only gone a short distance down the street when it stopped again.

Jim scowled as he watched Alex Marlow step from the Mercantile and tip his hat to Beth Richmond. The damned dude, with nothing better to do than hang around his pa's store, keep his button shoes polished up and wink at the girls that went by.

Jim walked on. In his room at the hotel, he looked at his battered features in the mirror. If he hoped to make any headway with Beth, he would have to change his ways.

After he had washed and put on clean clothes, Jim started to pour himself a drink from a bottle he kept in the room. Then he set the glass down and made a decision: no more drinking, no more brawling. He would behave himself and cut Alex, the storekeeper's worthless son, right out of the running.

As foreman of the Red Bird mine, a good deal of Jim's time was spent underground, working along with the others. It was a rough, dangerous job, but because he was always willing to pitch in when a hand was needed, Jim had won the respect of most of the miners.

A few troublemakers were always hoping to prove Jim wasn't as good as some claimed. At least once a week, he had to take on one of the miners, but seldom were there hard feelings and after the fights he and the boys usually went over to the Gold Nugget and had a drink.

If he was going to avoid trouble, Jim decided he would have to stay away from the saloon and take a job in the mine office.

"Seems kind of tame for a man like you," the superintendent said. "But you've been a good troubleshooter and I don't want to lose you, so if you're dead set on making a switch, I'll find somebody to take your place."

Over at the Gold Nugget, bartender Pat Robbins began making bets that Jim Shannon wouldn't last a week on his new job.

"You had better watch out," Nora Lurton said, sipping from a glass of strawberry soda pop while she watched Pat count the money he had taken in. "That banker's daughter has Jim so far gone, he don't know which end is up."

"It won't last long," the bartender said confidently. "You mark my word."

Pat Robbins ended up losing a whole month's pay because Jim Shannon stuck it out, and what was more, not once did he drop around to the Gold Nugget to have a drink or to say howdy.

Jim was proud of himself. He visited the barbershop more often and in the privacy of his hotel room, he tried on the new button shoes he had bought along with the best suit of clothes he could find in town.

He was doing all right. Beth's father, the most important man in Central City, was beginning to notice Jim for the first time and some of the churchgoing folks had stopped putting their noses in the air when they passed.

That night Jim and Beth went for a buggy ride down the steep road to Blackhawk. The moon was up and it was a nice night to stop along the creek and look out at the sluice boxes where men were working the stream for gold.

Beth was wearing a blue dress and her yellow hair smelled good as usual.

"I'm awful proud of you, Jim," Beth said. "At first Papa didn't think you could change, but I knew different."

"Shucks," Jim said. "It wasn't nothing."

Beth permitted him to kiss her before she suggested they start for home.

Jim Shannon figured he was the happiest man in the Colorado high country. When they got back to Central City and pulled up in front of the big Richmond house, Beth told him she was having a party Saturday night and that he was invited. She even let him kiss her again before she jumped out of the buggy and ran up the walk.

On the way to the livery stable with the rented rig, Jim whistled and wondered how an ornery cuss like him could be so lucky. Imagine, an invite to the banker's house.

But it was only Beth that he wanted to see and be with, and when he thought of rubbing elbows with the town's upper crust, he didn't feel as good as he had at first. Whether he liked it or not, he could see no way out of going.

After he had returned the buggy, Jim started for the hotel. It was early yet and the crowd in the Gold Nugget Saloon was whooping it up.

Stopping to roll a cigarette, Jim looked at the saloon and listened to the noise. The boys must be having a fine time. Then it got quiet in the barroom and Jim could hear Nora Lurton's low, throaty voice lifted in song. It was a number he hadn't heard before, so Jim leaned against the front of a building, smoking and listening to Nora sing.

He had an urge to see the girl, and Pat, the friendly bartender. He had known them both a long time and always enjoyed visiting with them. All the boys loved Nora; Jim used to tease her about it. He remembered how mad she would get sometimes at the hoorahing, and to get even she would smile at Porter Hobson, because she knew Jim didn't like the gambler.

But Nora was understanding, and it would be good to see her, have a beer, and talk over old times. Of course he wouldn't want to let on that he wasn't satisfied with his new job that kept him confined to the office.

If he walked into that saloon, though, there was a good chance of becoming involved in a brawl, so Jim forgot it and went on to the hotel.

The next day while Jim Shannon was going over some assay reports at the Red Bird mine, Ben Young, the superintendent, came into the office, scowling.

"What you so long-faced about?" Jim asked.

"I didn't know we had such a ornery bunch working in the mine,"

Young said. "The fellow I hired to take your place didn't last a week."

"I tried to give him a few pointers," Jim said. "Told him he couldn't be too hard on them to start with, but he wouldn't listen."

"I know, so they busted his head with a pick handle and run him off the job." Young shook his head worriedly. "There's some mean ones down in that hole, Jim, and they'll steal us blind if we don't ride close herd on them."

Paper work bored Jim and he was tempted to tell Young that he would take his old job back. But he had made too much progress with Beth to spoil the setup now.

Jim was edgy, and glad when quitting time came. Fighting the need for a drink, he passed the saloon and went on to his hotel room. With Beth's party coming up tomorrow night, he didn't have much time left to break in the button shoes. Trying the new footwear on, Jim made a face, and for the first time wondered if Beth was worth all the discomfort.

In a bad mood, he left the hotel, and turned into the first saloon he came to. He ordered a drink and downed it fast. Looking at himself in the bar mirror, he noticed that most of the battle scars on his face were beginning to heal. The scabs on his knuckles were about gone, too.

Jim swore under his breath. The first thing you knew, he would be as soft as Alex Marlow.

He left the saloon by a side door, and it bothered him to think that he was slipping around in order to keep Beth's old man from seeing him. He cursed again. Damn it, Jim Shannon was used to barging in and out of any place he was of a mind to.

Walking through the town that was known as the richest square mile on earth, Jim was able to unwind a little. He thought of Beth Richmond, beside him in the buggy, her mouth pressed against his.

A high-class woman like that was worth a little suffering.

Saturday, Jim spent half a day getting ready for the party. A trip to the barbershop for the closest shave he'd ever had. Then for a long while he lay and soaked in the wooden tub. At least an hour was spent in his hotel room, smearing grease on his unruly red hair.

During the long day, Jim must have smoked two sacks of tobacco. By the time night came he was as nervous as a tinhorn in church. A drink might settle him down, but he didn't want to go to the party smelling of whiskey.

He finished dressing, waiting until the very last to put on the button shoes. He grimaced. As uncomfortable as the shoes were, Jim wondered how he would ever make it through the evening.

Slipping into his new coat that was too tight across his broad shoulders, he left the hotel. On his way to the Richmond house, Jim passed the Gold Nugget Saloon. If he had stopped to think he would have gone by on the other side of the street, because if some of the old crowd came out and saw him in this getup, they would surely laugh.

Jim was about to hurry on when Porter Hobson stepped out of the saloon and bumped into him.

"Sorry," the tall gambler said, but he had that smirk on his face that always made Jim want to hit him.

"Out of my way," Jim said.

Hobson frowned. "I'm in a rush, too. Getting married tonight."

Jim shouldered past the gambler and went on down the street. He didn't want to be late for the party, but he wished he had waited long enough to find out who Porter Hobson was going to marry. Everyone in Central City knew how no-account the man was, so where would he find a woman that would have him?

By the time Jim reached the Richmond house, other guests had arrived and in the huge parlor a three-piece orchestra was tuning up. Beth, looking lovely in a white lace dress, introduced him around and somehow Jim got through it, but he could feel the sweat staining through that new broadcloth shirt.

When he and Beth were finally alone at the punch bowl for a minute, she smiled at him and said, "I'm so glad you could come, Jim."

"Nice of you to invite me."

Before he could ask her about opening a window so some fresh air could get in, other guests arrived and Beth left him alone at the punch bowl.

While Jim was mopping his damp brow with a handkerchief, Alex Marlow stepped up, amusement on his handsome face. "A little out of your class here, aren't you, Shannon?"

Jim wondered how Alex would like to have his head shoved in the punch bowl, but before Jim could do anything about it, Beth returned, along with another girl who took Alex by the arm and led him away.

"Like the punch?" Beth asked.

"Fine," Jim said, but he wondered why someone hadn't thought to mix a few bottles of likker in with the sweet-tasting stuff.

At that moment, the orchestra struck up a tune and several couples moved onto the floor. Beth stood close to him, smiling. "We've never danced together."

It was a waltz, something Jim figured he might get through without too much stumbling. The only trouble was those button shoes were pinching his feet. Still, he wasn't doing bad and it was good to hold Beth in his arms as they moved in time to the music.

Everything was fine. He and Beth were out in the center of the big room, right under that huge cut-glass chandelier when Alex Marlow and his partner danced by. Alex came close, showing some fancy footwork and at the same time jostling Jim.

It was done deliberately and Jim knew it, but Beth was smiling at him, so he went on dancing. Alex seemed to be enjoying himself. He came gliding in again and this time his foot slid in front of Jim's.

"Sorry," Alex said.

The floor was slick and Jim's feet went out from under him. He turned loose of Beth, not wanting to pull her down with him, and landed on his back with a jar that shook the room.

Alex Marlow couldn't hold back a snicker. Someone laughed and even Beth was smiling in amusement as she looked down at him. That did it, made Jim Shannon forget all about ever becoming a gentleman.

He got to his feet, grinning. The fall had caused his coat to split down the back. Everyone was laughing now, Alex louder than the rest.

Without a word, Jim walked over and grabbed Alex Marlow, put one hand on his collar, the other on the seat of his pants. Beth gasped and Alex's partner cried out in protest, but Jim marched the young man across the room and shoved his head in the punch bowl. When Jim turned him loose, Alex staggered back, then slipped and sprawled across the table which collapsed with a crash.

As Jim headed for the front door, he paused to glance back and saw that Beth Richmond had run over to kneel beside Alex who was still struggling to get up. Beth was humiliated, and her concern for Alex let Jim know that it was all over between them.

Outside the house, Jim filled his lungs with clean fresh air. He took the torn coat off and left it hanging on the gate of the Richmond house. On his way downtown, he reached up and ripped the collar off his shirt and no longer had the feeling he was choking to death.

By the time he got to town, he was limping. His feet hurt so badly that he sat down in a doorway and removed his button shoes. Standing again, he threw the shoes as far as he could into the darkness and went on in his sock feet.

When he came to the Teller House, Jim saw Porter Hobson standing on the steps of the church. The gambler's wedding night, Jim thought, remembering what Hobson had told him earlier. Jim couldn't have cared less, not until he looked down the street and saw

Nora Lurton and Pat Robbins, the Gold Nugget bartender, walking toward the church.

Jim stopped, his mouth open as he stared at Nora Lurton. That veil and fancy white dress she was wearing told him she was the girl Hobson was waiting for. Jim was stunned. Nora was too fine a girl to get mixed up with that tinhorn.

Jim Shannon turned and hurried over to the church.

"Glad you could make it," Hobson said, smirking. "The ceremony will be taking place as soon as Nora and Pat get here."

"I don't know what you did to sucker Nora into this deal," Jim said. "But you just as well forget it because the wedding bells aren't going to ring tonight or any other night, as far as you and Nora are concerned."

"You've got a lot of gall," Hobson said.

Jim started toward him and the gambler stepped back. His hand darted inside his coat. Light from the open doorway of the church shone on the snub-nosed revolver that appeared in Hobson's hand.

Before the gambler could fire, Jim closed in on him and knocked the gun out of his hand. "Get going, tinhorn, and make it fast," Jim said. "If you don't, I'll pick up that pop gun and cram it down your throat."

Hobson hesitated, his face pale. Perhaps he was remembering what he had seen Jim Shannon do with his bare hands. With a glance at Nora Lurton, the gambler left the church and ducked down an alley.

Nora and Pat came running up. "What happened?" Nora asked. "Where did Porter go?"

"Said he had a date down at Blackhawk," Jim said with a straight face. "I don't think he'll be back."

Nora stood there in her lace dress, angry as she looked at Jim Shannon. "You ran Porter off," she said accusingly. "Just who do you think you are?"

"I don't know what happened to you, Nora, but you were fixing to make a fool of yourself."

"The way you've been acting . . ." Nora cried. "And you have the nerve to talk about me making a fool of myself."

Pat Robbins didn't say anything. He stood there grinning.

"You're getting yourself all worked up," Jim said. "Why don't you calm down and we'll talk this over."

Nora's lips trembled. "Damn you, anyway."

Before Jim could say anything, she turned and ran back down the street.

"What's eating her?" Jim asked. "And why was she fixing to marry that tinhorn?"

Pat Robbins shook his hand. "You big, dumb cluck. If you hadn't let all that high-priced perfume of Beth Richmond's get your head fogged up, you might have been able to see how Nora felt, that she was going to marry Porter to spite you."

"Well, I'll be damned," Jim said.

He left Pat standing there and ran after Nora who was still hurrying along the dark street. She didn't stop and she wouldn't look at him when he came alongside.

"All right," Jim said. "So I got off the track for a while, but I woke up tonight. Tomorrow, I'm taking my old job back. Everything's going to be like it used to."

She didn't answer right away, but finally she said, "Are you sure?"

"Never was surer of anything in my life," Jim said. "And if you'll let me stop at the hotel long enough to get my boots, we'll go to the Nugget and have us a real celebration."

"You wouldn't fool a girl, would you, Jim?"

He shook his head, grinning as he took hold of her arm. "I'll start off by buying you a bottle of strawberry soda pop," he said. "What could be better?"

MAN WITH TWO LIVES

Joe R. Lansdale

It was July the Fourth and Nacogdoches, the oldest town in Texas, was hung with banners declaring the holiday. The old man read them and continued walking. He was not in a festive mood at all. It was too hot and he was too old. He continued around the square toward the general store.

Yes, too hot and too old, but he kept going full steam ahead, for this was how he had always lived, and he knew no other way.

Sometimes, especially when it was hot he had noticed, he thought perhaps it would have been better had he really died in that saloon facedown on the card table; really been buried in a good hard box in that dark, rocky ground.

Certainly it would have been better than this. Less painful than this; wasting away of old age, being a man out of place and time, a nobody. Considering the fact that in his first life he had been very important made this all the worse.

Once he had carried a brace of revolvers, but now it was all he could do to carry himself down the street.

Once his calm voice was enough to quiet violent men in a Wild West saloon, but now he did well to talk above the screams of his grandchildren.

Sometimes he considered telling family and friends who he really was. But who would believe him? They would think he had finally gone over the lip.

No. They would not believe him and there was no way for him to prove otherwise. Even digging up the grave wouldn't help. Inside they would find a rotted corpse, and though not his, how would he prove to the contrary? There just wasn't any way he could convince people he was that famous man about whom stories were told and books were written.

John Spradley, sheriff of Nacogdoches, strolled by and nodded at him. "How're you doing, Jim?"

"Fine, fine," he said, but wanted to yell, "miserable, that's how I'm doing. I was a famous man in my time and now no one even knows who I am."

But he said nothing beyond his false reply. Just walked on, toting his memories like a pedlar toting his sack.

God, but it was hard to believe he had begun a new life thirty-eight years ago. Here it was 1914 and he remembered that day as if it were yesterday. He should. He had had the rare honor of attending his own funeral and walking away.

In those days he had been a famous gunhand, a man known far and wide as a great pistoleer. But his hand was slowing and his eyes were dimming. Not so unusual for a man in his late thirties, but very disconcerting for a man whose life depended on the speed of his draw, the accuracy of his aim.

He was in Dakota Territory in those days, and as always, his reputation had proceeded him. It was a newly formed mining town where he stopped, and immediately his arrival set some concerned parties to buzzing. In the past he had had a reputation as a town tamer, and that just wouldn't do. Not when a handful of folks had it going good for them with illicit gambling and vice. They feared he'd clean up the town, institute law and order.

Rumor of that got around to him and he chuckled. No, he was through cleaning up towns, he'd had his fill of town marshaling. But he decided to use that to his advantage.

There was a guy named Varnes who probably had the biggest bite in the town, and more to lose than anyone should law and order be established and enforced. He went directly to Varnes and did not mince words.

"Varnes," he had said, "I'll tell you this, and tell you straight. I'm thinking about cleaning up this rathole and making it decent. But I can make a deal with you. I'm a bit tired of all this, and to tell you the truth, I fear this just might be my last camp. So, before one of your hired guns kills me, I'm going to arrange it so you can get it done proper."

He could still remember the way Varnes looked at him, mouth open, eyes startled.

"No," he told Varnes, "I'm not about to commit suicide. I won't make it that easy for you, but I do have a plan. A plan that'll leave the town to you and free me of my reputation."

The plan was simple: Varnes was to help him fake his death. For insurance, in case Varnes decided to make it for real, Varnes was to sign out a statement of his involvement beforehand and leave it with

Charlie Utter, a friend of Jim's. Once the deal was pulled off, Charlie was to return the paper to Varnes to do as he chose.

If Charlie did not return the paper, and should Varnes appear to be in hot water, he could always have the body exhumed to prove that the man in question was not there, and had not actually been murdered.

To do the deed, and to keep his hands out of it, Varnes had hired a cross-eyed drunk to do the shooting; gave him a snootful of whiskey and a gun full of defective cartridges, though the one that would fall under the hammer was designed to go pop. That would make the assassination appear real to any witnesses in the saloon.

The old man laughed thinking back on it. He remembered how he had sat with his back to the door for the first time ever, and how right on schedule the drunk had entered and walked up behind him. "Take that," the drunk had said pulling and firing his pistol, and he, the great gunman, who had some acting experience from a Wild West show, fell forward on the table with a moan.

So he lay there on his side until the doctor came in—a man on Varnes's payroll. The doctor quickly pronounced him dead, and with the aid of Charlie, carried him away.

A few days later, after hiding out in Charlie's tent, playing hand after hand of poker, he had to perform an even greater acting job—be the corpse at his own funeral.

Charlie, the doctor and Varnes helped him into a coffin and carried him out to be put on display. It was an odd feeling to have all those people passing by, and him trying to concentrate on shallow breathing and not moving a muscle, but Charlie had helped by not allowing viewers to linger, kept saying, "Move on, please, there are a lot of folks that want to pay their respects." He could still hear some of the talking as they passed.

"Isn't he lifelike?"

"He has a smile on his lips."

"Oh, did you see that? Didn't he breathe?"

"Hell no, he didn't breathe. He's dead and he looks it."

"Prettiest corpse I've ever seen."

And then they placed the lid on him and put him six feet down, with Charlie and Varnes supervising.

It was no mean trick to relax in the darkness, breathe easily and calmly while dirt clods sounded on the lid of the box, while it grew warm and sweaty within. He still remembered that moment, remembered wanting to kick and yell, scream out, "The deal is off!"

But he had remained calm, and shortly thereafter he heard the sound of spades, then hands on the box, and up he came.

Once out of the coffin, he had Charlie return Varnes's affidavit, and made Charlie promise to let him, "stay dead."

"You've got it, old pard," Charlie told him. "You're a corpse from here out."

And Charlie had lived by his word. For that matter, so had Varnes. And why not? He had gotten what he wanted most, control of Deadwood, and to reveal that the great gunman was still alive would have made him a fool.

A few years later Jim had read a newspaper account of "his" body having been dug up—due to the expansion of Deadwood—and re-buried. The body had been examined for some ghoulish reason, and good old Charlie had been on hand to state that "The body still maintained its features, and even the pleatings in the dress shirt were intact."

Since there were a number of witnesses present, Jim wondered just whose body Charlie had put in that coffin to substitute for him. He sort of hoped it was Varnes.

Yes, Charlie had been a true friend to the end. And perhaps that was what he missed most, friends like Charlie. He had never seen him again after that day at the grave site, for he had left Deadwood, shaved his mustache, cut his long hair, and ventured down South to eventually end up in Nacogdoches, Texas.

If anyone had told him that someday he'd give up his guns and meet up with some Texas farm girl and become a farmer, he'd have shot them on the spot. But that was exactly what had happened. He and Mattie had married, raised a beautiful daughter who married in turn and was raising his two lovely grandchildren, a boy and a girl.

Sometimes he wished he'd told Mattie who he really was, instead of making up a past for her. She would have believed him.

But he hadn't told her, and now she was gone.

God, but he missed her.

He strolled into the general store and bought a bag of hard rock candy and a few peppermints.

"Thank you, Mr. Butler," the storekeeper said.

"You're welcome," Jim said, and he strolled out, thinking, in my prime folks used to stand and stare when I walked in. Not only because of my reputation as a gunman, but because I was a fine figure of a man, tall and clear-eyed. Now I'm bent and half blind and do good to get a nod and a smile.

Sometimes he wished he'd really died that day in Deadwood, gone out at the top of his form.

He walked around the square and headed north down the treelined streets, toward his daughter's house.

After a while he stepped into her yard and started for the door, sighing heavily as he went.

"Grandpa!" came a voice from the side of the house. Turning, he saw nine-year-old Jimmy darting toward him, and not far behind came his five-year-old granddaughter, Lottie, who was now saying, "Gwanpa, Gwanpa," fast as revolver fire.

Stooping, his old bones creaking as he did, he took them in his arms, hugged them close.

"What you got in the sack, Grandpa?" Jimmy asked. "What you got?"

"Sack?" the old man said, as though he had not noticed it before. "What sack?"

"Oh, Grandpa," Jimmy said.

"Oh, Gwanpa," Lottie echoed.

Jim laughed and stood, opened his bag and poured candy into the two sets of hands that greedily reached up.

"You'll spoil them," came a voice, and he turned to see his daughter standing in the doorway. My, but she was the spitting image of her mother, a beautiful woman. Especially with her hands on her hips like that, and that half-concerned look on her face.

"I certainly hope so," Jim said. "What grandbabies are for."

She smiled. "Children, put the candy up until after supper. Come into this house, all three of you. Let's eat. Right now! Time for supper."

The children ran ahead of him, and he watched them with pride. Following them inside, he went to the dinner table, hung his hat on the back of a chair as he sat. His son-in-law, Bob, was already at the table and he said, "Hi, Dad. Got your favorite today, mashed potatoes."

"Bring 'em on," the old man said with a grin.

After dinner, while June washed the dishes and Bob fed the chickens out back, he seated himself on the front porch swing and lit his pipe.

The evening had brought a bit of a cool spell with it, and it was a comfortable contrast to the muggy heat of the earlier day.

The grandchildren came out on the porch to bathe in the aroma of his pipe smoke. Little Lottie, making quite a chore of it, climbed up on his knee and hugged him. Jimmy sat beside him on the swing.

"Going to stay the night, Grandpa?" Jimmy asked.

"I think so."

Somewhere, not far away, a horde of firecrackers went off in celebration of the Fourth of July. They sounded like gunfire, and for a moment the old man's thoughts went back to the old days; back to when he had pulled his revolvers and heard them sing.

Yes, sometimes he wished he had died that day in the Ten Spot saloon.

"I wuv you Gwanpa," Lottie said.

And sometimes not, he thought smiling at the pretty little girl.

"Grandpa," Jimmy said, "tell us a story."

The old man smiled, and said in a conspiratorial whisper, "I'll tell you a story, a secret one. Did you know that I'm really Wild Bill Hickok?"

"Oh Grandpa," Jimmy said. "He's dead."

The old man laughed again. "Yes," he said taking Lottie under one arm and Jimmy under the other. "I suppose he is."

"I wuv you Gwanpa," Lottie repeated.

"And I love you too," the old man said, and he told them a story. But it had nothing to do with Wild Bill Hickok.

GRAB, ROOT AND GROWL
Gary McCarthy

James Stanford ached with humiliation and a real sense of loss as the buggy turned north onto the high desert trail which would deliver him in two days at the railhead in Elko, Nevada. The wind was blowing hard and the cold, raw day matched their dispositions.

Beside him, Katie's eyes were frosty and her lips pinched down at the corners in disappointment and he couldn't help but remember how they'd looked when they'd first met only fourteen months ago. It had been autumn and she'd stood alone on Brandy Hill overlooking the New York boarding school to which she'd been sent by her father. There'd been a gentle sadness in her that day—and a beauty too. With her long auburn hair shimmering in the wind like burnished copper, he'd thought her incredibly beautiful. And he still did.

Now, a year later and finished with medical school, he'd come west to marry Katie but he'd lost her instead.

"Hey," he ventured, breaking the silence which hung between them, "you don't have to drive so fast."

"Yes, I do," she countered. "It's a long road between here and Benton's Crossing. They'll put us up for the night there. Next day, we'll still have nearly thirty miles to Elko."

"You could have had one of your cowboys take me back. Why didn't you?"

She blinked and stared into the gray desert distance. "It wouldn't have been right. You came on my account, it's only right I do this."

"Right?" he echoed in hurt bewilderment. "What does 'right' have to do with any of this madness? Why are you driving me out of your life? Is it just because I refused to play cowboy with your father and his ranch hands? Does that somehow brand me as less than a man?"

"I never said that!"

"You didn't have to. I could see it in everyone's eyes. But yours were the only ones which counted." He swallowed dryly. "I thought we knew each other well enough to become man and wife."

"We were mistaken, James. This life isn't for you and I'd never be happy with a man who was afraid to grab, root and growl."

"Grab . . ." He threw up his hands in exasperation. "What are you talking about!"

"It means *grit,* James. It means you grab hold of life with both hands, root your feet in the dirt, and make it clear to everyone you've made a stand. That no one is going to push you where you aren't willing to go."

"I see." He turned away to hide the bitterness. "What about the growl? That's necessary too, is it?"

"Absolutely! Out here nothing comes easy. In town, or on our ranch, there's no room for a quitter."

He took a deep breath. "And that's what you people have decided I am, isn't it?"

Her stony silence was answer enough. James lapsed into brooding silence. The word "quitter," which he'd never been called in his life, suddenly was an oath as they crawled across the sun-blasted land.

"You . . . you wouldn't even *try!*" she blurted angrily, after an hour passed.

"Try." He spat the word out like an oath. "You mean when your father kept demonstrating how to shoot and I kept missing?"

"Yes!"

"Did it ever enter your mind that having ten cowboys lounging around, whooping and laughing every time I missed, might have had something to do with being unsteady? Or that my real father shot himself to death one night when I was only eight and I've hated guns ever since?"

The color drained from her face but he couldn't check the torrent of words. "And then there was that 'plow horse' they saddled that threw me to the ground."

"You could have ridden him," Katie said in a small voice. "No one wanted you hurt and he'd have quit after a few more jumps. Always had. But you did first."

He rubbed his face wearily. "Anything else? I want to hear it all. Maybe . . . aw, hell, maybe I can write an account for an eastern newspaper. It ought to be good for a few laughs."

"Stop it!"

"Why should I? Every time I made a mistake your father and the crew laughed."

"That's their way, James! Out here, men *are* tested. They take their knocks and laugh and get laughed at. If you had grabbed hold, they'd have respected and helped you."

"I didn't want their help. I just became a doctor, remember? I'm

not a cowboy, a rancher or gunslinger. You knew that when we became engaged. What happened? Did you expect me to live out on the
ranch? Bust broncos and wear chaps?"

"No! But I'd hoped you'd learn our ways," she countered accusingly. "Even my father, who's always wanted me to marry a Neva-
dan, said he'd treat you like a son and teach you our ways if I loved
you and you had grit. Well, I *did* love you, James. But it wasn't
enough!"

He clamped his mouth shut, because he had his own ideas about
how hard Mr. Regan had tried. Hard enough to drive doubts in Katie's mind about his manhood. But what good would that do? The
hurt was already deep enough.

All afternoon the wind grew stronger and, finally, it hurled a dust
storm twisting out of the Independence Mountains like a cyclone,
blowing tumbleweeds stampeding across the land like berserk
buffalo. They slammed into the buggy, tore underneath the horse,
causing the animal to bolt and run in terror. Katie sawed on the
lines. She tried to hand them to him but, in the blinding dust, they
fell and were lost.

James gripped the buggy and Katie and hung on as they charged
onward. When he tried to see, his eyes were raked raw by the blowing sand and, when he shouted for the girl to hold on tight, it was
like having a fistful of dirt shoved down his throat.

A rear wheel cracked ominously as one side of the buggy catapulted skyward and hung for a terrifying moment before crashing
back down to right itself.

"We've got to jump!" Katie yelled. "There are deep ravines every-
where!"

He wasn't about to argue. Maybe the horse couldn't run much farther, but if they flipped, they'd be crushed.

The moment they jumped, the buggy lurched violently and he
knew that something was desperately wrong. They both kept falling.
And, when he did hit ground, it was to carom downward in a shower
of rock and gravel. Things tore at him, cut and bit and pelted him,
until blessed insensibility drove him into darkness.

He awoke in the night, awash in a sea of pain, but yelling, "Katie?
Katie! Where are you?"

She mumbled something unintelligible and he scrambled deeper
into the ravine, tearing through brush until he knelt beside her in the
wan moonlight. Katie was bent all wrong, like a battered doll pitched
into a corner; her right leg was twisted at an unnatural angle.

Her pulse was shallow, respiration quick and light. He cradled her
head into his lap and she whispered, "I tried to find you but . . ."

"You can't move," he said gently. "Don't even try. I'll have a look."

He folded her skirt up to the knee and his dread was confirmed as he touched bone and knew it was a compound fracture of the tibia. James tried not to sound alarmed. "It's just your normal, everyday fracture."

She clenched her teeth in pain but a wiry shape formed on her lips. "That's fine, Doctor. But I'm not impressed. How bad?"

There was enough moonlight to see the jagged bone edges protruding through the skin. James told her that infection was the real danger.

"What happens if it does become infected?"

He took a deep breath. "You could lose your leg but we aren't going to think about that because there'll be no infection. I may be an inept greenhorn out here, but I'm a damned good doctor and what I must do now is find the buggy and retrieve my medical bag. I've just enough sulfa powder to temporarily arrest an infection."

"I'll be fine, James. Don't worry about me. But be careful, we may be miles from the road and water."

He hesitated. "Is there a chance your father will find us?"

She tried a smile that didn't succeed. "It'll be at least two days before he realizes something went wrong. Another couple to locate our tracks if they haven't all been blown away."

"We'll be fine," he said heartily. No use in telling her the sulfa would last just forty-eight hours before the wound would demand cleaning and remedicating.

Forty-eight hours. It wasn't much time. No time at all.

He felt his own knee burn from a deep laceration but made himself ignore it. This wound would heal with time. Katie's leg needed something more.

"Rest easy. The buggy has to be nearby."

"James?"

"Yes?"

"Stay close. You don't know this land and would just get lost."

He shut his eyes tightly. Bit back the anger. When her breathing told him she'd fallen asleep, he crawled away into the night with the word "quitter" burning into his brain. For what seemed like hours, he crabbed over the ground in a circle until he found the wheel ruts. His knee had swelled up like a melon and his surgeon's fingers were raw meat. Dawn found him on the lip of a shallow canyon staring down at what had been a horse and buggy.

James edged down to the wreckage, noting with professional relief that the horse had died instantly. Wasting no time, he retrieved his suitcase, replacing his clothing with two canteens, a tin of peaches and some dried jerky. In addition to his medical bag, he also took a lariat which had been coiled under the seat, a loaded Winchester rifle, and a knife, along with the tangled reins from the horse which he thought might do to wrap a splint.

He returned to Katie before the glow of sunrise faded and had a fire going shortly afterward. Then he knelt down beside her. "I've got to cut back a small flap of skin," he explained, eyeing the canteen of boiling water and the empty peaches tin he intended to use as an instrument tray. "It's not a difficult operation. I saw one last year in medical school. I can do it."

She said nothing out loud. But her eyes reflected her uncertainty. "All right," she said at last. "You are a doctor."

When the sedatives took effect, he poured the boiling water over the instruments, needle and sutures resting in the smoke-blackened tin. Then he grabbed the scalpel and felt it burn his skin as he began to recount aloud how they'd met and fallen in love during the autumn days when brown and gold and scarlet leaves sailed under blue October skies.

The incision was neat and, though she went stiff and white, his voice seemed to lift her above the present. And, gradually, she relaxed, even as his fingers worked with the perfect dexterity he'd always known they possessed. James found the pieces of loose bone and removed them. Next he applied pressure to fit the fracture together and it meshed beautifully.

His voice was a soft drone in her ears and a smile formed across her lips at times when he recounted some of the crazy things they'd laughed about and seen together. He used all the sulfa, then sutured the skin and bandaged the incision.

It was done.

"James?"

"Yes?" he asked shakily.

"I didn't feel a thing. Honest."

"Good. You'll be fine." He stood up and surveyed the land. He'd seen horse droppings. They needed a horse. "Katie, I'm going to catch a mustang," he said, not daring to let her see the uncertainty he felt.

"What!"

"A mustang. We can't wait for help. The sulfa won't last."

"But . . ."

His voice roughened. "Katie, don't say it. Maybe I am a tenderfoot. But I'm a man too! Now, how do I catch one of the damned things? Tell me about mustanging. Everything you know."

As he listened, James rejected the idea of attempting to stun one with a bullet low across the neck, knowing he'd either miss entirely or kill the poor animal, but felt a stirring excitement when she told him about a man named Mustang Grey whose horse broke a leg and stranded him on the prairie. Grey had finally captured a horse by waiting up in a tree over a waterhole. Katie thought it seemed believable because horses apparently weren't able to detect the scent of a cougar hiding up on a tree branch.

He'd appreciated the idea because he'd only have to drop a loop from overhead. But, late that afternoon, when he finally trailed the mustangs' path to the nearest waterhole and even scaled a big cottonwood tree beside it, the entire idea seemed as shaky as the limb he'd chosen.

He waited nearly four hours until sunset when they arrived—a big dun-colored stallion in the lead and perhaps a dozen mares right behind. He froze. Pressed himself down on the limb and tried to melt into its bark. His loop was ready and tied around his waist in a slipknot, just in case he had to get free quickly.

On they came. Silhouettes really, like unearthly things, they snorted and shuffled, ears flicking, nostrils testing the wind. The stallion was huge as it passed underneath, with rippling muscles along its shoulders, back and rump.

Next came the mares, some with foals. He waited until a smallish animal moved underneath, then he dropped the loop perfectly, and jumped for its back.

He belly flopped across the withers and his lungs flattened as the mare threw him into the brush, retching for air. All hell broke loose. Horses exploded in every direction and one got tangled in the rope. The impact catapulted him into the sky and he tried desperately to plant his feet.

But his feet were overhead and somehow everything was upside down. He lit on one shoulder as the horse sprang over piñon and mesquite like a crazed jackrabbit going to high ground.

He never had a chance and, in his last lucid moment, he pulled the slipknot and the mare shot off into the night to thunder after her friends.

Head buried in brush and feeling as though he'd touched the hand of death, James listened as the stallion trumpeted a challenge from some distant hilltop. Or maybe it wasn't a challenge—probably just wild horse laughter.

Thirty-six hours. Tomorrow. If he failed tomorrow, Katie's leg . . .

James didn't sleep that night. Time was running out before the leg would become infected. So he chose another method of mustanging and dug himself a man-sized hole, then found a stout log and threw it in before burying a loop across the wild horse trail. Finally, he brushed the entire area with sage to hide both tracks and smell. Then he climbed into the hole, pulled sage overhead, and huddled with the log until dawn crept over the hills and mustangs would begin to seek water.

He must have dozed because he wasn't aware of their silent procession until he felt the tremor of their weight. Not even daring to peek, he waited until the dust from their feet drifted over the hole. Then he yanked the rope on his foot trap.

A wild squeal filled the air and the rope-tied log he'd bedded down with flew up through the brush like a circus man shot out of a cannon. He followed with a whoop and lit out, chasing the mare who was bucking off through the sage dragging the log for all she was worth. She ran a hundred yards before the log jammed and twisted her to the earth. She was on her feet in an instant, biting viciously at the rope which cut off her air, threatening to choke her to death or break her neck. James knew either spelled disaster so he jumped for the mare's head, trying to blindfold her. The mustang's teeth flashed and James screamed as flesh tore away from his upper arm and the horse clawed erect to stagger into a run.

But her strength was bleeding away quickly now and she soon toppled again. He collapsed on her neck and tied his shirt over her eyes.

The mustang gasped for air and threw its head crazily in blind fright. James ignored a wave of pity and tied one foreleg up against its foam-flecked body.

"Easy," he crooned. "Easy."

The mare smashed her head into him and he went flying sideways.

"Easy, dammit!" he yelled, picking himself up from the dirt and glancing at the sun. Ten in the morning at least. *Twenty-four hours*. It would take him four of them to get back to Katie, even if nothing went wrong.

Fortunately, nothing did. He returned to camp wondering who was worse off, himself or the mustang. No matter. That afternoon he returned to the wrecked buggy where he tore away the pair of long wooden shafts. With Katie's help, they made her a travois. It took longer than he'd thought. He checked her leg, smiled and said it was fine, then went to face the mustang.

She fought him viciously. Over and over, she knocked him spinning when he tried to rig the travois to a makeshift harness. He had to roll as she stomped in three-legged fury in a desperate attempt to crush out his life.

At first, Katie had begged him to give it up—but he hadn't listened. He'd just grabbed hold of the neck rope, planted his feet and fought the mare right back until they both swayed with exhaustion. To his undying relief, the mare quit first.

She'd stolen two more hours. Maybe, he reasoned wildly, maybe the sulfa would stop a bone infection longer than he'd been told. But maybe not. It was night. *Twelve hours give or take.*

Katie crawled onto the latticework of reins they'd tied between the shafts, while James held the mare. When he pulled her forward, she tried to run him down but he looped both arms around her head and hung on for his life as his weight forced her to a stop.

The mare's teeth snapped but she missed and he chomped down hard on her ear, spitting hair, and mad as hell. Minutes later, they were moving north, the horse and the man content in a temporary truce because both hurt so damned much.

Try amputating Katie's leg, he thought. Understand real pain.

A drummer with a converted mud wagon, garishly painted to depict his own brand of medicine, met them on the road. He was a big man, gruff when not selling, and little inclined to errands of mercy. *Four hours.*

James yanked him from his seat and fought him to the ground where they battled until the drummer was knocked unconscious. Then, he lifted Katie into the wagon and raced toward Elko.

He must have broken every bottle of snake oil elixir in the wagon before he slewed it around the corner of the first street and braked to a halt at the dentist's office. When he picked her up, she was delirious with fever. Dark purplish lines were fingering out from the leg's fracture.

Two days later the train puffed into town as he eased into a chair by her side. "The ordeal's over," he said wearily. "Stay in bed a few weeks before you go home to the ranch."

"I'm not going back," she told him quietly.

"I don't . . ."

"Not if you still love me."

He started to speak but Katie placed a finger across his lips, silencing him. "It's like my leg. I never realized how much I wanted to walk with you until . . . until I thought I might never again. Can you forgive me?"

His throat ached as he choked out a simple, "Yes."

She looked deep into his eyes and he saw mirrored there something he'd thought lost; it glowed like a warm fire on a cold night as she reached up to cradle his face in her hands.

"Then isn't it wonderful that I've got to stay in bed?" she asked shyly. "Send out for the preacher, James. 'Cause I do love a man who can grab, root and growl."

BIOGRAPHICAL NOTes

STEPHEN OVERHOLSER is the author of a number of novels, including *A Hanging in Sweetwater* (Doubleday), named winner of the Spur Award by the Western Writers of America for best novel of 1974. A second-generation writer of novels of the West, he carries on the tradition of his father, Wayne D. Overholser, who is represented in this anthology with his first short story in many years.

To date, ELMER KELTON has published twenty-four novels and has won the Western Writers of America Spur Award for best novel of the year with *Buffalo Wagons, The Day the Cowboys Quit,* and *The Time It Never Rained.* In addition, Elmer has twice been named the recipient of the Western Heritage Award from the National Cowboy Hall of Fame. He and his wife, Anna, live in San Angelo, Texas.

CARLA KELLY won the Western Writers of America Spur Award in 1979 for Best Short Story, and in 1981 she was a finalist for the same award. She has published stories in *Far West* and written historical articles for *American History Illustrated* and *The American West.*

ELMORE LEONARD is well known for both his novels and his screenplays. Author of *3:10 to Yuma, Valdez Is Coming,* and *Hombre,* he has also written scripts for *The Return of Will Kane,* a sequel to *High Noon,* and *Joe Kidd.* Two of his detective novels, *Cat Chaser* and *Split Images,* were recently published by Arbor House.

WAYNE D. OVERHOLSER, a charter member of the Western Writers of America, has written one hundred novels and over four hundred novelettes and short stories. He has won awards from the Colorado Authors League in 1950 and 1960 for Best Adult Fiction as well as two Spur Awards for Best Western Novel in 1953 and 1954. In 1969 he won the Spur for Best Western Juvenile with *The Meeker Massacre,* written in collaboration with Lewis B. Patten. Wayne has worked on many WWA committees and served two terms on the

Board of Directors. He was chairman of the first WWA convention held in Denver in 1954. He lives with his wife, Evaleth, in Boulder, Colorado.

JEANNE WILLIAMS is the author of many short stories and novels, including *The Horse Talker* and *Freedom Trail,* which both won Spur Awards for Best Western Juvenile; the first also won the Golden Saddleman Award from the Western Writers of America. *The Valiant Women,* published by Pocket Books, is the first of a trilogy on Arizona, and won the Spur for Best Western Novel in 1981. *Eden Richards,* published in Fawcett's Frontier Women Series, was published under her pen name, Jeanne Foster. In 1983, Avon will publish *The Cave of Always Summer,* a story of the Basques from prehistory to the present.

BENJAMIN CAPPS received the Golden Saddleman Award from the Western Writers of America in 1965. His work has been honored by Spur Awards from WWA and by Wrangler Awards from the Western Heritage Center for both fiction and nonfiction. His novels, including *The Trail to Ogallala* and *The White Man's Road,* appear on required reading lists of university courses in Western Literature. Recently his novel *Woman Chief* was a nominee for the first American Book Awards.

Ben's grandfather was a mustanger, going out to capture wild horses in west Texas, Oklahoma, and New Mexico during the years after the Civil War. His father broke and trained horses for the D's, one of the great ranches in northwest Texas. Ben himself rode horseback to a one-teacher school as a child.

FRANK RODERUS is the author of more than twenty Western novels, including *The 33 Brand, Hell Creek Cabin,* and *Jason Evers, His Own Story.* Frank lives with his wife, Betty, and family on a horse ranch near Colorado Springs, Colorado.
"Ed" is his first, and only, short story.

JUDY ALTER, a past board member of the Western Writers of America, is the author of *After Pa was Shot,* a juvenile novel, and is coauthor of *The Quack Doctor,* a Texas memoir. In addition, she has written *The Texas ABC Book* for children and studies of authors Dorothy Johnson and Stewart Edward White for the Boise State University Western Pamphlet Series. She holds a Ph.D. in English from Texas Christian University.

BILL GULICK is the author of sixteen novels, among them *Bend of the River, The Hallelujah Trail,* and *Showdown in the Sun,* that were made into feature-length films. His most recent novel, *Treasure in Hell's Canyon,* was published by Doubleday. Bill also writes nonfiction books, having published *Snake River Country* and *Chief Joseph Country: Land of the Nez Perce* with Caxton. He has won two Spur Awards for his short stories that originally appeared in the *Saturday Evening Post.* Bill has been president and board member of the Western Writers of America.

BILL BURCHARDT is the author of numerous short stories and articles and nine Western novels. He is a past president of the Western Writers of America and a native Oklahoman. For twenty-three years he edited *Oklahoma Today* magazine. Bill has received the Western Heritage Award presented by the National Cowboy Hall of Fame, the University of Oklahoma Professional Writing Award, and has twice won the Tepee Award of the Oklahoma Writers Federation for the Best Novel of the Year by an Oklahoman.

JOHN R. ERICKSON has published one hundred and seventy-five humorous stories and articles about cowboy life, in addition to three nonfiction books, *Through Time and the Valley* (1978), *Panhandle Cowboy* (1980), and *The Modern Cowboy* (1981). He has managed and worked on ranches himself and now makes his home in Perryton, Texas, with his wife and family.

Author of many books, short stories, and articles on a variety of topics, WAYNE C. LEE is a past president of the Western Writers of America. Two novels he has recently published with Ace Books are *Petticoat Wagon Train* and *The Violent Man.* Nonfiction books he has published with Caxton are *Scotty Philip, The Man who Saved the Buffalo,* and *Trails of the Smoky Hill.* Wayne lives with his wife, Pearl, on a farm in western Nebraska that was homesteaded by his parents.

NATLEE KENOYER, who will serve as president of the Western Writers of America in 1983, is the author of many books including *The Western Horse* which won a Spur Award. She has published over one hundred articles in various horse magazines. Natlee makes her home in Santa Rosa, California.

BILL PRONZINI has written twenty-five novels, a nonfiction book, and two hundred and fifty short stories, articles, and essays in a vari-

ety of fields. This year two of his novels in the "Nameless Detective"
series were published, along with *Gun in Cheek,* a satirical look at
the mystery genre, and *The Gallows Land,* a Western novel he co-
authored with Joe R. Lansdale.

WAYNE BARTON's short story "One Man's Code" (*Far West,* Winter, 1980) was awarded a Spur Award for best short story of the
year by the Western Writers of America. A native of west Texas,
Wayne has published forty short stories and articles about the Old
West. In 1981 Doubleday published his novel, *Ride Down the Wind,*
and will soon bring out his next novel, *Return to Phantom Hill.*

GERALD KEENAN, managing editor of Pruett Publishing Company
in Colorado, is a writer as well. Author of book reviews and articles
that have appeared in many magazines, he has a long-time interest in
the history of the West.

RAY GAULDEN has written many magazine stories, but for some
time now has concentrated on novels. Two of his titles, *Red Sundown* and *Ride a Crooked Trail,* became movies. *Glory Gulch* was
filmed as *Five Card Stud,* one of the few original paperback Westerns
ever to be made into a major motion picture. Ray's most recent
novels are *A Man Named Murdo* and *Rough Road to Denver.*

Short stories by JOE R. LANSDALE have appeared in several magazines and anthologies. Joe has also written a number of articles for
Frontier Times and *True West.* His Western novel, *Blood Dance,*
will be published this year by Ace Books. Joe lives in Nacogdoches,
Texas.

GARY MCCARTHY is the author of a dozen Western novels, includ-
ing The Derby Man series published by Bantam Books. Among
Gary's other books are *Winds of Gold* and the novelized screenplay,
The Legend of the Lone Ranger.